Mary Due Scott
Jan, 2020 Great Book

Mischief on the Mountain

A Novel by
Rebecca Monhollon

Rebecca Monhollon 2-26-16

Cover Art by
Zrondra Monhollon Wilson

Kids At Heart Publishing LLC
PO Box 492
Milton, IN 47357
765-478-5873
www.kidsatheartpublishing.com

First published by Kids At Heart Publishing LLC 7/23/2015
ISBN # 978-0-9964962-1-6
Library of Congress Control Number: 2015944043

Printed in the United States of America
Milton, Indiana

This book printed on acid-free paper.

To order more copies of this book go to
www.kidsatheartpublishing.com

The books at Kids At Heart Publishing feature turn the page technology. No batteries or charging required.

Dedication

To my grandmother, Lucielle Watson Boggs and to my husband for always being there and encouraging me.

A special thank you to Diana Medler for all her help and advice, which was greatly appreciated.

Chapter 1
Milking Flossy

Lucy awoke from a dream; she smelled bacon frying and the hint of cinnamon apples drifting into her room. She looked outside the window just as the first rays of light from the sun started to peek over the mountain and pierce the black sky. She watched the morning light turn to grey, then to yellow, as the sun climbed past the top of Grapeyard Ridge and shined in the little community of Turkey's Roost in Gatlinburg, Tennessee.

She had a hard time waking. She felt tired from yesterday's adventure. Her parents took her to visit friends that lived in Cade's Cove. They started the day with a ride in the wagon and arrived just in time to attend the morning service at the Baptist Church. After the services were over, she played games with the children. In the graveyard, they crouched behind the tombstones and played hide and seek. A shiver ran down her back as she remembered the tombstones marking the people's names buried there who had been killed in the Indian massacres.

She watched as the trees became illuminated and her imagination soared. She looked toward the top of the mountain as the sun brought the tree line to life. She imagined that the trees were Indians. The first tree on the ridge looked like a chief and the shadows made the fall leaves look like his war bonnet of feathers. The tree behind it looked like another Indian and this one carried a tomahawk and wielded it over his head. The wind rustled the leaves and magically the trees were Indians doing a war dance.

Her mother's voice interrupted her daydreaming. "Lucille Watson, time to git up. We got lots of work ta do today. Times a wastin' Lucy, come on now," yelled her mother from the kitchen.

Lucy pulled the quilt up over her head and squirmed farther down in the warm bed. Cold air engulfed the cabin this late October morning because the fire in the fireplace went out during the night. She heard the fire crackling this morning, but the warmth had not made it into her room.

"Lucille Watson, I means today not tomorry. Now, I need some milk and Flossy is belerin'," her mother hollered.

"Oh, Ma, why do I have to milk her? I hates that old heifer. She's mean. How's come Jeb ain't milkin' her?" Lucy yelled.

"Jeb went to Gatlinburg to meet the train. Yer Uncle Little's a comin' today. Come on now don't be lollygaggin' this mornin'," yelled her mother.

"Why don't ya let Ben do it this mornin'?" Lucy shouted and snuggled back down in her bed.

"I reckon ya know Ben is too little ta be a milkin' that cow, I need it for the gravy this mornin'. I won't tell ye again," her mother warned her.

Lucy hurried out of bed and changed her nightgown into her work clothes. Her room was the farthest from the fireplace in the living room and her mother's wood cook stove in the kitchen. She watched her breath turn into a cloud as she raced to the living room.

"How's Pa?" she asked as she landed on the stone hearth of the fireplace.

Her little brother Ben came over and stuck his tongue out at her. Lucy shook her fist at him.

"He's blessed to be a livin'. The doctor is comin' today. We be knowin' one way ta the other though afore the doctor gets here I reckon," answered her mother.

Lucy watched her mother preparing their breakfast. She thought her ma always looked as if she were going to church. Her ma kept her long brown hair pulled neatly in a bun and her work dress always seemed as if she had recently pressed and starched it. Lucy touched her hair. She wished she had inherited her father's black hair, like her older brother Jeb and her younger brother Ben. She didn't like the plain brown colored hair she inherited from her mother.

Their cabin stayed the same way, neat and clean. The rocking chairs always sat in their place facing the fireplace. No dust settled on the furniture; her mother kept it wiped clean.

Her mother started putting the breakfast on the table. Lucy grabbed a piece of bacon and started munching on it.

"What was the snake got him? Is he waked up yet?" asked Lucy.

"No, he's still sleepin'. The fever's still got a hold on him. Most likely t'was a copperhead, the swellin's not as bad as a rattler. I reckon I done told him a thousand times that them snakes is still out even if it's cold of a night. They come out ta sun in the day this time a year. It'll be awhile afore they goes away fer the winter. I want ya ta be mindful of that when yer outside." Her mother cracked an egg in the skillet, "I'm worried about his leg. It's broke in two places from that tree falling on him best I can tell. He don't need you a pesterin' him, so go on and git that milk," replied her mother.

Lucy rolled her brown eyes and made a face.

Before she could speak, her mother scolded, "Now, don't be a givin' me no backtalk just go and do it this one time."

Lucy gobbled a piece of the bacon and got up to put on her coat. She found her scarf and wrapped it around her head. Her eyes and the tops of her cheeks were all that was exposed to the cold morning air. She carried the milk pail muttering the whole way under her breath.

The morning mist hung thick in the air, so she had a hard time seeing. The mist settled on her cheeks; they became red. She loved the mist of the mountains. It looked like smoke from a distance. She knew it was actually clouds that made the illusion of smoke. She remembered her father saying he had heard talk in town that plans were being made to make a national park of the mountains and call the park The Great Smokey Mountains. He said people had taken notice of the way the mountains looked with the clouds hanging over them.

The guineas busied themselves pecking for seeds and bugs. They made a tremendous racket. The rooster crowed and the hens clucked as she passed by the chicken coop. She didn't pay any attention to the sounds. She only dreaded trying to deal with that old cow.

She found the rope halter and went to open the pen to find Flossy. The gate creaked as she opened and closed it back. She stopped and turned to made sure the gate was latched behind her; she didn't want Flossy to escape. Flossy had played that trick on her the last time she was forced to do the milking.

"Alright now, Flossy, I ain't aimin' to put up with none of yer nonsense this morning. Come on over here like a good cow and let me git's ya," Lucy crooned to the cow.

She held the halter behind her back wishing this time that Flossy would not notice it. She sneaked around the pen pretending not to be interested in the cow. Flossy stood in the corner of the pen keeping an eye on Lucy. Lucy eased up close to the black and white spotted cow. Flossy wasn't in the mood to be caught, so at the exact moment when Lucy got close enough to put the halter on, she ran to the opposite side of the pen. Lucy threw the halter down and stomped her foot.

"Ooh, I can't stand ya. If'n t'was up ta me, you'd be supper instead of a milker," she hissed at the cow.

Lucy picked up the halter and tried again."Come on now, nice cow. We got to git's that milk," she said as she slowly inched toward the cow.

This time, Flossy let Lucy put the halter on her and then whoosh, she turned and started running with Lucy hanging on to the halter. Flossy gave one jerk and Lucy hit the ground in a belly flop. Lucy lay face down in the dirt trying to catch her breath. When the pain subsided, she stood up and dusted herself off shouting at Flossy.

"Do that again and yer gonna git it!" she yelled while shaking her fist at the cow.

Lucy's Mother watched the commotion from the kitchen window. She raised the window and yelled, "Lucy, quit aggrervatin' that cow. Yer gonna make her milk sour. Git some corn and she'll follow ya rite in the shed."

Lucy dropped her bucket and ran to the barn to get some corn. She came back shaking the bucket so Flossy could hear she had some corn for her. The crafty old cow turned and started for the feed. Flossy followed Lucy into the milking shed trying to take the corn from her along the way. Lucy slammed the door shut as Flossy entered the stall.

"Got's ya!" she yelled. Lucy tied the rope to the barn pole and the old cow knew she was caught.

Lucy went to the pump and filled a pail with water. She moved over to clean the udder. She kept an eye on the cow. She knew full well what that cow was capable of; she'd been the target of it many times.

"Now, Flossy, we kin do this the easy way or the hard way," Lucy said as she placed the bucket of water under the cow to wash the udder. "I'm a tellin' ya, be good or I'm gonna knock ya in the head with this bucket," she warned.

Flossy mooed loudly and kicked the bucket of water in Lucy's face. To add insult to injury, Flossy flicked her tail and hit Lucy smack in the mouth. Dirt and manure landed on Lucy's face.

Lucy wiped the muck off her face blinking back tears.

"Ooh, I hates ya! Do that again and I'll clobber ya!" shouted Lucy.

Lucy went to the pump and filled another pail with water, she waited until Flossy was eating again, then she sat down and finished washing the udder. While Flossy ate the corn, she began to milk the cow. As soon as she filled the pail, she readied herself for what she knew was coming next. She didn't turn loose of the teat until she was ready to grab the bucket of milk. When Lucy let go, Flossy kicked at the bucket of milk.

Lucy jumped to the side and felt the foot go past her leg. Flossy landed a swipe of her tail against Lucy's face, again.

"Ooh, I cant's stand's ya. Yer the stupidest critter on God's earth. I can't see what Ma sees in ya," she cried.

Lucy hurried back to the house and ran straight to the water basin to wash the muck off her face. She didn't have much of an appetite now.

As soon as they had finished eating and washing the dishes, Lucy and her mother went out to the corn field and started picking the corn that was to be food for the livestock through the winter. The day went from cold in the morning to hot in the evening sun.

Lucy put an ear of corn in her basket. "Ma?"

Her Mother yanked at the ears of corn. "Yes, Lucy?"

Lucy stubbed her toe on a rock. She picked it up and threw it out of the garden. "Tell me again how Pa and Uncle Little got their names."

Her mother stopped picking the corn and wiped her face. "Ya heard that story a thousand times."

Lucy walked down the row of corn to where her Mother was. "I know but tell me again."

Her mother reached up and started yanking at another ear of corn. "Well, yer Nanny says when yer pa was born, he was the scrawniest child she ever did see. Pa said they'd just have ta name him Big, they was a hoping he would grow into his name. When yer Uncle Little come along, he was the fattest child they ever seen, so they decided to name him Little. I reckon they figured if namin' yer pa Big would make him grow, they figured namin' his brother Little would keep him from getting too fat."

Lucy giggled; it was funnier when Pa told it. He told about all the fights they were involved in on account of them names. She sat down to rest. She wiggled her toes in the dirt. She loved the feel of the moist dirt between her toes. She stood up and stepped on a another rock, but it didn't hurt her feet. They were tough from going without shoes all summer. She picked the rock up and threw it in the pile at the end of the row of corn.

Lucy started pulling the corn from the stalk beside her mother. "Will Macy be a comin' with them?" she asked.

"Well I reckon they ain't gonna leave her," her mother replied.

Lucy tossed her corn into her mother's basket. "I don't remember much about Macy. Is she as old as me?" she asked.

"She'd be a couple years older than ye. That'ud make her about thirteen." Her mother started yanking at another ear of corn.

"Does she really have red hair?" Lucy asked.

Lucy's mother said with a laugh, "She sure does. Nanny says she don't know where that come from or how she come out with red hair. Yer nanny says that Macy has the temper to go with that hair, too."

The basket was full and they picked it up to carry it to the corn crib. "First cousins can be almost like a sisters cain't they?" Lucy asked.

Her mother looked at Lucy and shook her head, "I reckon they could be."

Lucy started daydreaming about the adventures she would have with Macy. "I always wanted a sister," she spoke her thought.

They emptied the basket in the crib, then took it back to the corn patch.

Lucy screamed as a locust landed on her shirt. Its prickly legs held on to her shirt while its bulging red eyes stared at Lucy. Her Mother swatted it off her shirt!

Lucy covered her ears with her hands. "Them locust bugs shore are makin' a racket this year. I don't like that noise they make." Lucy looked around to make sure no more locusts flew about in her row of corn. The locusts terrified her.

Her mother bent down and picked up a rock. She tossed it in the growing mound from the stones that kept surfacing in the garden. "I reckon this must be a seventh year fer them. Maybe a forty nine of the seven years. They're worse in the forty nine year," she told Lucy.

Lucy looked around for the bugs and whimpered, "They scare me with them big red eyes they got. Ma?"

"Oh Lucille, quit your pesterin' and git ta pickin'," demanded her mother.

Lucy reached up to pull another ear of corn and put her hand on a saddleback caterpillar. "OOOOWWWWW!" she screamed.

Lucy's mother let out a sigh, "What is it now?"

Lucy held out her hand to show the red welts that were already forming. "I jist got bit by a packsaddle. It hurts! It's the second one ta git me today I cain't see how somethin' so purty could be so mean," she cried.

Lucy knocked the green caterpillar off the corn and watched it crawl away. She picked up a rock and held it over her head. "Ya dern packsaddle! I reckon I see where ya git's yer name, with yer green things a stickin' out a yer head and yer brown spot on yer back. I ort ta squish ya with this rock even if'n yer purty! she hissed at the caterpillar. She watched it crawl into the weeds. She couldn't kill it though and she lowered her hand and tossed the rock in the pile.

Her mother turned Lucy's hand to look at the sting. "Purty things are mean too. If ya watched what ya was doin' them worms wouldn't git ya. Alright, go on down to the creek and rub some touch me nots on the sting. You come straight back though, this corn ain't a gonna pick itself," she told Lucy.

Chapter 2
Skinnin' Cats

The noise of the locust and katydids singing in the trees drowned out all other sounds. Lucy didn't even hear the sound of her own footsteps as she stepped on leaves and branches on her way to the creek. She thought the trees were glorious with brilliant colors. The yellow hickory trees and the red, yellow, and orange sugar maples mixed with the green of the pines made this a beautiful walk. She found a patch of touch me not flowers. She loved to pinch the green pods and feel them explode between her fingers. While Lucy was absorbed in pinching them, she didn't hear Macy walking up to her.

"Ya ever skinned a cat?" asked Macy.

Lucy jumped and nearly fell. "What?"

"Ya ever skinned a cat?" demanded Macy.

Lucy knew right away this had to be Macy. She had never seen hair quite that color. Macy's hair was almost as orange as carrots and hanging down her shoulders in two long braids. "No, ya ever ate a crawdad?" she asked Macy. Lucy didn't want to be outdone.

Macy reached her hand out and started popping the touch me not pods and making them explode. "Yeah, lots of them. That ain't nothin'. Want ta learn how ta skin a cat?" she asked.

"No I don't want to hurt no kitty cat," Lucy replied as she put her hands on her hips.

Macy laughed, "Oh, ya ninny, look over yonder. See that hick'ry tree? The one beside that big pine. See it?"

Lucy looked in the direction Macy pointed. The tree stood out in the forest. The yellow leaves mixed with the green of the pine made it easy to spot. "Yeah," she replied.

"Well, what ya do is, ya climb that pine and jump out of it into that hickr'y. It'll bend down real gentle like and ya touch the ground. It's a game called skinnin' cats," Macy said with a hint of mischief in her eyes.

Lucy looked from Macy to the tree. "Sounds ta me like ya might git kilt a doin' that." She stared at Macy feeling a sense of adventure.

Macy shook her head, "Nah, it's fun. Want ta try?"

Lucy became frightened and decided she didn't want to climb the tree. "No I'd sure git hurt," she told Macy.

Macy dared her, "Are ya chicken?"

Lucy's heart skipped a beat because she was afraid. "No, I ain't no chicken. I just ain't never done nothin' like that afore," Lucy blurted out.

Macy grabbed Lucy's hand and pulled her up the hill to the hickory tree. "Oh, it's easy I'll show ya."

Lucy had second thoughts about climbing the tree. "Ya ever did it?" she asked.

"I seed my brothers do it lot's of times. Come on, let's try it," Macy said.

Lucy backed up a couple of steps when Macy let go of her hand. "Oh I don't know if I want to do that or not. Them locust are in the trees. I'm scared ta death of them when they holler phaaarrrooo!"

Macy gave Lucy a look of disbelief. "Them locust bugs don't git in pine trees, come on," she insisted.

Lucy swallowed hard. She didn't want her cousin Macy to think she was afraid. "Okay, but ya got's ta go first."

Macy shook her head. "No I'm gonna give ya the first try. The trees ain't as springy after the first time and it's not as fun." Macy patted the trunk, "Now, all ye do is climb this tree, when ya git up so's yer even with the top of the hickr'y, jump over to it. Ya grab the top and let it bend down with ya."

Lucy looked up the tree, again. She put her hand on the lowest branch. "I don't know maybe ya should show me first."

"Go on now." Macy gave Lucy a boost to get her started and she began climbing the pine tree. When Lucy reached the top, Macy yelled and motioned with her hand, "Now, just jump out and grab the top of that hickr'y."

Lucy swallowed hard, "I think I'd better climb back down, it's awful high."

"Ya done the hard part and made it that far, t'aint' nothin' to jump over ta the other one. Just jump and grab the top. It's fun," Macy insisted.

Lucy closed her eyes and said a little prayer trying to get up her courage. She moved her hand up a few inches, she opened her eyes and looked up, there sat a locust with it's red eyes staring at her. Lucy's heart fluttered with fear and she lost her balance. She felt herself begin to fall and grabbed wildly for a limb. She missed the limb and touched the locust. It's eyes bulged and the bug screamed making a loud noise as it flew up. Terrified, Lucy made a wild jump for the hickory tree. The next thing she remembered was hearing the tree limbs snap. She got scraped and scratched from her head to her toes as she fell hard to the ground. Macy watched in disbelief as Lucy hit the ground, then Macy ran over to her.

"That ain't how it works. Yer 'posed to grab that other tree top, not jist fall."

Lucy had the breath knocked out of her and was only able to say, "Locust."

Macy tried to help Lucy sit up, but she fell back down. "Are ya kilt? Wait right here. I'll go git yer ma!" Macy turned and started running.

Lucy hurt all over from the fall. She tried to sit up but fell backwards and lay there not moving.

After a little time, she began to breath normally. She made herself sit up. Lucy looked down the trail and saw her mother and some other people she didn't know running towards her. "I declare child, what possessed ya to do sich a thing?" her mother asked, as she bent over Lucy.

Lucy rubbed the scratches on her arm, "We's playin' a game called skinnin' cats. Ya jump from one tree ta the next."

Lucy's mother helped her stand, "Playin' a game! Why that's the stupidest thang you've ever done. Ya don't go jumpin' out'a trees. Have ya lost your mind, child?"

"Macy said it was fun. I don't feel so good," Lucy whimpered and tried to put weight on her ankle. It hurt and she quickly lifted it.

Her mother dusted the leaves out of her hair. "I reckon ya don't and ya hurt yerself at harvest time, too. Yer pa's laid up. Yer nanny's on her death bed and ya go and jump out'a tree," her mother shook her head in disbelief.

Macy went over to stand by Lucy. "I'll do her share till she picks up," she told Lucy's mother.

Macy's mother crossed her arms with an angry stare for Macy. "I reckon ya will. I reckon yer pa's a gonna give ya a good whoopin', when he hears 'bout this." She turned to Lucy's mother, "Linny, I'm so sorry. I don't know what gets in ta this child of mine. She's a'las stirrin' up somethin'. I reckon it's that red hair of her'n. I don't know where that come from. My family has blond hair and her pa's got black hair, same as Big."

Macy took one of her braids and began switching it back and forth under her nose. "It weren't my fault, Ma. She was 'posed to grab that other tree. How's I ta know she'd jist jump out and fall?"

Macy's mother held her hand up at Macy, "Hush, now, well talk about it later. " She turned to help Lucy,"Come on Lucy, let's git's ya patched up."

They all helped carry Lucy back and put her to bed. Lucy stayed in bed the rest of the day. Bruised and sore all over, every breath she took caused her pain. She wiggled around until she had a comfortable spot that didn't hurt and she fell asleep.

Macy came to see her as soon as it was light the next morning. She opened the door just a crack and peeped in the room. She smiled big at Lucy. "Hi cuz, how ya feelin'?"

Lucy turned her head away from Macy and didn't answer.

Macy pretended not to notice that Lucy wasn't going to speak to her. "Guess what? Ma's got a letter she needs ta post. I git ta take the rowboat ta Gatlinburg ta post it. Wan't ta come with me? We can go ta Townsend and watch'um run the sawmill and we can go watch'um grind the corn at the mill. Ma says they got's some new shops in the Gatlinburg. It'll be fun and we can make a whole day of it."

"No," Lucy said flatly.

Macy continued talking as if Lucy hadn't said anything, "I mean when yer feelin' better, then we can go. Ya ain't hurt that bad. It won't take ya long to feel better I reckon. That's when we'll go, how's that?

"She didn't give Lucy anytime to reply. Macy shut the door.

Since she couldn't find a place on her body that was not bruised, bitten or scratched, Lucy decided she didn't know if she was going to like Macy or not.

Lucy's stomach started growling so she forced herself to get out of bed and she limped down the hall to the kitchen.

Everyone was out working in the garden and the little cabin was quiet. The only sound came from the fire that crackled in the fireplace.

The smell of breakfast hung in the air. She opened the door of the stove, found a biscuit and a piece of sausage left over from breakfast. She went to the cupboard and found a jar of jelly. She smothered the biscuit in the jelly and sat down in front of the fireplace to eat it. She ate the biscuit and jelly quickly.

She heard her father stir in the next room. She tiptoed over and knocked on his door. "Pa, you awake? Can I come in?"

"Shore honey, I'm awake," she heard him say.

Lucy opened the door a tiny crack and peeped in the room. Her father put down the book he was reading and took his glasses off. He let out a whistle, "I heard ya had an adventure yesterday. Ya shore look like it." He patted the bed for her to come sit down.

Lucy went over to the bed and climbed up beside him. "Ya don't look so good yerself, Pa."

"How do I look?"

"Well, ya look wooly."

Her father laughed, "I reckon I do. I ain't shaved in three days. I reckon I look sickly to ya also, don't I? Tell me about yer adventure."

Lucy picked at a string on his quilt. "It was Macy's fault, she tricked me into jumping out'a tree."

He gave her a knowing look, "Now Lucy, did she really trick ya?"

Lucy looked into his brown eyes and dropped her head, "Well, I guess not. It sounded like fun, I would'a done it too, but one of them dern locust scaret me and I jumped afore I was ready."

Her father laughed, "Want ta know a secret?"

Lucy perked up and answered, "Yes."

"I played that game, the one ya tried and we called it skinnin' cats, too. Blame if I don't know why we called it that," he gave Lucy a wink. "Ya want to know somethin' else? I did the same thing ya did. I jumped out'a that tree and pert near kilt myself."

Lucy asked laughingly, "Yer not just a foolin' me, are ya Pa? Did a locust scare ya too, first time?"

Her father got tickled and told her, "Oh, I was scared. I did jump, but not cause of them locusts. I jumped because yer Uncle Little was a dar'in me to. Yer nanny was very angry at us. If I weren't that banged up, she'd a give me a clout on the head for sure," her Pa laughed as he remembered. He leaned over and whispered in Lucy's ear, "The trick is, ta climb the tree yer a tryin' to skin. It'll bend over slowly when ya git ta the top. If ya jump from another tree like ya did, yer gonna miss and fall ever time."

Lucy let out a little giggle as she replied, "That's what I did."

They both burst out laughing and then her pa got very serious, "But promise me ya won't try that again anytime soon."

Lucy crossed her heart and promised her pa, "No, Pa I won't do that anymore. What ya readin'?"

"I'm readin' the bible, bout when Jesus got lost," her dad replied.

Lucy was instantly interested, "Jesus got lost?"

"He shore did, well now that ain't exactly true. He weren't lost, he knowed exactly where he was and what he was a doin'. His ma and pa, though, they thought he was lost. They were awfully mad at him. On account of they loved him ya see, that made them afraid something had happened to him. He was very close to yer age when that happened. That's why yer ma's mad at ya. She was afraid ya was hurt."

"I never thought of that. I'm still mad at Macy."

Her father patted her on the arm. "I know ya didn't think of that. Ya shouldn't be mad at Macy though, ya had as much a hand in that as she did. Besides, Macy's a tryin' to make up for gettin' ya hurt. Ya make friends with yer cousin and don't be a skinnin' no cats for a while, ok? Go on I need some rest."

Lucy hugged him and started to leave the room. She stopped and turned around. "Ok, Pa, I won't. I'm glad yer feelin' better Pa," Lucy said as she scurried out of the room.

Chapter 3
Learning to Swim

Lucy went to the living room sat down in front of the fireplace. When boredom took her over, she walked over to look out the window. She saw Macy working hard in the corn trying to make amends. Her mother had told her she didn't have to do any work until she felt better. But the more she watched everyone yanking at the ears of corn, the more guilty she felt. She decided she needed to help, even if it was only to carry the baskets from the garden to the barn and empty them in the corn crib. She limped down the hall back to her room, changed her clothes, and went out to join the others.

Macy's face lit up when she saw her, "Hey Lucy, what'cha doin' out'a bed? I thought you's laid up for sure."

Lucy made her way over to the row of corn that Macy was picking. "Oh it ain't that bad. I'll help ya carry the baskets and empty them. It'll make this go faster," Lucy told her cousin.

Macy had filled a basket with corn. She picked up one end and Lucy took hold of the other end. They started carrying it to the corn crib. "We 'bout got the pickin' done. This'll be the worst of it. Next, it's just puttin' stuff up."

Lucy had laid out the drying strings for the beans on the table before she came outside. "I know's it, I got the strings ready for the shucky beans. They's my fav'rite."

Macy looked down the garden to the bean patch. "My brother's 'bout got the beans all picked."

Lucy hobbled along beside Macy. "I seed'um from the winder. It's how's come I went ta gettin' the strings ready."

Macy became very excited. "Ma says I kin go post a letter for her. We can go tommorry if'n ya feel like it."

They emptied the corn and started back. Lucy limped along behind Macy. "I feels alright. Just a little sore. I don't reckon I can make it all the way ta Gatlinburg on this ankle."

Not to be deterred, Macy argued, "Why not? We'll take the rowboat most'a the way down the river, it'll be fun. I ain't never got ta see'um grind the cornmeal and I want to go to the old mill to watch'um work. Sides, we can find us a place ta catch us some big ole cats." Macy paid no attention to Lucy's earlier words.

"I'm afeered of them catfish," Lucy shuddered.

Macy put her basket down and looked at Lucy in amazement. "Yer afeered of ever'thin'. Yer gonna have ta git out of that girl."

Lucy rubbed the welts from yesterday's caterpillar sting. "Well, they got's them big ole whiskers and they stings ya if'n ya git too close. I've been stinged enough. Look here at these packsaddle stings," Lucy showed her arms to Macy.

Macy jerked Lucy's arm and inspected the red welts. "Wheewweee that looks bad, I been a watchin' for them critters. I shorley don't want them stings. Makes me cringe just a thinkin' 'bout it."

"Ma says she'll make me a poultice tonight. I shore hope it helps," Lucy rubbed her arm.

Macy slapped Lucy on the back and said, "That'll fix it and we'll go in the 'morrow ta town and post Ma's letter."

"Well maybe," Lucy consented.

The two of them worked hard at harvesting the corn. Macy's mother looked with pleasure at the work Macy had done. They all made their way back to the cabin to prepare supper. "Linny, I never seed my girl work sa hard. Yer Lucy is good fer her," she nodded at Macy and Lucy who were walking ahead of them.

Lucy's mother nodded in agreement, "Well, Betsy ta tell ya the truth I figured that girl of mine a'stayed in the cabin as long as she'd git away with it. They's good fer each other I reckon. Lucy's been a sayin' maybe her and Macy might be like sisters."

Macy's mother smiled, "Yeah, Macy's a been sayin' the same thing ta me the whole trip up here. We's awful glad we come. What with Nanny bein' sick and all. It'd be just plumb awful we didn't git ta see her afore she passed."

They walked up on the porch and washed the dirt from their hands in the old wash tub. Lucy's mother started the fire in the stove and got the bread dough that had been rising and put it in the oven. "I want ya to know that we's all mighty grateful fer ya. What with Big laid up like he is," she told Macy's mother.

Macy and Lucy huddled around the fireplace playing checkers and listening to their mothers talking.

"Ya reckon Nanny'll last the week?" Macy whispered to Lucy.

Lucy chose the red checkers and began lining them up on the checker board. "Hard ta tell, I've seen her be sick and git better. But, somethin' ain't right this time," Lucy whispered back. "I'm scaret Nanny's gonna die."

Macy arranged her checkers and made the first move. They took turns and in no time Macy jumped two of Lucy's checkers and picked them up off the board. "It's prob'ly why they's sendin' us ta town."

Lucy hadn't thought of that, "Ya think so? Oh I hope not, Macy." Lucy took her turn and moved her checker, not thinking of how she had made the move.

Macy jumped two more of Lucy checkers. "Yep, I reckon it's so's they can git the burial ready."

Lucy stared at the checker board and the few checker pieces she had left on it. Macy laughed at Lucy's bewildered look. "I reckon I've won this game," she bragged.

Supper was ready and put on the table. Everyone ate in silence and after supper they sat around the fire with sad hearts. With thoughts of their sick grandmother, no one wanted to tell stories or laugh.

Macy's mother and father left as soon as supper was over and went to stay at the cabin with Nanny Watson, Macy and Lucy's grandmother.

Macy shared Lucy's room and they knelt down beside the bed to say a prayer for their nanny before going to sleep.

As soon as the sun sent its rays across the ridge, Macy shook Lucy to wake her. "Wake up sleepy head, we best get's goin' if'n we gonna git back afore dark."

Lucy rolled over and pulled the covers up over her head. "I don't think I'm gonna go with ya, I don't feel good."

Macy yanked the covers down. "Ya have ta. I ain't got's no one else ta go with me. Come on now, it'll be fun."

Beginning to be skeptical of Macy's idea of fun, Lucy told her, "I'm just gonna stay here and help with the cannin' and stringin' the shuck beans."

"What do ya want to do that fer? Ye got's ta come with me, Ma says I can't go by myself. Now git up." Macy grabbed the covers and yanked them off the bed.

"Hey, what'd ya do that fer? It's cold in here." Lucy jumped out of bed, grabbed the quilts and threw them back over her.

"Lucy git up! Cause we best be a goin'. Come on, hurry let's go 'afore my brothers git's wind of it. Then, I'll not git's to go," Macy pleaded.

Lucy dragged herself out of bed and dressed as fast as she could. Macy bounced around the room in excitement.

They raced to the kitchen and grabbed some ham and biscuits for their lunch. They put on their coats and started down the trail that led to the boat dock by the Little Pigeon River. As they went along and passed other cabins, they were followed by several children from the mountain.

"Hey Lucy, where ya goin'?" Bob Blaylock and his little brother Jeff came running to them. Bob tripped over his overalls and fell. The hand-me-down clothes were too big and he had a hard time walking. Jeff tripped over Bob and fell on top of him.

Lucy went over and helped them up. She swatted at the leaves and dirt that covered Bob. Jeff and Bob's white hair was a dingy grey from the dust that had settled on their heads. The more Lucy batted at the dirt on their clothes, the more dust came up. She gave up and went back over to Macy. "We's goin' ta post a letter in Gatlinburg," Lucy said proudly.

"Who's that with ya?" Jeff asked her as he peeked around Bob to look at Macy.

Lucy puffed her chest out. "This is my cousin Macy. She's come all the way from Kaintuck," Lucy said as her and Macy turned to continue toward the river.

"We wants ta come with ya," Bob said and they started following them.

The group made their way down the trail. When they came to the Tinker's cabin, Ann Tinker and her two brothers Charles and Ray came running from the house. They stopped at their gate.

"Where ya goin', Lucy?" Ann asked them.

"We's a goin' ta post a letter," Lucy told her but she didn't stop walking trying to keep up with Macy.

They started following Macy and Lucy, also.

Macy looked over her shoulder at the growing group of children. She had never seen anyone that looked exactly alike. She was fascinated by Anne and her brothers. They all had the same brown hair, same brown eyes, and their faces all had freckles.

"We wants ta come. Can we go with ya?" Charles asked.

Lucy stopped and looked at the little group of children that had followed. "I don't know, yer gonna have ta ask my cousin Macy if'n ya can come."

Macy crossed her arms at the little group of five kids. She looked hard at them, "I don't know, can ya be good and do what I says?"

"Oh yeah, we's good at mindin'," Ann spoke up for the group and assured Macy.

Macy nodded to them, "Well, ok I reckon ya can come then."

Macy and Lucy led the way to the Little Pigeon River and the boat dock. There were three paddle boats tied to the dock. Macy untied the rope to one and pulled the boat close to the shore. She motioned for the children. "Ever'body git in the boat," she ordered.

All the children scrambled over the side and settled in the bottom of the boat. Macy pushed off from the bank and set out paddling down the river. She paddled them out to the current and it took the little boat downstream.

"See, I told ya this'ud be fun," Macy laughed with glee.

Lucy held on to the side of the boat with a fierce grip. "This ain't fun fer me, I can'ts swim," she muttered.

Macy put her paddle down and stood up. "Did I hear ya rite? Did ya jist say that ya can't swim? Why that's the dumbest thing I ever her'd. Ever'body needs ta know how ta swim."

"I can't swim either," Bob Blaylock said.

Macy looked from him to Lucy and shook her head in disbelief.

"Me neither," Jeff said.

"Me neither," all three Tinker children said together.

Macy made up her mind she was going to make them learn to swim. "Well now, I'll jist tell ya, it's 'bout time ya learned," Macy grabbed each one of the children one at a time. Starting with Lucy, she threw them in the river. "Swim'er drown whichever one ya wants!" she yelled out at them.

Lucy panicked as soon as she hit the icy water. "Help, ayeee it's cold! Help!" she splashed and yelled.

All the children began screaming, "Help I can't swim! It's cold, Macy, help us out!"

Macy began to think that throwing the children in the water wasn't such a good idea. She watched in horror as the little boat moved with the current, she paddled furiously trying to make it back to the children splashing in the river.

"Ya 'fraidy cats, grab a hold of a fist of water and pulls it to ya," she reached her arms out and pulled them back to show them how. "Like this."

"Help! Help!" they all yelled louder swallowing mouthfuls of water and splashing in the cold water.

Macy began to become very scared and she yelled, "I can't the water's too swift. It's a pullin' me downstream!" She began paddling as fast as she could, but the current pulled her farther away from them.

Macy's brothers, Louis and Jack, came along trying to catch up with Macy. They wanted to send her after some sugar and yeast. From the hill, they saw all the commotion in the water and heard the cries for help. They started running to the river bank. They burst into the clearing at the dock and saw all the turmoil in the water.

"What in the world has come over ya young'uns. It's too cold ta be a swimmin'. Git out'a that water right now!" Louis shouted to them.

When she heard his voice, Macy looked up. She saw Louis and she thought that he was her pa. Relieved, she stopped paddling. She looked again and saw Jack, she recognized that it was her brothers and not her pa. She started paddling again trying to reach the splashing children.

Louis and Jack were two years apart but they looked like twins. From a distance, it was hard to tell them apart. They had all the features of the Watsons. They were tall and skinny with black hair and blue eyes.

Lucy screamed, "Macy throwed us in, help we can't swim. Heeeellllppppp!"

Realizing what was happening, Louis and Jack both jumped in the river to save the children. They fished Lucy and all the other kids coughing, sputtering, and shivering out of the river.

As soon as they helped them to the bank, all of the children that had followed Macy and Lucy started running for home.

"I'm gonna tell my pa on ya, Lucy Watson," Bob warned her.

"I weren't the one ta throw ya in, I'm near drowned myself," Lucy hollered back at him.

"I don't care, I'm a gonna tell. I hopes ya both git a good lickin' fer this," Bob yelled back over his shoulder. He ran for home, with all the other children running close behind.

Macy managed to paddle the boat over to the bank downstream. She tied the boat to a tree and came running to where her brothers and Lucy stood on the bank. Louis scowled at her as she came running to them, "I swear Macy, what's ya gonna do, let them there kids all drown? Yer cousin Lucy, too. Why she's a gonna think yer a heathern."

"I most already do, she's tried ta kilt me twice, now," Lucy said through shivering teeth.

Macy shrugged her shoulders and held her palms out. "I was just a tryin' ta teach'um ta swim, on account a they said they didn't know how. Ya know yerself ever'body needs ta know how ta swim," she turned to Lucy. "If'n ya'd a listened ta me you'd be a swimmin' rite now," Macy shook her finger at Lucy.

Lucy jumped up and started running for home. "If'n I'd a listened ta me, I'd a not come with ya. I don't thinks I will next time," she yelled back at Macy.

Louis held out his hand to Macy and demanded, "Give me that there letter. I'll be a takin' it ta town myself. Yer gonna have ta go back with Lucy and 'splain what ya did."

"I reckon if Pa don't whup ya this time, I will," Jack told her.

Macy gave her brothers a warning stare. "Ya try it and see what ya git, Jack Watson. Ya don't want ta git me on yer bad side I reckon," Macy challenged him.

Lucy ran shivering back up the little dirt road to her warm home. Macy followed a short distance behind her, not saying a word. She practiced what she would say to explain.

Her thoughts turned to fishing for a catfish and halfway to the cabin Macy wasn't able to stand it anymore, "Slow down will ya Lucy? I got an idea. I thinks we needs ta go fishin' tomorry. I seed a big ole cat whils't ya was a tryin' ta swim. I'm bound ta catch him."

"Oh, Macy, hush up. I don't want ta talk with ya no more the rest of the night. I weren't a tryin' ta swim I was a drownin'," Lucy said and she ran the rest of the way home. She busted in the door ran over to the fireplace.

Lucy's mother dropped the bowl of beans she was stringing. "Land sakes, Child, what'cha a doin' all wet? Did the boat turn ya out?" her mother grabbed a blanket and wrapped it around her., "Let's git these wet clothes off afore ya catch yer death of cold."

Lucy's teeth chattered. "It was Macy, she throwed me out'a the boat."

Macy's mother jumped up and asked, "WHAT? How come she done that? I swear that child of mine is gonna be the death of me." Macy's mother's face became flushed with anger.

Macy came dragging into the cabin. Her mother snatched her by the arm. "Macy Watson, what is wrong with ya girl. Are ya tryin' ta kill yer cousin?"

Macy trudged over to the fireplace. "No, I ain't a tryin' ta kill her. She says she can't swim and I was a gonna teach her."

Macy's mother became furious. "I can't believe ya threw her out of the boat, and it as cold as it is. I swear ya don't use yer head for nothin' do ya? I think yer past due a good lickin'. Go outside and pick me a switch. Mind ya now, git a good one or else I'll git one and ya don't want me ta do that," she warned.

Lucy heard her father laughing from the next room. She didn't care if Macy did get a switching. Her mother handed her a hot cup of coffee and it made her feel a tiny bit better after she drank some.

They dried Lucy off and her mother sent her to her room. "Back ta bed with ya, Lucy. Mind me now, stay in that bed. Yer gonna be sick with a fever I'm afeered."

"Ok, Ma." Lucy was cold and hungry, but too tired to stay up any longer. She slept the rest of the evening and when she woke up, the room had become dark.

Macy opened the door and came in, carrying a lantern and a plate of food for Lucy. "Ya missed supper, yer ma says fer me ta bring ya this here plate."

Lucy's stomach grumbled with hunger, but still furious with Macy, she refused to eat anything. "I'm not hungry, take it back."

Macy sat the tray on the bed beside Lucy. "Ma says fer me ta tell ya I'm sorry. She give me a good lickin' with that switch. Look fer yer'self." Macy dropped her overalls for Lucy to see where she had been striped.

Lucy looked at the red stripes on Macy's legs and she felt sorry for her. "Oh that looks like it hurt, she got ya good, didn't she?"

Macy buttoned her overalls back over her shoulder. "Naah, not too bad, the trick is find a keen limb, one that ain't too flimsy. Them skinny'uns hurt worse than them that got some strength to'em. Them skinny'uns are like whips. Besides, if ya dance around and yell, they don't stripe ya as hard."

Lucy giggled. She had been sent after her own switch many times and knew what Macy was talking about.

Macy sat down on the bed beside Lucy. She felt bad about what had happened. "Lucy, I'm sorry, I wants us ta be friends. I don't know what gets in'ta me sometimes. I don't mean no harm, it jist turns out that way."

Lucy's anger at Macy began to subside and she decided to forgive Macy. "It's alright, I 'cepts yer apology. We'll start afresh in the mornin'. How's that?"

Macy's face lit up and she smiled at Lucy, "I been thinkin' 'bout that. Let's go fishin' and catch some big cats fer supper. Ever'body'll like that."

Lucy didn't know if she wanted another adventure with Macy. "I'll think 'bout it Macy. I thinks I can maybe eat some now," Lucy grinned at her.

"Yeah, good. Here ya go. We'll git an early start in the mornin'," Macy smiled and placed the tray of food on Lucy's lap.

Chapter 4
Fishing

Macy awoke before the sun started rising across the ridge. She rolled out of bed and fumbled about in the dark room looking for the matches. She found them after a few minutes and lit the lamp. She made a lot of noise while she changed into her overalls. She was trying to wake Lucy.

She tried to brush her wild hair enough to braid it. After she finished braiding her hair, she banged the hair brush on the dresser. When that didn't wake her, Macy started shaking Lucy. "Hey get's up. It's time fer fishin'. We got's worms ta dig."

Lucy struggled to awaken. "Oh Macy, let's jist stay in bed a little while longer, 'sides the grounds likely froze. It'll be hard ta dig worms," Lucy tried to discourage her. She didn't want to get out of their warm bed.

Macy kept pestering Lucy, "Come on, I seed a good place fer'um under the hen house. They's a big ole rock there. I bet'cha them night crawlers are a plenty there. Hurry now, git dressed. Times a wastin'. I can't wait ta catch that big ole granddaddy catfish." Macy rubbed her hands together.

Lucy dragged herself out of bed and dressed in her old work clothes. Macy fidgeted, trying to get her to hurry. After she changed, Lucy found her coat and shoes and carried them to the door with her. "I'm ready, They's a ole coffee can in the barn, we use for scoopin' the feed. We can use it ta carry the worms and I know's where we can git some cane poles. They's a big patch of cane on the way to the river. But, ya got ta promise me I won't have ta touch them whiskers or no parts of them catfish we catch or else I ain't a goin'."

"I promise," Macy crossed her heart with her finger and held it up. "Cross my heart and hope's ta die."

"Okay, then I'll go with ya," Lucy consented.

They took a lantern and started to the barn before the sun began to rise. Lucy retrieved the coffee can from the feed barrel and showed it to Macy. "This'll work won't it?" she asked Macy.

Macy inspected the can for holes. "Yep, they ain't no holes in it fer them worms ta sneak out of," Macy nodded her approval.

They carried the lantern around to the hen house to dig for worms. They turned over a big rock and started digging in the frozen ground. It took a few minutes to dig deep enough to find the worms.

"Wheeweee, would ya look at them fat ones," Macy squealed and handed Lucy the coffee can. "If'n I'm gonna touch the fish, ya have ta carry the worm can, and the poles. That's only fair."

Lucy held the lantern so she could get a good look at the worms trying to get back in the ground. "I don't like them squirmy worms. It's yer idea, yer gonna have ta get'em."

Macy pushed the can back at Lucy. "Fair is fair, I get's the fish ya get's the worms."

Lucy took one look at Macy's frown and realized she wasn't going to talk Macy into getting the worms. She put the can down and went to the shed, she came back with a trowel. "This ort'ta do it. We can dig'em up with this. That way we'll not have ta touch'um," Lucy began digging again. She dug up a lot of the dirt with the worms in it. Lucy paused her digging, she had thought of something else to tell Macy, "I'll carry the worms but I ain't a baitin' no hooks with'em. I ain't a goin' if I has ta do that."

Macy watched as Lucy scooped the dirt and worms into the can. "Well, I guess that's fair, ya can carry ever'thin'. I'll bait the hook and take the fish off."

Lucy stopped, looked up at Macy and warned her, "I ain'ts a skinnin' none of them fish neither."

Macy gave Lucy a wink, "We'll let my brothers do that. They's good at that."

Lucy inspected the can of worms. "I reckon I got a whole can full of these worms this ort'ta be enough."

They picked up the can of worms and the lantern and started down the trail back to the river. Lucy and Macy stopped at the patch of cane that Lucy had told Macy about. They pushed their way through the cane and briars searching for the right stalk to use for their fishing pole. They chose the tallest one in the patch for their pole. Macy took her knife out of her pocket and cut it down. "Ya wants me ta find ya one too?"

Lucy turned and started walking for the river. "No, I'm just gonna watch ya catch'em. I'm carryin' the trappins."

They reached the river as the sun cast its light through the valley. The light reflected on the water, turning it to a golden color. The swift and rushing water drowned out all the other sounds of the mountains.

Macy looked at the sunlight reflecting on the river. She shook her head and shouted over the roaring of the water, "This won't do, it just won't do a'tall."

"What Macy? What's wrong?" Lucy stared at her with a puzzled look.

Macy looked up and pointed to the sky. "The sun, he's a makin' shadows from this side. Pa says if'n we can see'um, so can the fish. We'll have ta go under the bridge and across ta the other side."

"Looks mighty swift, we'll have ta be careful else we'll fall in," Lucy eyed the water remembering how cold it was.

"Jist foller me, and step wheres I steps." Macy began leading the way across the river, jumping from rock to rock.

Lucy tried to step exactly where Macy was stepping. She lost her balance and made a giant leap from one rock to the other, when swhoosh, she lost her footing on the slick slimy rocks and fell in. She came up sputtering water and gasping for breath.

The current began sweeping her downstream. She panicked and started hollering for help, "Macy, I've fell in again! Here help me out!" She reached her hand toward Macy, but the current swept her farther downstream. She managed to grab a limb and hang on. "It's more cold than it was yisterdy. I've hurt my backside. I'm gonna have ta go back home. Git me out of here!" she wailed.

Macy threw her fishing pole down and ran down the bank to catch up with Lucy. She waded out to where Lucy clung to the limb and pulled her out of the water. "Ya ain't hurt none, are ya? Are ya alright?" She didn't give Lucy time to answer. Macy grasped Lucy by the arm and started dragging her to the other side of the river. "Jist ya sit over yonder on a rock and the sun'll warm ya directly. I jist know I'm gonna catch that big ole granddaddy catfish today."

Lucy sloshed her way over to the rock Macy was pointing to. "Oh Macy, I'm cold and I've hurt my foot, too. I can't stand on it, yer gonna have ta help me home," Lucy whimpered.

Macy tied a piece of twine around her pole, fastened the hook, and baited a worm on it. She threw the worm in the river. "I will, I will. Just let me git one throw in, alright?"

Lucy took off her shoes and rung the water out of her socks. She sat there shivering, "Ok, but jist one throw, I've done scaret all the fish when I fell in anyways. Ya ain't a gonna catch nothin', now. 'Sides I've drowned the worms anyhow."

Macy pulled her line out of the water and ran over to where Lucy was sitting. "Oh no, let me see. Maybe I can save a few of'um." Macy grabbed the can from Lucy and looked to see if there were any worms to salvage. "I think's they's 'bout three or four in here still yit."

Lucy started shivering violently from the cold, she pulled on her wet socks and shoes. "Well hurry, I think I'm 'bout ta faint."

Macy determined in her mind that the catfish needed to be caught. She picked up her pole and tossed the line back in the river. She sat down beside Lucy to wait for the fish to bite. "It won't be long now. Them fish'll be hungry this mornin'."

Out of nowhere, a big rock came sailing off the bridge and splashed water all over them.

Macy jumped up. "Hey, who done that?" she hollered up to the bridge.

No one answered.

She sat back down. "Reckon they's anybody up there on the bridge?" Macy asked Lucy.

Lucy looked up to the bridge. "I don't see nobody."

Macy pulled her line in and the worm was gone. "Would ya look at that. That sly ole fish done stole my bait," she said as she fixed another worm on the hook and tossed it back in.

She sat back down beside Lucy. "I think I feel him a tuggin' at the line."

Another rock came sailing down and wet them again.

Macy stood and backed up trying to see where the rocks were coming from, "I know's they's someone up there. Ya might as well show yerself," Macy yelled up at the bridge.

John Taylor had been watching the girls. He doubled over laughing.

He thought it was the funniest thing he had ever seen, Lucy falling in the river and Macy trying to fish. He wasn't able to resist throwing the rocks at them. He stood up to let them see him. "John Taylor is who it is, and if'n I throw rocks, what'cha gonna do about it?" he challenged Macy.

"Who's John Taylor?" Macy asked Lucy.

Lucy whispered to Macy. "He's the mill owner's boy. And he's mean as all git out. Better leave him alone," she warned.

Macy looked up at John. "He's the one better leave me alone. He throws another rock down here and he's gonna regrit it," she whispered back to Lucy. She yelled up at John, "Throw 'nother rock down here and I'm comin' up there ta throw ya off'n that bridge."

Macy fixed her hook with the last worm and threw her line back in the water.

John searched around for the biggest rock he could find. He sent it sailing over the side of the bridge.

This rock made a tremendous splash and water soaked both girls. Macy threw her cane pole down. "That done it, yer gonna git it now!" she yelled up at John. She ran across the river and up the bridge. But, John was ready for her. When Macy made it to where he stood, he picked her up and threw her off the bridge. Macy's body hit the river with a loud splash.

Macy came up out of the water choking and shivering from the cold. "Oohhhh this is cold!" she exclaimed.

Lucy hobbled over to help Macy out of the river. "I told ya, it were cold. I reckon you'll go home now, huh?"

Macy stood in the river soaking wet and shaking all over. She was very angry, but she didn't want to get thrown off the bridge again. "I reckon we better afore we both catch our death from the cold water. Come on, Lucy I'll help ya home," she vowed to get even with that boy though, if it was the last thing she done.

Macy helped Lucy limp back to the cabin. They were both soaking wet and dripping water the whole way home.

When they opened the door and came inside, their mothers looked at each other. "I ain't even gonna ask," Lucy's mother said to Macy's mother.

Macy and Lucy dried off with blankets and wrapped quilts around themselves. They spent the rest of the day by the fire sipping hot coffee. Macy schemed what she needed to do to get even with that boy.

Chapter 5
Mourning

Lucy and Macy worked hard alongside their parents preparing the harvested vegetables for the upcoming winter. Everyone had their job to do in the preparations.

Both of their brothers took charge of getting the sweet potatoes and regular potatoes in the bins in the cellar. The girls spent the days boiling the jars of beans and corn to can, while their mothers made jams and butters from fresh picked fruit. They watched the smoke from the canning fire curl up in the air mixing with the clouds.

"I shore like the smell of apple butter a cookin'," Lucy said as she sniffed the air.

Macy added another piece of wood to the fire under the pot. "Me too, I don't know why they stuck us here with the green beans."

"What I hate most is fixin' the kraut. Sheewweee, I don't like the smell of kraut and greens a cookin'," Lucy commented as she wrinkled her nose.

"Yes, and it attracts them dern green flies, too," Macy told Lucy. She had a big fly swatter knocking it at the flies when they came buzzing around. "Ya'd think them flies'ud be dead by now it's been so cold at night."

Lucy batted at a fly. "I know, but just as soon as it warms up in the day, here they come."

"I wish they'd hurry up and freeze. They's a tryin' ta ruin all this food," Macy said. Then, she swatted at another fly.

Lucy picked up a stick of wood and threw it in the fire. "I like the pickled corn, but I reckon my fav'rite is the shucky beans. It's fun ta sit around the fire and string'em. Nanny used ta tell the best stories. While we fixed'um," Lucy said with sadness in her voice.

"Nanny ain't a doin' sa good. I peeked around the door yes'terdy and she was a just layin' there." With very sad eyes, Macy told Lucy. "I heard Ma and Pa a talkin'. They says it can't be long now 'till the Lord be a callin' her home."

Tears welled up in Lucy's eyes at Macy's prediction. She wiped them with her shirt sleeve.

Lucy's mother came out to make sure they were keeping the fire hot enough to boil the beans and corn they were canning. "Why the long faces, girls?" she asked them.

"We's sad for Nanny," Lucy replied.

Lucy's mother checked the jars, the water was bubbling and the jars were beginning to seal. "I know, but we cry's for us when we lose our loved ones. They's rejoicin' in heaven soon as they take's their last breath. Nanny's real sick and she ain't got no kind of life now," Lucy's mom tried to console the girls.

"Macy say's it wouldn't be long now 'till she dies," said Lucy as the tears came streaming down her face.

"Well now, we don't know that, it's up to the good Lord for all of us. We'll just pray and we have ta 'cepts what he decides." She started back to the house to check the apple butter she was cooking. "I think these jars are ready to come out'a the water. Ya girls start carryin' them in the house and set them on the kitchen table," she told them and went back inside the cabin.

Macy and Lucy had a set of tongs they used to lift the hot jars out of the water and put them in a washtub. When it was full, they carried it to the house and sat the jars on the table. They made four trips back and forth to get all the jars out of the boiling water and into the house. They set up the checker board by the fireplace and listened as the jars sealed themselves with a pop as they cooled.

As usual, Macy won all the checker games they played before they went to bed.

The next morning, Lucy and Macy knew something was wrong as soon as they awoke. The normally busy house seemed subdued, visitors milled about in the kitchen and on the porch. A hushed quietness that could be felt, hung in the air.

Up this time first, Lucy shook Macy, "Macy, are ya awake?"

Macy rolled over, "I am now. What is it?"

Lucy tiptoed to the door of her bedroom and opened it. "Somethin's wrong, too many folks 'round about."

Macy stumbled out of bed and started changing from her night clothes into her work clothes. "Are they a bringin' food?" she asked as she pulled on her shoes.

Lucy peeked down the hallway, "I think so, I see the preacher and his wife, too."

Macy went to the door, "Oh no, I'd say it's Nanny, I'd say she's passed. Come on let's go see."

They tiptoed their way down the hall to the kitchen.

As soon as they came into the kitchen, Lucy saw that her mother had been crying. She went over and knelt down beside her, "Ma, what's wrong?"

Lucy's mother wiped her eyes and sniffed. "It's your nanny child, the Lord's called her home and she's passed on," she told them.

"Aunt Linny, where's Ma and Pa?" Macy asked.

Lucy's mother stood up and went to the stove. "They's went to the cemetery to see about the burrin'. They'll be back directly. We gots a lot of folks ta greet today, so ya girls be on ya best behavior, alright?"

Lucy took Macy by the hand and they started for the porch. "We will, Ma, we'll just go out back and sit on the porch," she promised.

Lucy's Mother wiped her eyes again. "That's good, Lucy, they's gonna be a lot of people here today and I'll need ya and Macy to help watch the little young'uns so's the grown-ups can visit with us."

Lucy and Macy nodded to her. They trudged with heavy steps out to the back porch and sat down on the steps. They were both crying for their Grandmother.

The visitors that came to show respect brought their whole family with them. They went into the cabin and left the children to play in the yard. Macy watched the children as they were running and laughing.

She wiped her face and the more she watched the children, the angrier she got. "This is making me mad!" she shouted.

Lucy jumped, "What Macy? What's a makin' ya mad?"

Macy pointed to the children. "Watch them young'uns, they ain't got no respect. No respect a'tall. Nanny a layin' there in the parlor dead," Macy turned around and pointed to the cabin.

Lucy wiped her eyes and looked at the children who were running and playing games. "They's just little Macy, they don't know what they'er a doin'."

"Well it's 'bout time they did." Macy jumped up and ran over to the group of children. "Ain't ya got no respect for the dead?" she shouted at them. "My Nanny's a layin' in there dead and yer out here a makin' light of it runnin' and playin'."

The children stopped and stared at Macy. "We didn't know, we don't mean no harm," Charles Tinker said. He dropped his head and kicked at the ground. He dusted the dirt off his pants and didn't look up at Macy.

Macy jerked him by the arm. "Well, it's 'bout time ya learned some manners. Now, what we're a gonna do is show ya how to respect and mourn somebody's passin'. Come here and line up," Macy pointed to the door. She arranged all the children and lined them up, from the tallest to the smallest.

Macy crossed her arms and turned to the group of children she had lined up, "We's gonna mourn Nanny. What we're gonna do is, go in that parlor and each and ever one of ya is goin' ta cry and mourn real loud. We're gonna march around that death bed and show's some respect. Or else that ole hairy man named Lucas Makukus is bound ta come and git ya."

"Who' s Lucas Makukus?" one of the children asked.

Macy bent down and whispered as if she were afraid to be heard, "He's a big ole hairy man, lives in the caves and he comes ta git little mean girls and boys that don't show respects." She made a scared face and looked around expecting the buger man to emerge from the mountain.

Scared for real, now all of the children started crying.

"Now ya follow me, and ya do what I does," Macy commanded as she led the way.

The children were scared to go in to where the casket was, but they were more afraid of Macy and Lucas Mackukus. They kept the line straight and silently filed into the parlor. The screen door made an eerie creak as each child passed through. It shut with a bang and all the children jumped.

Macy was first in the room. The room had been cleared of all the furniture and chairs were placed around the walls for the mourners. The pine casket had been placed on a table in the middle of the room. The lid now remained closed. Macy walked over to it and lifted the lid. She looked down at her grandmother and she crossed her arms over her chest. The house was quiet and the boards on the floor made a loud creak as the children walked over them. The sun slanted through the window and illuminated dust particles floating in the air.

Macy turned to the line of children and instructed, "Now cross yer arms and ya begins yer cryin' and mornin'."

Lucy brought up the back of the line. She became afraid as any of the children. She crossed her arms in solemn silence.

Macy made them all march in a single file around the casket seven times. Each time they marched around, the floor creaked and popped. The children became more frightened and cried louder. When the crying became very loud sobs, the adults came into the parlor to see what all the commotion was about.

Lucy's mother came into the room first. She looked at the children marching around the casket and sobbing. "What in the world is a goin' on here?" Lucy's mother demanded.

The children jumped and turned their frightened eyes in her direction.

Lucy spoke up, "Macy is a showin' these youg'uns 'bout respect to the ones that have passed. We's a mournin' Nanny and all these here young'uns is a helpin' us."

Lucy's mother put her hands on her hips and walked over to the door. She opened the door and pointed to it. "I never heered such a racket. Ya git's outside now and stop all this nonsense."

All the children made a mad dash for the door and to their parents. There was no playing and laughing now, only frightened sobs. The children could not be consoled and one by one their parents took them home.

Chapter 6
Ghost Stories

The next day the funeral procession made its way in a slow march from the Watson's cabin to the White Oak Cemetery in Roaring Fork.

Big and Little Watson led the way with their mother's casket. They placed the casket on a wagon that was being pulled by a mule. Lucy's father had regained most of his strength, but he still needed a homemade crutch to help him walk.

All of the people that lived on the mountain came to show their respect and share their sorrow for Mrs. Wartson. She was called Nanny Watson and was loved by the all. These folks walked behind the wagon.

A screech owl hollered as the mourners walked by disturbing it's sleep. The sound gave chills to the mourners and they walked faster.

A grave side service started with the preacher's wife singing Amazing Grace, tears flowed from already red eyes. The preacher had a short message, words of comfort to the family. The group of mourners listened in silence. Everyone stayed with Big and Little Watson until the grave was covered and the flowers placed on the mound of dirt.

For the next week, neighbors stopped by with food and sympathy. The visits sometimes lasted long into the night.

Lucy and her cousin loved to sit and listen to the memories people shared of their grandmother. One evening, as they sat around the fireplace, Big and Little Watson began telling stories about their mother.

"Ya know, Ma used ta tell us 'bout a ghost she seed one time," Big, Lucy's father, said to all the children that were there.

Lucy's mother frowned and made a huffing sound. "Oh now, ya know yer ma never believed in ghosts," she told him.

Lucy's father nodded his head. "Well, I know's she saw a spirit or ghost or somethin'. For she told us lots of times 'bout it. Didn't she, Little?" he asked his brother.

Macy's father put down his whittling stick and took a drink of coffee. "She shore did and it sent chills down to my toes ever time," he said. Then, he picked up the stick of wood and began peeling off the shavings.

Lucy's Mother huffed again. "Ya know yer ma thought it were prob'ly an angel, that's what she told me. Ya know's 'bout angels unaware," she scolded him.

"Well, she never told us it was an angel," Little, Macy's father answered her.

Macy became fascinated, "Ya never did tell us that'n Pa. Tell it to us."

He began whittling again and started the story. "Well now, as I recollect, she says when she's a little girl they's was a comin' home from church." He lowered his voice and leaned forward, adding, "The night was jist 'bout like this. The mountains were full a mist. It were dark like only these mountains can be. Ma said they was walkin' 'long and all the sudden, the night birds go quiet and stopped their singin'. They look's up, and ahead in the road, jist out a nowhere, they's an old woman a standin' in the road. They didn't know where she come from. She was jist there."

Lucy and Macy held their breath and leaned in a little closer to hear the story.

Lucy's father picked up the story. He talked in a hushed voice, "Ma say's, her ma tried to speak to the old woman, but she never turned 'round. Jist went ta walkin' across in their path back and forth, back and forth. She was a keepin'em from goin' 'round her. They didn't hear her footsteps ner nothin'. Jist a quiet whisper goin' back and forth."

He paused to take a drink of his coffee and then continued, "She say's her ma say's 'how'dy do? Where ya a goin'?' to the old woman. But, she never says a word, jist walkin' back and forth, in the road not a lettin'em pass." Then he nodded to his brother Little.

Macy's father took his turn telling the story. In a low whisper he said, "So, all of'um get's mighty skeered; they decide's maybe they should go back. They turn's 'round to leave. As soon as they turn's 'round to go back to the church, they looked back and that old woman was gone. They think's maybe, they's jist a seein' things. They decide's to start for home. When they turn's 'round to go on up the road, there she is again a goin' back and forth across the road in front of them.

Them whip'o'will's go ta hollerin' and they heered the screech owls. I reckon they git's real skeered when them night birds starts a hollerin'." When he finishes speaking, he nodded to Lucy's father.

Lucy's father looked around to make sure he had everyone's attention, "Yer nanny say's they get's real skeered, they turns 'round and goes back to the church and they don't look back this time. They come's ta find out the next day, that jist up ahead in their path, they's a man drunk on corn liquor. He's a shootin' at ever'thin' that comes along. They'd a been kilt for sure, if they'd gone any further up that road."

The girls sat with big eyes listening to the story. "Is that true, Pa?" Macy asked.

He stopped his whittling and replied, "It is fer a fact."

Lucy's mother snorted, "I say's, that proves it were an angel, not no ghost or spirit. Ain't no ghost a gonna help protect nobody. Now if'n ya girls want's ta, ya can build a fire tonight and roast some chestnuts and pop some popcorn. This being Sat'rday, we's prob'ly gonna have a lot of company," she said this to Macy and Lucy, after seeing the fear in their eyes. She tried to take their minds off of the story.

Macy jumped up and said, "Hey that'll be fun! Let's go git some chestnuts." Then, she pulled Lucy to her feet and they ran to get their coats. Macy snatched their coats out of the closet then she dragged Lucy outside.

Frightened by the ghost story, Lucy stopped on the porch to look around. Dusk started to settle in the mountain and the mist was thicker this evening. "Where we gonna git chestnuts 'round here Macy?" she asked. Every time Macy said FUN, Lucy got weary. She put on her scarf and gloves. Her breath showed in the cool evening air.

Macy jumped off the porch and started down the path that led to Roaring Fork. "I seed some on the way from the grave site," she said excitedly.

Lucy saw the direction Macy was headed. She picked up an old bucket from the porch and just started shaking her head. A whip'o'will started singing, and the hair on the back of Lucy's neck stood up. "I know's the one's yer a talkin' 'bout and I don't want nothin' ta do with that. Ole spinster Bevins she's mean and I ain't a goin' in her yard," Lucy stammered.

Macy ran back over and tugged at Lucy. "Who's spinster Bevins? We don't have ta go in her yard. I seed lot's of'um 'cross the fence we can gather up. Come on, we got's ta git's some for all them kids a comin' here tonight," Macy told Lucy.

Lucy didn't want to go, but she went with Macy in spite of her reservations. The sun began sinking when they started; it had almost set by the time they got to Spinster Bevins' house. They started gathering up the chestnuts that lay all around in the road and putting them in their bucket.

Macy picked one up, nodded her head and stated, "Look here, these ole chestnuts are scrawny and got worms in'um. Look at'm in the yard there. They's jist fell from the tree and are real fresh. Let's climb this fence and git's the one's over there."

Lucy's eyes flew open wide and she shook her head no. "Ya climb over there if'n ya want's to, Macy, but I'm jist stayin' on this side."

Macy looked over the fence and pointed at the chestnuts in the yard. "I have ta have some help. Yer gonna have ta go over the fence and throw'em to me and I'll catch'em as ya do. Jist look at them fat ones, jist layin' there ta rot. Hurry now, it's almost dark and I didn't bring a lantern."

Lucy looked at the chestnuts laying all around in the yard. "I hate they's a gonna rot, Pa says it's a shame, she don't eat'em. Then in the spring, she has them little trees pulled up and burned. I'd shore like ta have one of them little saplin's," Lucy replied as she eyed the chestnuts again that lay all around that tree.

Macy knew she had Lucy hooked. "Well, ya need ta climb over the fence and help me get'em." Macy looked toward the house and assured Lucy, "I don't see her, likely as not, she's in the bed by now and we can be real quiet."

Lucy started climbing over the fence. "Alright, but we'll have ta hurry afore she see's us."

Lucy climbed the wood fence, then jumped from the top and landed in the grass. She started throwing the chestnuts over the fence as fast as she could. Macy picked them up from the ground.

The front door of the house busted open. "Who's that out there in my yard?" Ms. Bevins hollered. "I sees ya John Taylor. I'm gonna come give ya a lickin', I don't know how many times I've caught ya stealin' from me!" she yelled. Then, she saw Lucy in her yard. When she saw Macy in her overalls on the other side of the fence, she thought it was a group of the boys come to pester her.

Lucy's heart leapt up in her throat. She dropped the chestnuts she had in her hands and ran for the fence. As she jumped over the fence, her dress became caught on the top. It tore with a loud rip, but not all the way so she was stuck on the fence. "Help, Macy, I've got my dress caught!"

"That's what I'm a tellin' ya 'bout wearin' overalls and not dresses," Macy whispered back to her and yanked her off the fence.

They grabbed their bucket and took off running up the road as fast as their legs would go. Macy stumbled over a limb and Lucy ran into her. They both fell down.

"I'll be a tellin' your pa for that, ya scalawags. Ya stay off'n my property," Ms. Bevins yelled and shook her fist at them.

Macy jumped up and grabbed her cousin by the arm. They ran until they were out of sight and stopped to catch their breath. "That ole biddy, she's that mean! Someone's a needin' ta teach her a lesson!" Macy exclaimed as she stuck her tongue out in the direction of Ms. Bevins' house.

Lucy shook her head and uttered, "Yeah, I know's it. But, she hates ever'body. All she does is take that store-bought mop and clean that porch of hers."

Macy had an idea and stated, "Hey, it's time for trick or treat. We ought'ta put some cuckle burrs in her mop fer her. That'd teach her."

Lucy giggled, "Oh Macy, that'd be so funny. But, Ma and Pa don't believe in trick or treat. I'd git in trouble shore and I ain't a goin' back there noways!"

Macy stopped suddenly and Lucy ran into her. "I am," she declared. We got's chestnuts over that fence ta gather. Come on let's go," Macy grabbed Lucy and dragged her back with her.

They found a patch of burrs beside the dirt road on the way back to Ms. Bevins' place. They gathered two handfuls of burrs and started giggling. They put them in the bucket and sneaked back to Spinster Bevins' house.

Lucy refused to go back over the fence. Macy gave up and went over it by herself.

Lucy gathered the chestnuts they had thrown over the fence from before. She scrambled to pick up the new ones. Macy sneaked over to the porch. She found Ms. Bevins' mop and scrunched all those burrs in it. They were still snickering as they ran back up the road.

They laughed and giggled all the way home. When they reached the cabin, they saw a huge fire blazing in the middle of the yard. They took their place in the circle of children that had gathered by the fire. Lucy's mother had started the popcorn. Lucy and Macy put the chestnuts in a pan and set them in the fire.

The fire cracked and popped as sparks shot up in the night sky. The light made shadows behind the story tellers and illuminated their faces with an orange glow.

"Been fishin' lately?"

Macy looked across the fire and there sat John Taylor. She shot him a dirty look but didn't say anything to him. There was a ghost story being told.

"And they say that ole man still runs the mountains at night to this day, but he's in the shape of a big black varmit a some kind. Nobody knows quite what it is," Helen Blaylock finished her story. All of the children gasped in horror.

Helen's brother Tom leaned forward and added to the tale, "They say they's people's kin, that can turn's theys'self inta other critters certain times a year."

Sam Creech wiped his sweating hands on his overalls and started another story, "I heered a panther scream once, sounded like a baby a cryin' and next it sounded like a woman a screamin'. My pa says they's a ghost down by the big rock, down by the big rock. It's a man that was kilt a tryin' ta find his sweetheart. Ta find his sweetheart. They say's he goes back and forth across that rock a lookin' fer her. A lookin' fer her.

That's why they call's it the haunted rock. Haunted rock."

"What's a the matter with him?" Macy whispered to Lucy.

"What ya mean?" Lucy whispered back.

"He says everthin' twice," Macy softly said.

"I don't know, he's a'las done that," Lucy alleged.

"That's kind a funny, the way he does that," Macy whispered.

"Yeah, I guess it is. I jist never paid it no mind, he's a'las done that," Lucy told her.

"I'm skeered," one of the little children whimpered and started to cry.

Macy's brothers sat on the porch watching the children at the bonfire. "Listen to them kids a tellin' them scary tales," Louis said to Jack.

"Yeah, they's a skeerin' themselves silly," Jack scuffed his boot on the porch. "I think's we ort'ta give'um somethin' ta be skeered of."

Louis looked at the group of kids sitting around the fire. "How we gonna do that?"

Jack grinned at Louis and replied, "Let's git's some feed sacks and put over our heads, and git's some hay and stick it out of them sacks and 'round our shirt sleeves. Then, let's sneak up on'um."

"That'll scare'um silly," Louis said with a chuckle.

They snuck out to the barn and stuffed hay in their shirts. They put the feed sacks over their heads and stuffed hay around the collars. When they thought they had fixed themselves scary enough, they crawled along the ground from the barn to the fire. The children were very involved with the tales they were telling. Each one trying to make a scarier tale than the last one. They didn't hear Louis and Jack sneaking up on them.

When they reached the fire, Macy's brothers stood up behind the little circle of children without saying a word.

"And they say's…," Lucy was starting her tale, when she looked up and saw Louis and Jack standing there like two scarecrows. Frozen with terror, she slowly raised her arm and pointed to them, "EEEEYYYYYEEEE!" she screamed as loud as she could. She screamed at the same time the popcorn started popping and the chestnuts started exploding.

Everyone jumped and snapped their heads around to look in the direction Lucy pointed. When they saw Louis and Jack, they all leapt up and started screaming and running for the cabin. Lucy fainted. Macy grabbed a stick from the fire and went after her brothers. She swung the stick wildly at Louis and Jack, trying to defend Lucy and the other children.

Louis put his hand on her head to keep her from hitting him. She swung the stick of fire at him as hard as she was able. "Whoa now! Macy, it's Louis, put that stick down. Ya want ta burn us up?" he shouted.

"Louis?" she asked, as she stopped swinging. "Oh, yer so mean. I ort'ta knock ya in the head with this here stick of fire. Y'uns scaret' us all ta death."

Her brothers dropped to the ground laughing. All of the children had made it to the porch with their parents, even John. He outran everyone and made it to the porch first.

Jack picked Lucy up and carried her to the cabin. Her mother came out of the door. "Land sakes, what's happened?" she fretted over Lucy.

"We scaret' them kids. They was all tellin' ghost stories and we sneaked up on'um," Jack said between laughs.

"Lucy was that skeered and she fainted Aunt Linny," Macy told her.

"Hurry Macy, run fetch some water," Lucy's mother said.

Macy ran to find some water. She brought it back and dropped some on Lucy face.

Lucy opened her eyes and jumped up yelling, "Run, run, they's bugars after us!"

Macy's brothers started cackling again.

"It was jist my ole brothers, Lucy. They's dressed up ta scare us like they did," Macy told her as she shook her fist at her brothers.

"It worked, too," Jack said between holding his side and laughing. "I never seed such a ruckus."

"Yer gonna git your's and back and then some, I'm a tellin' ya," Macy spat back at him.

A full moon cast shadows from the trees. Parents tried to comfort the crying children with no success. They gave up and took their scared and sobbing children home. Lucy and Macy went to bed making plans of how to get even with Macy's brothers.

When they were tucked in under the layers of quilts, Macy rolled over on her back. "I'm a gonna git Jack and Louis back fer a scarin' ya like they did."

Lucy sat up and curiously asked, "What ya gonna do, Macy?"

Macy sighed, "I ain't rightl'y figured it out yit. But they's a gonna git theirs."

Lucy yawned and laid back down and said, "I'm sleepy let's talk 'bout it in the mornin'."

Macy turned down the lamp. "Okay, night."

"Night, Macy," Lucy mumbled as she fell asleep.

Chapter 7
Spinster Bevins

The next morning started with lots of work. Chores had to be done before the sun shed its light to start the day. They wanted to get all the work done before Sunday church services, so they could have fellowship all day long. Sunday was the one time Macy wore a dress. She pulled and scratched at the dress as they walked the few miles to the church.

"Miss Macy, leave that dress alone," her mother scolded her.

Macy twisted and pulled at the dress. "But it's a itchin' me somethin' awful, Ma."

"Macy, I declare ya might at least not complain as much on Sunday and the mornin' as purty as it is," her mother said with a sigh.

Lucy's mother had been humming a hymn. "That is so right. Betsy, would ya look at all that color this mornin'. It's as if God took these mountains and made them a painting," she said to them as they walked along.

Lucy's father still used the birch wood crutch and hobbled along beside them. "My favr'ite is the maples, they change from green ta red, yellow, some orange, and some have all three colors. Why even the pi'son oak is red."

Macy's father looked with wonder at the beauty of the mountain. "This is truly a blessed time of year, brother. We's mighty glad we come ta be with ya. I loves the hickr'ys, they shine such a bright yeller. Look at them beech trees yonder they's yeller too." He pointed down the lane at the trees.

They all marveled as they walked along. Lucy's mother loved to think how ordinary lanes turned into God's paintbrush. Yellow, red and orange leaves glittered in the morning frost. Big was right, even the poison oak and poison ivy glowed brilliant red in the warm sunshine. The gusting wind blew the leaves around. They looked to Linny as if they were something alive scurrying across the road.

Lucy's mother turned her thoughts to Thanksgiving and a time of worship, a special time to be with family. She nudged Lucy's father encouraging him to speak to Little.

He nodded to his wife and turned to his brother. "Have ya made up yer mind yet Little? Are ya a gonna stay on here?" Lucy's father asked his brother.

Macy's father stopped walking to look at a nest of hornets. "Would ya look at that, Ma a'las said if them hornets built their nest in the tree high like that, we's gonna have a bad winter," he turned to Big. "Me and Betsy have talked it over and we'd like ta stay. We'd be a takin' Ma and Pa's cabin. They's room fer us and the boys if'n Macy kin stay with ya."

Lucy's father let out the breath he had been holding. He had been praying that his brother would choose to stay. "That's shore good news ta me, brother, I purely didn't know what I was a gonna do with both these places ta keep up. If'n yer a mind to, we kin start in on the timber in the spring. It should fetch a right big sum."

"Yes, brother we can, and maybe we can start a new ground after it's cut. A'las good ta plant a new ground," Macy's father agreed.

Linny hugged her sister-in-law. They were both very happy. "Be soon ta eat the Thanksgivin' supper. Just about two weeks. Little, I reckon ya and Big better git ta scoutin' out a turkey fer us," she told them.

"That's fer shore, and maybe ya kin fix us a ham ta go along with it," Big Watson laughed rubbing his stomach.

They all laughed together with him.

Macy started picking at her dress again and stated, "I hate's wearin' these dresses. They let's the cold in."

Macy's mother smacked her on the rear. "Hush now, Macy, yer a gonna wear a dress ta church if'n it kills ya. The house of the Lord is a place for ya ta show respect. That is one thing yer gonna do."

"Oh Ma, I got's clean overalls. Ain't that what matters yer decent and clean?"

Macy's mother laughed at her and replied, "Decent yes and ta me that means a dress. Clean don't really matter that much. Of course, it's nice in the summer time when it's hot if'n everyone is clean."

Lucy and Macy giggled. They had sat through many services where someone needed a bath.

They came around the bend in the road that went by Ms. Bevins' house. They saw her out on the porch and as they came closer, they saw John Taylor and Sam Creech with their fathers on the porch with her.

They heard her arguing, "And I know's it was them what dun it. Fer I shaked my mop at them and they's run's out'a my yard leavin' them chestnuts they was a tryin' ta steal. Would ya look here, fer my trouble, they comes back and puts burrs all in my mop. It ain't fit for nothin' now." Ms. Bevins threw the mop on the porch and put her hands on her plump hips.

The girls began walking faster. Their parents looked at each other and then back to them.

"Macy Watson, stop and come right back here," her mother said sternly.

Macy turned around. She knew she had been caught and was in trouble. He mother had the look on her face she had seen many times. Her normally round mouth was set in a thin line and her blue eyes were blazing. Macy dropped her head and started walking back to her mother.

"Ya come here too, Lucille," Lucy's mother demanded.

Lucy knew she was in trouble, her mother only called her Lucille when she was angry. "I want ta know where's ya got them chestnuts ya was a roastin' last night?" Lucy's mother crossed her arms and waited for Lucy to answer her.

Macy and Lucy didn't say anything. They just stood there with their heads down kicking at the gravel in the road.

Macy's mother put her hand on Macy's chin and lifted her head up, "Uh huh, it were both of ya what put them burrs in Ms. Bevins' mop. Not these boys, weren't it?"

Lucy looked up at her mother, "It weren't my fault Ma, it was Macy's idea."

Macy punched Lucy on the arm. "It weren't all my idea. Ya had a hand in it, too."

Lucy shook her head, "I'd a never come down here if'n ya didn't drag me."

"I'd didn't have ta do too much a draggin' and yer all talkin' 'bout how ya want's one of them sapplin's," Macy challenged her.

"That's enough, girls. It don't matter who started it. Yer both ta blame," Lucy's father hushed them up with a stern voice.

Ms. Bevins watched from her porch with her arms crossed across her plump chest. She lowered her head to look at Macy and Lucy over her horn-rimmed glasses.

Lucy's father went over to the gate and took his hat off, "Ms. Bevins, I don't think it were them boys what did the mischief. I think it were these two girls of our'n. "

She uncrossed her arms and let out a grunt. She pushed her glasses up on her round nose, "Well, if'n ya'd teach them young'uns some manners in the first place this'd a not happened. I declare I don't know what's gits in'ta these young'uns nowadays. Why in my day, we'd a been afeered of the strap too much ta do any of that kind of devilry."

Lucy's father darted a warning look at Macy and Lucy. He turned back to Ms. Bevins, "Yes ma'm, I'm mighty ashamed of our girls, but we'll figure out somethin' fer'em ta do to make it right, ya can be shore of that."

"See I told ya, Pa, it weren't me," John told his father and glared at Macy and Lucy.

Macy's father turned Macy and Lucy around and pointed his finger toward the church. They started walking with their heads down not saying a word.

The thought of what was to come made the service last extra-long for the girls. The wood pews seemed harder than normal to them. They squirmed and fidgeted in their seats, while their parents darted warning looks at them. After service, the worshipers filed out and shook the pastor's hand. Macy and Lucy followed behind shuffling their feet. The closer they got to Ms. Bevins' house, the slower they walked. Lucy's mother turned around and hollered for them to catch up. They were almost to Ms. Bevins' house and it was the first thing that their parents had been spoken to them since they went by her place that morning.

"Big, I think's these girls need ta pay Ms. Bevins for that mop they ruin't," Lucy's mother said to Lucy's father.

He stopped and rubbed his beard, "Yeah Ma, I think that's a good idea. Lucy that's jist what yer a gonna do."

Macy's father nodded in agreement. "I reckon that means ya too, Macy," her father told her.

When they reached Ms. Bevins' house, they stopped and Lucy's father hollered across the gate, "Ms. Bevins."

The door opened with a screech and she came out on the porch.

Lucy's father went over to the gate and took his hat off again, "We got's two girls here that are mighty sorry fer what they done. They's say's if'n you'll forgive'em, they'll work fer ya 'til ya say that mop has been paid off."

"Oh Pa," Macy whined.

"Hush now, that's ta be yer lot and that's the end of the matter," Macy's father told her.

Ms. Bevins looked hard at Macy and Lucy. "That seems fair ta me. They can start tomorr'y. I got's lots of dustin' and moppin' ta do," Ms. Bevins said in a huff and went back in her house and slammed the door with a loud bang.

"They'll be here bright and early in the mornin'. Ya can be a lookin' fer'em," Lucy's mother yelled at the closed door. She turned to Macy and Lucy, "I'm mighty ashamed of ye both," she turned and marched home.

Macy and Lucy dragged their feet all the way home kicking the dirt as they walked. The path from the community at Turkey's Nest to their cabin seemed like it went on forever. Their parents didn't say a word to them the rest of the evening. They were sent to bed right after supper.

"Macy, are ya asleep?" Lucy asked, several hours after they had gone to bed.

Macy raised up and turned up the lamp. "No, I'm mad at Pa. I'd a rather taken a whoopin' than have ta go work fer that ole woman."

Lucy let out a sigh, "I know's it. I reckon it were mean of us ta ruin her mop."

Macy turned the lamp out and laid back down. "She's the one's mean. She's stingy and mean and I don't aim ta do much work fer her."

Lucy squirmed down under the covers. "Pa say's we have ta work till she say's so."

Macy gave a grunt, "That'll prob'ly be ferever. She ain't gonna git much out'a me I tell's ya."

Lucy rolled over toward Macy and leaned up on her elbow. "I guess I'll work real hard, then maybe she let's us go quick like."

"Ya do what ya want's, I ain't a goin' to," Macy had already made up her mind.

"This mess were part yer fault, Macy. Yer 'alas a gettin' us inta somethin'," Lucy fretted.

"Ya don't have ta go along with me. Oh hush, and go ta sleep. Ma'll be a yellin' fer shore come mornin'," Macy huffed.

The next morning, as Macy predicted, both their mothers came into the room very early to wake them up. "Come on, girls, ya got's ta go ta Ms. Bevins and start a workin'. Come on now, breakfast is ready. The sooner ya eat, the sooner ya can git started."

Lucy's mother pulled the quilts down to get them out of bed. She turned and marched off to the kitchen.

Macy and Lucy forced themselves to get out of bed and get dressed. They came dragging their feet down the hall and into the kitchen. "Ma, I'd just rather take a switchin'," Macy said to her mother as she plopped down at the table.

Macy's mother was kneading dough for bread. She didn't look up from her task. "I know's ya would, that's the very reason yer a gonna go work fer Ms. Bevins. Could be that'll learn ya a lesson."

Macy poked at the food on the plate Lucy's mother had set in front of her. "But she's that stingy mean woman and she don't need no help."

Her mother stopped her kneading and looked at her, "What she didn't need was two girls a 'stroyin' her stuff. Now yer gonna git down there and be real sorry or else I'll tell her ta make ya stay and work 'till Christmas." She turned and went back to her task of kneading the bread dough.

After they had eaten, Macy and Lucy put on their coats, gloves, and scarfs and started for Ms. Bevins. They both kept silent for the whole walk to Ms. Bevins' house.

When they arrived at Ms. Bevins' house, she had been watching for them. She opened the door and came out on the porch. She tapped her foot impatiently, "Yer late, the sun's 'buot ta git up and we ain't started workin'."

Macy and Lucy looked at each other.

She motioned for them to come up on the porch, "Come on, come on. The day's a wastin'. One of y'uns can do the scrubbin' and t'other can do the rinsin'. When ya git's this done, ya come tell me, I got's lots of things need's a doin'. "

She dropped a scrub brush and a mop bucket on the porch and pointed to Macy. "What's your name, girl?" she asked Macy.

Macy scuffed her foot on the porch. She didn't look up, but she told Ms. Bevins her name, "Macy."

Ms. Bevins turned to Lucy, "I reckon I know yer name Miss Lucy Watson."

Ms. Bevins looked at them for what seemed like to Macy and Lucy forever without saying anything. Finally, she spoke, "Macy, yer the biggest, I reckon yer gonna be the one ta scrub the porch. Lucy, ye can rinse it fer her. Mind ya now, I 'spects it ta be clean." She marched back in the house and slammed the door.

They both stood there staring at the closed door. Macy took the scrub brush and bucket. "She shore is a sour old biddy. Come on Lucy, let's git started."

Lucy took off her gloves and cupped her hands and blew into them. "It's mighty cold this mornin'. She knows it's hard ta clean when water makes yer hands feel like ice."

The curtain moved in the house and Ms. Bevins tapped on the window.

They started scrubbing the porch with the cold water and soap that Ms. Bevins had left for them to use. They discovered quickly that they were not going to get the porch clean in the cold morning air. Their hands became red and chapped. The more she scrubbed, the more the water turned to ice. Macy became very aggravated. She picked up the bucket of soap water and threw it all over the porch. Lucy picked up the bucket of rinse water and threw it on top of the soapy water. They both took the scrub brushes and tried to push the water off the porch before it froze.

Ms. Bevins watched them from behind the curtains in the front window. She decided to go out to inspect the work. She walked over to a spot they had cleaned and tapped her foot on the floor, "Ya missed this spot. Clean it again." Then, she stomped back inside and slammed the door with a bang.

Lucy stuck her tongue out at her back as she went inside, "I shore hope's Pa don't make us do this fer long."

Macy stuck her tongue out at the house too, "It ain't up ta him, it's up ta her. I don't know how she 'spects us ta wash this porch without no water. Do ya see a pump where we can git's some more water?"

Lucy looked around, she went to the backyard and looked for a water pump or well. She came back and shook her head, "I don't see's one nowhere's."

Their hands were getting numb; they went to the door and knocked.

Ms. Bevins opened the door a tiny crack, "Well what is it?"

Lucy was shivering, "We got ta have some more water ta git's the porch scrubbed again."

She walked out on the porch. "It don't look ta me like ya know's how ta scrub a Porch," Ms. Bevins said as she bent down to inspect their work.

Getting angry, Macy raised her hands in the air with frustration, "We did the best we was able. It's cold and ya can't scrub with cold water.".

Ms. Bevins straightened up. She gave them a hard stare for a few minutes. The stare melted Macy's resolve to be angry. "Come in the house, then. I got's some dusters. Ya can start in the parlor," she told them.

They followed her into the house. She opened the cupboard door and took out two feather dusters. She handed the girls each a duster. Macy and Lucy looked at each other and then back at the feather dusters.

Ms. Bevins let out an exasperated sigh, "Ain't ya never seed no feather duster?" She grabbed Lucy's out of her hand and started batting at the tables. "This is how ya do it. Now mind ya git ever speck of dust." She thrust it back at Lucy and stormed off into her kitchen.

They began dusting with the feather dusters. Lucy started at the mantle over the fireplace. The fireplace was huge and the fire crackling in it felt good to her. She felt icy cold all over from scrubbing the porch. She put the duster down and spread her hands out toward the fire. She looked up on the mantle and saw a small purple box. "Hey what's this?" Lucy picked up the box to examine it.

Macy looked up from dusting the tables, "I don't know, but put it back afore she see's ya. Else she'll accuse us a stealin' somethin' too. We'd be bond to her all our life if'n that happened shore as I'm a standin' here."

Lucy put the box back in its place. She was fascinated by all the trinkets and pictures in the big room. They dusted for about an hour and they thought everything looked clean. "We's done," Lucy yelled at the kitchen.

Ms. Bevins came back in the parlor. She ran her finger over the coffee table and held it up to look. "It's still got some dust on it. Do it again," she stomped back off.

Macy and Lucy both stuck their tongue out at her back.

In a few minutes, Ms. Bevins came back in the room. "Since yer so fond of my chestnuts, when ya gits finished with this dustin', I want ya to go out and pick up the new ones that has fell and put them in a pile," she handed them a bucket and stormed back out of sight.

Lucy looked at the bucket and then out the window at the leaves blowing in the wind. She shivered. "We just got warmed up, ain't there somethin' in here we could do?" Lucy called after her.

Ms. Bevins stopped and turned around. She came back in the parlor. "They's lot's ta do, but I want's ya ta go out and clean up the yard," she pointed to the door.

The girls retrieved their coats from the coat stand by the door. They put them back on and went outside to start gathering the chestnuts that had fallen from the tree.

Macy decided to keep the chestnuts they had gathered. "If'n we gots ta pick'um up, I'm a gonna keep'um," Macy said and started throwing the chestnuts over the fence.

Helen Blaylock and Loretta Creech were walking by Ms. Bevins' house. They saw Macy and Lucy working in the yard and came over to make fun of them.

Helen nudged Loretta as they walked over to the fence. "We heer'ed ya got into some trouble, Lucy," Helen smiled sarcastically.

Macy and Lucy kept working, while trying to ignore the girls.

"I reckon I can see why she thought Macy was a boy. Look how ugly she is, wearin' boy's overalls and all. I want ya to look at that ugly colored red hair," Helen said to Loretta.

"I know, I never seed hair the color of a pun'kin afore," Loretta laughed.

Lucy stomped over to the fence. "Macy ain't ugly, yer the one's ugly. Yer hair looks like the color of some varmit," she shouted at them.

Loretta balled her hands up in fists. "Well, ya ain't one ta talk, Lucy Watson, with that stringy brown hair of your'n."

Macy came over with Lucy, "Ya quit talkin' bout my cousin or yer gonna be sorry." Already angry from having to work, she was ready for a fight.

Ignoring Macy, Loretta went on talking to Helen, "My hair is as black as a raven's wing. My pa says so. John does too, he say's it's so black that it looks blue." She twirled a strand of her long hair around her finger.

Helen turned to Loretta and flipped her blonde ponytail as she smoothed out her calico dress. "Ya know, Loretta, that Mr. Taylor has said he's gonna clear a place in the warehouse for a square dance after the church dinner next week."

"I know. John's done told me 'bout it. He say's he wants ta dance the reel with me and not ta dance it with nobody else," Loretta twirled around as if she was dancing all ready.

Helen pointed to Macy and Lucy. "Who else would he want ta dance it with? Shorley not these two they's too young and they's homely, too."

Loretta stopped her twirling and came back to the fence, "Yeah, they's jist babies. Ya know I turn sixteen in a few days." She turned to Lucy, "How's old are ya now, Lucy?"

Helen laughed, "Why I bet she's not even nine yit."

Lucy put her bucket down. "I'm eleven and Macy is thirteen, just so ya know."

Helen clucked her tongue, "Oh how sad, still babies right, Loretta? I'd be amazed if'n they's even knowed how ta dance, being they's such babies. They's ugly ones at that." Helen made a sad face and they both laughed.

Macy had taken all she was able to stand. "My nanny done told me how ta make a soap that'd make my hair as dark auburn as the lilies. I might jist use it and we'll see who git's ta dance the reel."

Helen and Loretta stopped their laughing. "That ain't true or you'd a done it afore now," Helen challenged Macy.

Lucy chimed in, "Oh, it's the truth and she showed me how ta make my brown hair soft like corn silks. We's jist a waitin' ta use it afore the church dinner, on account of we jist got enough fer me and Macy. Come on, Macy, we need's ta git back ta work." Lucy linked her arm in Macy's and they stuck their noses in the air. They walked around the house out of sight of the two girls.

"We ain't a believin' ya," Loretta yelled at them.

In the door watching the exchange, Ms. Bevins felt sorry for Macy and Lucy. She went out back where they were gathering the chestnuts. "I think that's enough for today, girls. Ya can come back tomorr'y and finish."

The two girls didn't say a word. They left the bucket of chestnuts and took off running for home as fast as their legs would carry them.

The next day started much the same way. Ms. Bevins had water ready for them and they began scrubbing the porch using the cold water. They were scrubbing and almost finished their task, when they heard a very loud crash come from the house.

"What were that?" Lucy jumped up.

Macy jumped up and ran over to the door of the house. "I don't know sounded like somethin' fell. Ms. Bevins, ya alright?" Macy yelled through the door.

"I don't hear nothin. Reckon she's alright?" Lucy went over to look through the window. She saw Ms. Bevins on the floor and ran over to the door. "Macy, it's Ms. Bevins. She done fell and is a layin' there in the middle of the floor. We better go in and see's if'n she's alright!" she said nervously.

They flung open the door and ran over to Ms. Bevins.

"Ms. Bevins, are ya alright?" Macy asked as she bent down over her.

Ms. Bevins lay face down on the floor not moving.

"Reckon she's done had a heart attack?" Lucy moved closer.

Macy leaned down to listen for Ms. Bevins to breath. "She's not breathin'! Go run fer the doctor. I'll stay here and see's if'n I can do somethin'."

Lucy took off in a run for the doctor. She ran as fast as she could make her legs go. She ran all the way without stopping. When she got to the doctor's house, she ran up on the porch and banged on the door.

Not many of the mountain people called for the doctor's services. He wasn't from Turkey's Nest and the people of the mountain were weary of strangers. Dr. Wilson sat in his parlor reading a magazine, not expecting anyone to be banging on his door. He heard Lucy knocking and dropped the magazine on the table. He jumped up and started searching for his coat. Lucy kept knocking on the door. "I'm comin,' I'm comin' hold your horses," Dr. Wilson yelled. He ran to the examination room to find his doctor's coat. He scanned the room and located his white coat. He grabbed it and tried to quickly put his arms in the sleeves. He knocked his glasses off his nose, then he dropped to the floor trying to feel around for the them. He picked them up and put them back on.

Lucy knocked louder. "Dr. Wilson, are ya in there?" she yelled through the door.

Dr. Wilson jerked the door open. He saw Lucy standing there out of breath. "I declare what's the rush child?"

Lucy sucked in a deep breath. "It's Ms. Bevins," she said between gasps of air. "Somethin' bad's happened. She's a layin' on her floor not movin'. Come quick."

Dr. Wilson always had his horse hitched to the buggy, in case of an emergency. He grabbed his bag off the table and they ran to the buggy. "Did you see what happened?" he asked Lucy as they climbed in the buggy.

Lucy flopped back in the seat, "No, we's a scrubbin' her porch and heard an awful noise. We went in and she's a layin' there not movin'."

He flicked the reins and the horse took off at a gallop. He prodded the horse to go faster all the way to Ms. Bevins' house. Lucy had to hold on with both hands as the buggy bounced along the road. Dr. Wilson pulled back on the reigns and the horse skidded to a stop in front of the gate. Lucy nearly flew out of the buggy. Dr. Wilson jumped out and dropped the weighted hitch. He handed Lucy the reigns and told her to tie the horse. He took his medical bag and ran for the house. Lucy looped the reigns around the hitch and bounded after him. Dr. Wilson ran up on the porch and inside the house with Lucy close behind him.

Dr. Wilson burst through the door. He paused to catch his breath. He saw Ms. Bevins sitting in a chair sipping water. He went over to her and placed his hand on her shoulder. "Are you alright Ms. Bevins? Lucy said you had fallen on the floor. Do you know what happened?" he asked and took out his watch to take her pulse.

Ms. Bevins took another sip of water and stated, "I shorely do know what happened. I took a big bite of a apple and I got's a piece hung in my neck. I couldn't breathe, I was a chokin' ta death. This here child seed it right off and she slammed her fist on my back and out popped that apple."

Dr. Wilson nodded to Macy. "That was quick thinking, girl," he said as he examined Ms. Bevins. "If that's what happened, I don't know if I could have got here in time."

Macy sat on the floor beside her and Ms. Bevins patted her on the head. "That is shorely what happened and this is a smart girl alright."

Dr. Wilson checked her heart and her blood pressure. "Well, it looks as if you're a gonna be right as a fiddle. You take it easy the rest of the day and don't be eating any more apples for a while, unless you cut them up good first, okay?" He began putting his things in his bag. "You be sure and send for me if you feel worse or need me for anything." He closed the medical bag and started to leave disappointed.

He kept hoping for the chance to help someone, so that the mountain people would trust him for their care.

Ms. Bevins waved her hand at him, "I thank ya, doctor, I'm sorry ta be so much trouble."

He stopped and turned around. "It's no trouble. I didn't do anything. Well, If you are sure you're alright, I'll be going now," he left thoroughly disappointed. Not much happened to need a doctor in Turkey's Roost.

As soon as the doctor left, Ms. Bevins turned to Macy and Lucy. "I reckon that squares us away with what ya owe me, girls. I'd consider it a great pleasure if'n you'd both stay and have supper with me," she smiled at them.

Lucy and Macy looked at each other. They couldn't believe she was being nice to them. "We'd like that just fine," Macy spoke up.

Lucy walked over to the fireplace to warm her cold backside. She noticed the purple box and picked it up. "What is this, Ms. Bevins?"

Ms. Bevins pulled herself up out of the chair and went over to the fireplace. She took the box from Lucy and opened it. She turned it toward Lucy so that she could see what was inside. "That's a medal my sweetheart won fer bein' in the war."

Lucy looked at her with curiousity. "Ya had a sweetheart?" she asked as she peered at the Purple Heart medal.

Ms. Bevins laughed, "Well, now, I weren't a'las an old wrinkled woman. I was very purty in my day." She looked at Macy and Lucy's stunned faces. "Oh, ya needn't ta look at me like that. One a these days, I'll find a picture ta show ya ta prove it."

Macy took the box from Lucy to look more closely at the medal. "What happened that ya and yer sweetheart didn't git married?" Macy handed the box back to her.

Ms. Bevins sat the box back in its place on the mantle. She went to her chair to sit down. She felt tired and very sad. "We did git married. He was my husband. I reckon he was a'las my sweetheart, though. He was kilt, or so they say's. I never seen his body and they never found him. I don't really know. They send's me that there medal."

Lucy came over and sat at her feet. "How come ya never got

married again?" she asked her.

Macy flopped down beside Lucy. "Didn't ya have no young'uns? Where's yer family, don't ya have no brothers or sisters?" The questions popped out of her mouth.

Ms. Bevins sighed, "We was that in love, I jist was never able ta take ta no one else. We weren't married long enough ta have young'uns. I did have a sister though, she was my twin, born just a minute after me. She were born blue though, the doctor tried ever'thin' he knowe'd how, but they couldn't revive her. My ma buried her out by that ole chestnut tree. That tree weren't as big then as it is now. I reckon the years has got goin' too fast on me. T'weren't long after I lost my husband, that my ma and pa both took the fever. I keered fer them as hard as I knowed how but t'wernt enough and they both died. That left me alone. I buried Ma and Pa alongside my sister. Come on out in the yard with me and I'll show ya."

They followed Ms. Bevins outside to the big chestnut tree. She pointed to the headstones made of rock that marked the graves.

Macy had not noticed the headstones before. She looked in Ms. Bevins sad face and she felt bad now for the things she had done to Ms. Bevins. She looked and saw four headstones. "I thought ya said they was three buried here, Ms. Bevins. Who is this'un fer?" Macy asked.

Ms. Bevins bent down and picked up a chestnut and threw it off the grave of her sister. "I had that one made fer my husband. I know's he ain't there but it's somethin' ta remind me." She pulled at a sapling that was beginning to take root. "I want ya to look here at these trees a sproutin' and it winter. Help me clear them off'n the grave, will ya girls?" She bent down and pulled the little tree out of the ground. "I reckon I should chop this ole tree down, but my ma loved it so. She says to me, 'Someday Beulah, we'll have chestnuts ta roast fer Christmas. Now it's just a trouble ta me ta keep them pulled of'n the graves. I jist can't bring myself ta cut it down."

Macy and Lucy helped her pull the sprouting trees out of the ground and throw them over the fence.

When they were finished, Ms. Bevins started for the house, "I got's somethin' I wants ta give ya girls, come on back in the house with me."

They followed her back in the house. She motioned for them to sit on the couch. "Wait here, I'll be back in a jiffy," she said. Then she disappeared into a room off the kitchen.

She came back with a small glass bottle in her hand. "Here it is. Look here girls. It's called parfum. Course I've had it ever since I got married. My Joseph gave it to me on our weddin' day." She opened the bottle and sniffed, "Whew! Of course it's mighty strong smellin' now. I reckon if'n ya mixed it with some water, it won't smell as strong."

She handed the bottle to Macy. "Mind ya now, don't mix it with no polk berries, they's bound ta turn your skin purple if'n ya do. Or don't mix it with beet juice. That'll turn yer skin a bright red," she winked at Macy. "Now, let's see what we got's in the pantry fer supper."

Macy looked at that little bottle and back to Lucy. They both grinned at each other. An idea had already formed in their minds. They hooked arms and skipped in the kitchen to help fix supper.

Chapter 8
Thanksgiving

The community of Turkey's Nest came to life with preparations and decorations for the upcoming holidays. The gardens had been harvested and food stored for the winter. They used corn stalks tied with ribbon for decorations and these they placed beside the entry of their porches.

Thanksgiving was a day to celebrate and give thanks for blessings. The whole community prepared with excitement for a harvest dance and church fellowship dinner.

The church would be used now as a school house during the week. Macy and Lucy walked two miles from their cabin to Roaring Fork for the first day of school.

Ms. Bevins watched for them to come by her home. As soon as she saw Macy and Lucy, she came out of the house and met them at her gate. "Mornin', girls, I made ya few cakes of fried pies ta take ta school with ya. Here ya go," she handed them a basket of pies.

Macy smiled with glee because fried pies were her favorite. "Thank ya, Ms. Bevins. That were awful nice of ya," Macy took the basket from her.

Ms. Bevins smiled back at them, "Will both ya girls stop by on yer way home now and say hello to me? I want's ya ta call me Ms. Beulah."

Macy looked in the basket and then back to Ms. Bevins. "My pa'ud whoop us shore we called ya that," Macy told her.

Ms. Bevins waved her hand at Macy, "Nonsense, I'll have a talk with yer pa. Ya has my permission ta call me that. Have a good day at school now, girls." She waved goodbye to them.

They turned to leave.

"We will and thank ya fer the pies," Lucy waved back.

Lucy thought about Ms. Bevins as they walked along. "Ya know, Macy, she weren't mean and selfish like we thought she was."

Macy took one of the pies out of the basket and took a bite, "I know, I feel bad fer thinkin' such as we did 'bout her. She only keeps them graves cleared on account of she loves them that's buried there."

Lucy took the pie from Macy and took a bite of it. The cinnamon and apples tasted delicious to her. "Yeah, I reckon that's the very reason. She's not a spinster either. Do ya think you'll like this school?" she asked and took another bite of the pie and handed it back to Macy.

Macy stuffed the rest of the pie in her mouth. She swallowed the bite, "I don't know, I's a might behind in my learnin'. It's hard ta learn when yer on a train being bounced around."

Lucy remembered her mother telling her that Macy and her family lived in houses built on flatbed railroad cars and they went on the train from place to place for the logging companies. "What were it like, Macy, ta be livin' in a house on a train?"

Macy shook her head remembering living on the train, "I didn't like it much. That there train was a'las noisy and if'n ya stuck yer head out the winder when them smoke stacks were a belerin', it'd come back in black with soot. I's mighty glad Pa and Ma decided ta stay here."

They had walked almost to the Creech cabin. "I hope's we don't run into that Sam Creech this mornin'," Macy said.

Feeling the cold, Lucy walked a little faster. "No, we won't. His pa works at the mill and he rides in to school in his pa's buggy. Sam gets the fire goin' in the stove of the church, so's that way it's warm when we git there."

Macy thought about Helen and Loretta. "What about that Loretta? Her cabin is on the way ta school too. Does she walk with ya?"

Lucy walked faster, "No, her pa works at the mill, too. They go in with him. They are a'las the first'uns to the class."

Macy picked up the pace to keep up with Lucy. "I don't like them uppity girls. I'm glad we don't have ta walk with them. They think they're better'n everybody else on account of they's older'n we are. Well, they might be older but they ain't smarter. I say they best leave me alone or they'll be sorry."

The wind picked up and Macy watched as it blew the leaves across the road. "Ya know, Ma's right. Them leaves look like they's almost somethin' alive the way they scurry across the road with the wind."

Lucy laughed, "It's a might purty sight at that. I like fall. Last year, at school we found leaves and made pictures out of them." Lucy stopped and picked up a red maple leaf.

Mr. Jenkins, the teacher, rang the bell to start the school day. They heard the bell ringing as they came into the church yard and they started running. They ran up on the steps of the church and into the building.

Mr. Jenkins followed the students in and went to the blackboard. He adjusted his bowtie as he went to the blackboard and turned around to write his name on it. He was tall and thin, his suit jacket hung loosely from his shoulders. His hair was thinning on the top, making his forehead look very long. His straight thin nose stuck out almost like a pointer. He wrote his name with a flourish and turned around to address the class. He saw Macy and he realized he had a new student. He banged the ruler on the desk to silence the class. He turned to Macy, who had taken a seat in the back of the building with Lucy. "I see we have a new student. What is your name?"

Everyone turned around to look at Macy and her face became flushed. She didn't answer him.

Mr. Jenkins walked back to where Macy sat. "Hello, I don't think you have been with us in our class before, have you?"

Macy cleared her throat. She didn't like being singled out, "No sir, this is my first day in a school. My ma's been a learnin' me ever since I remember."

"It's teaching, not learning. She's been teaching you. Well that's alright. We'll do an evaluation and see where to place you. So tell me, what is your name?"

Macy looked around at the other children who stared at her. She wanted the teacher to leave her alone. "Macy," she stated flatly.

Lucy spoke up, "Macy's my cousin, Mr. Jenkins. She's come ta live with us and will be a comin' to school with me."

He nodded to Lucy and went back to his desk and took out a book. "We have a lot of catching up to do, does anyone remember where we left off before fall break?"

Helen stood up, "I believe ya had put me and Loretta in the top grade. We was a doin' better'n ever'one else."

He put the book down on the desk, "Okay, thank you, Helen. I think it would be best if I give everyone a test to see what we need to work on. I have one prepared. Helen will you come and help me by passing the tests out?"

"Why shore, Mr. Jenkins. I'd be pleased ta help ya," she stood up and tossed her blond ponytail.

Mr. Jenkins handed her the tests. She took them and placed one on each of the children's desks. Pausing in between Macy and Lucy, she stopped. When they looked at her, she gave them a haughty look and dropped Macy's test on the floor. Lucy made a face at her as Helen walked around the potbellied stove in the middle of the room. When she finished handing out the test to the children on the other side of the room, she took one for herself and sat down beside Loretta.

Mr. Jenkins waited at his desk as they filled out their answers. After an hour had passed, he rang the bell on his desk. "Okay, put your pencils down. We'll have a recess now. Everyone take a break. You have permission to go outside if you need to. I'll ring the church bell when it's time to come back inside."

No one wanted to go outside because of the cold. They gathered around the stove. Macy and Lucy went to stand with them.

Helen nudged Loretta in the arm, "See, I told ya they didn't have no special soap ta make their hair change colors, Loretta. I knowed they was a lyin' all the time and besides, nothin' is gonna make these two babies look purty. Ya have ta be purty ta start with afore anythin' can help."

Then, they both laughed.

Macy balled her hand into a fist, "We done told ya, we's a savin' it for the church picnic and Thanksgivin' dance."

"Prove it, show me the soap," Loretta taunted Macy.

Macy reared back and put her hands in her pockets, "Well now, Loretta, that's fer me and Lucy. We ain't a sharin' it with nobody. I reckon yer gonna find out come next week."

They stood there around the stove staring at each other in silence. Mr. Jenkins rang the bell and they all found their desks and sat down. They finished the test and after they were collected, school was dismissed for the day.

Macy and Lucy were the last ones to leave the schoolhouse. They looked across the yard to the trees to see if anyone was watching them. "We shouldn't a bragged about that special soap, them girls are just gonna make fun of us more when we get's to the church supper," Lucy told Macy as they started walking home.

Macy stomped through the woods in anger, "I know's it but I weren't a gonna let her git the best of me. 'Sides I got me a plan."

"What you gonna do Macy?" Lucy held her breath.

Macy stopped and scanned the woods, "I know's it's past time fer polk berries, but I'd say if'n we looked hard 'nough we can find some dried ones."

Lucy let out her breath, "Wha'tcha gonna do with polk berries?"

Macy shook her head at Lucy, "I swear sometimes I think yer jist dense. Didn't ya pay no attention ta Ms. Beulah? She said if'n we mixed that parfum with polk berries it'd turn us purple. That's what I'm a fixin' ta do."

Lucy's brown eyes flew open, "Turn yerself purple, what good'ud that do. They'd jist make fun of us shore fer that."

Macy stopped and leaned close to Lucy. "No, ya ninny, I'm a gonna make that Helen and Loretta use it," she whispered.

Lucy looked around to see if anyone was listening to them, "How ya a gonna do that? They know's better'n ta use polk berries on their hair."

Macy winked at Lucy, "We's a gonna mix them berries with that parfum Ms. Bevins give us and some a ma's lye soap. What we'll do is, mix in some smashed up beets ta see if'n that'll work too. We'll act like that's our special soap and see if'n we can trick them uppity girls in'ta usin' it."

"They shorely ain't that dumb, it won't work," Lucy giggled. "I can't believe they'd be that stupid."

They stopped at the river, the sounds of it rushing and gurgling over the rocks made it hard to hear. Lucy picked up a rock and tossed it in the water. She bent down and picked up another rock.

Macy grabbed her arm. "Look over yonder, ain't that some dried up polk stalks? Come on, let's go see if'n them mockin' birds left any berries," she yelled over the sound of the river.

Lucy dropped her rock and they ran over to the clearing. The wilted stalks were brown and dried. Macy and Lucy started picking up the dried stalks looking for pods of berries. They became excited when they found several pods still intact.

Macy began gathering the berries, "See, I told ya, they'd be some left."

Lucy picked up a stalk and discovered a whole pod of the plump purple berries. "Macy, look over here, they's a whole mess of 'um left. They ain't too dried neither. They still got lots a juice left in'um"

Macy ran over to Lucy. She clapped her hands, "That's jist what I's a lookin' fer. Be sure and git's all of'um. Don't bust none though and git's them on ya."

They picked all the berries and carried them home in Macy's straw hat. They were extra careful and didn't let the juice from the berries stain their clothes.

When they made it home, they scurried in the cabin and went straight to their room. They stashed the polk berries in a jar under the bed. Later that night, they crushed the berries in a bucket and added the lye soap. They poured that mixture in a glass canning jar and closed it tightly with a lid. They mashed the pickled beets they had swiped from the root cellar and mixed the lye soap with them. They poured that mixture into another jar. Then they opened the perfume Ms. Bevins had given them and mixed it equally with the polk berry and beet pulp mixtures. They sealed the jars with a lid and pushed them under the bed.

Lucy jumped in the bed and squirmed down under the covers. "Ya know's, we're a gonna git the lickin' of a lifetime fer this don't ya, Macy?" Lucy giggled in spite of the thought of getting in trouble.

Macy grinned at her, "No, we ain't. I got it all figured out. What we'll do is put a sign on these jars sayin' that they's po'sin and fer nobody ta use them. Them uppidy girls'll think we's a just tryin' ta fool'em. We'll say that we put a warning sign on it and they shouldn't ta used it. How can we git's in trouble if'n we do that?"

Lucy liked that idea and she snickered, "I hope's they are dumb 'nough ta fall fer this. But, I don't think they'll be."

They whispered and giggled themselves to sleep. The next morning they hid the jars in their lunch pail and sneaked them out of the house.

When they arrived at the school, Macy made sure that Helen and Loretta were watching her. She took the jars of purple mixture out of her lunch pail and stashed them in the opening in her desk. She started whispering to Lucy and pointing to the jars. True to her plan, Macy wrote po'sin do not use on a piece of paper and placed it on top of the jars. At recess, they didn't leave their desk. They took the jars and looked at them. Then put them back, and whispered to each other sheepishly.

"Look at them girls a lookin' at us. We need ta act like we don't want's nobody ta see what we got."

"Yeah, I know, but I still don't think it'll work," Lucy whispered back.

Macy rolled her eyes at her, "Lucy, I swear, of course it's a gonna work. After school, we'll just leave them in the desk and act like we forget's 'em. Them nosy girls bound ta come and look ta see what this is."

When the classes were finished for the day, Macy and Lucy put on their coats and made sure they went out of the school first. When they started up the trail to their home, they stopped and turned around. They acted as if they had forgot something and went running back to their desk.

Macy went over to her desk and started looking through it. "Lucy, did ya take my jars of ink?" she said loud enough for anyone close to hear.

"No, Macy, I forget's 'em myself. Are they not in the desk?" she yelled from the door.

They looked through the window and saw Helen and Loretta duck around the building with the the jars of the concoction tucked under their arms.

Macy motioned for Lucy to come look. Lucy started laughing as soon as she saw Helen and Loretta. Macy slapped Lucy on the back, "See's, I told ya it'd work."

Lucy shook her head, "You's right, but I reckon I still ain't fer shore they'll use it."

School was dismissed for the rest of the week for the upcoming holiday.

Early the next day, everyone in the community of Turkey's Nest kept busy cooking food and preparing the warehouse for the supper and square dance. Macy and Lucy helped put strings of popcorn in the rafters for decorations. The boys brought hay bales for people to sit on while they ate. They bundled the tall green and brown corn stalks together and tied with them with orange ribbon. The normally drab warehouse took on an atmosphere of celebration.

As the dusk settled on the mountain, everyone began to arrive at the warehouse. The mountain folks brought all the food they had prepared for the pot luck supper. The men brought their dulcimers, banjos and guitars with them. They gathered on the makeshift podium and began tuning the instruments for the dance.

Soon the warehouse became filled with people laughing and enjoying the fellowship together. The ladies put the food they had prepared on a long table, then called for the parson to say the blessing. Everyone took a plate and began loading it with the goodies.

Macy and Lucy fixed themselves a heaping plate of food and found a bale of hay to sit on to eat. They kept an eye on the door for Helen and Loretta.

Lucy swallowed her last bite of pie and put her plate down, "I don't see them girls, Macy. Reckon they'll be here?"

Macy had been watching the door.''Their ma and pa's here, let's go ask'em," Macy said between mouthfuls of pie.

They made their way around the dance floor and over to Mrs. Blaylock. Macy smiled at Mrs. Blaylock, "Evenin', Mrs. Blaylock, I were a wonerin', is Helen coming to the supper?"

Mrs. Blaylock took a sip of lemonade, she didn't want to be disturbed. She nodded to Macy, "She'll be here directly. She told me Loretta were a gonna help her git's ready. I reckon they were a takin' their time and gettin' fixed as best they could. I didn't want ta wait fer 'em and came on ahead to help with the table."

Lucy smiled at Mrs. Blaylock, "Oh, ok, thank ya. I hope's she gets here soon."

Mrs. Blaylock smiled back at Lucy, "That's sweet of ya, Lucy. I didn't know ya and my Helen were friends."

Lucy stammered, "Thank ya, Mrs. Blaylock."

Macy and Lucy scampered back to their hay bale and Lucy whispered to Macy, "I reckon yer a gonna be right Macy. Them girls are as dumb as ya said they were. I bet they's a tryin' ta use that stuff we mixed up."

Macy kept her eyes on the door. She fidgeted with her hair switching it back and forth under her nose. She was anxious to see what was going to happen, "I know, this'll be better'n I'd a thought if'n it's a takin' this long. They must be a using all that concoction what we made."

Lucy giggled, "That'd shore learn'um a lesson."

After the dinner, the food was cleared away and the musicians took up their instruments. Mr. Blaylock went to the podium to call the dances.

He tapped his cane on the podium, "Okay now, ever'one git their fav'rite girl and let's git's this dance a goin'."

The music started. "Grab your partner and promenade," Mr. Blaylock started calling the dance.

The dancers began walking to the music, holding hands and circling to the right. "Allemande left and a docy do," he called out the next move.

The doors of the warehouse were shoved open and Helen came in screaming. The music stopped and everyone turned to stare in her direction to see what was happening.

Helen stopped in the doorway and screamed, "Look at me!" Her hair glowed bright purple and her face shined scarlet red.

Helen's mother dropped her plate of food and ran over to her. "What has happened Helen?" She looked around frantically, "Where's Dr. Wilson? Hurry someone git the doctor." She turned back to Helen, "I declare child, what has happened to ya?"

Helen began sobbing. "That Macy and Lucy Watson, they lied to me and said they had a special soap. Said it'd make their hair turn like corn silk," she said between sobs.

Her mother grabbed a towel and started wiping at her face, "Well, what's that got to do with ya?"

The doors burst open again and Loretta came running in the warehouse. Her face was scarlet, the same color as Helen's and her hair had turned from black to a blueish purple.

She ran over to her mother, "Look what them girls done to me."

Loretta's mother grabbed some water and a towel and began wiping at her face. "Who, who's done this to ya?"

Loretta sank down on the floor, "It were Macy and Lucy Watson."

Everyone turned to look at Macy and Lucy. The girls looked at each other and backed up a few steps. Macy and Lucy's fathers watched the commotion from the other side of the room trying very hard not to laugh.

Macy took a deep breath and went over to Helen and Loretta, "I don't know what yer a talkin' 'bout. How did I do that to ya?" She said every word slowly.

Loretta looked up at her, "I reckon ya know full well what ya done. Ya lied to me and tricked me 'bout that soap."

Macy's mother turned Macy around to face her, "Macy, what did ya do ta these girls?"

"I didn't do nothin', Ma, honest. We found some polk berries and we decided ta make some ink, so's we could make a paintin' fer Mr. Jenkins. We put a sign on it that said po'sin and not ta use. We forgot it in our desks when we left school. We went back ta git it and it were gone," she blurted out the story she had been rehearsing just in case this happened. She looked back at Helen and Loretta and she let out a whistle. "So that's were it went," she shook her finger at Helen. "This ain't my fault if'n you's dumb 'nough ta wash their hair and face in that there ink we made."

"Is that right? Did it say not ta use, Loretta?" Loretta's mother demanded to know.

Loretta began crying again. "Well yeah, it did say that on the sign, but they done bragged they had a special soap. We thought it was what that stuff were," she said between sobs.

Loretta's mother gasped. "Why did ya believed her? Well even if'n ya did, ya should a know'd better than ta use somethin' said not ta use and was purple." Loretta's mother turned to Dr. Wilson, who was in a fit of laughing, "Is this dangerous?"

He took his bag and set it down in front of Helen and Loretta. "Did you drink it?" he asked them.

"No, we didn't drink it, we washed our hair and face in it. Look at me now," Helen wailed.

Helen's little brother Bob and his friends had been outside. They came over to see what the commotion was all about. They started laughing. "She looks like one of them there blue crawdads, what make's them holes in the ground," he said and his friends started belly laughing.

Dr. Wilson and everyone couldn't hold it in any longer and they started laughing. "Well no, it's probably not going to make you sick. But you're going to be stained that color for a while."

Loretta screamed and came at Macy. She grabbed one of Macy's braids and began pulling her hair. They fell down on the floor. Macy started hitting and fighting back.

Their parents stepped in and separated them. "Girls, girls, that ain't a gonna solve nothin'," Macy's father told them as he pulled them apart.

Macy touched her finger to her busted lip. "Honest, Pa, We went back in a lookin' fer them jars a polk berries. They'd done took'um. We didn't know what had happened to our ink. We decided we'd just make us some more. We never thought no one'd be dumb enough ta use it fer their hair," Macy looked over at Helen and Loretta and winked at them.

Helen gasped and started for Macy with her hands balled up in fists. Helen's mother grabbed and stopped her.

Macy's mother whirled her around and gave her the look that Macy had seen many times. "When we git home, we'll see 'bout that, young lady," she warned her.

Mr. and Mrs. Blaylock took a sobbing Helen and Loretta home to see if they would be able to scrub some of the color off of them.

Mr. Creech went back to the podium. "Well, that was fun, let's see we can have some more and git on with the reels, folks," he took Mr. Blaylock's place on the podium and the dance started again.

Macy and Lucy found a seat in the corner and tried not laugh. They knew if they did, they were going to be in more trouble than they already were.

That night they were awake long after everyone had gone to sleep snickering about the trick they had played on those girls.

"Macy, ya know them girls ain't a gonna forgit what we don to'um don't ye? They's a gonna be a tryin' ta git us back fer that we did," Lucy giggled.

Macy grinned back, "Yeah, I know's it. But we'll just be on the lookout fer what they might do."

"I wonder what Ma'll say in the mornin.' She wouldn't speak to me tonight," Lucy let out a sigh. "I 'spects we'll be in a lot'a trouble. Ma thinks I did it a purpose."

Macy sat up. "They can't blame us, we fixed it so's they was the ones in the wrong. They stole our stuff, 'sides if'n we get's in trouble it were worth it, did you see that color?" Macy flopped back down in the bed laughing hard.

Lucy joined her, "I did, whewee weren't that a funny site?"

The next morning, they waited for their parents to say something about the incident. No one said anything to them. Breakfast was cooked and put on the table, but not a word was said. Macy and Lucy started getting worried. They looked across the table at each other. Macy shrugged her shoulders at Lucy.

After they had finished eating breakfast, Lucy's mother called them outside. "Girls, someone used all my lye soap. Me and yer ma, Macy, have decided both of you need's ta learn how ta make it," she told them.

They looked in the direction she pointed and saw the lye and lard in a big kettle. Lucy's mother handed each of them a paddle to stir the kettle.

Macy and Lucy knew better than to say anything. They picked up the paddles and began stirring the strong smelling concoction. The two of them were stuck making soap all week. But every now and then, they were able to smell the pies and aromas coming from the cabin. Their mothers were busy preparing the Thanksgiving dinner.

"I wonder what Ms. Beulah is doing for Thanksgivin'?" Lucy asked as she took her turn stirring the soap.

Macy sat down on the porch and wiped the tears out of her burning eyes, "I don't know, she ain't got nobody. I'd say she'll be by herself."

Lucy felt sorry for Ms. Beulah. "Macy, that'd be a shame, reckon we ort'ta ask if'n she can come eat with us?"

Macy stood up. She had been thinking the same thing, "I think's we'd better do that. Let's go ask Ma."

They put their paddles down and went into the kitchen. Their mothers had dinner almost ready.

Macy started inspecting all the food that they had on the stove. She looked in the oven at the pies and bread that was baking. "Ma, we been a thinkin' 'bout Ms. Bevins, she ain't got nobody, can we go ask her ta eat with us?"

Macy's mother basted the ham and put it back in the oven. She turned to Macy, "Why Macy, that's real thoughtful. I think that'd be a fine thing. Ya girls go on and fetch her ta supper."

Macy and Lucy smiled at each other. They grabbed their coats and took off down the road. The fumes from the lye soap had scorched their skin and made their eyes water. They were glad to be away from it. They ran all the way to Ms. Bevin's house. When they got there, the fire was not lit and the house was dark.

They knocked on the door, "Ms. Beulah, ya home?"

No answer.

"Maybe she went somewheres else," Lucy said.

They knocked on the door again, no answer. They looked through the window and saw Ms. Beulah sitting in a chair.

"Reckon she's sick?" Lucy whispered.

Macy began to get worried, "I don't know, let's go in and see."

They opened the door and went over to Ms. Bevins. "Ms. Beulah, are ya alright? It's cold as ice in here. Why don't ya have no fire goin'?" Macy asked her.

Ms. Beulah looked at them blankly and for several minutes she didn't say anything. After what seemed like a long time to Macy and Lucy, she spoke, "I jist didn't have the heart to make a fire this mornin'."

Macy stood up, "Lucy, ya go git some wood and git's the fire a goin' and I'll find a quilt ta warm her up. Hurry now."

Lucy built a fire and in a few moments the blaze made the room warm. They helped Ms. Beulah to stand near the fireplace. Lucy smiled at her with excitement, "Ms. Beulah, Ma done sent us ta fetch ya ta eat the Thanksgiving dinner with us."

Ms. Beulah looked from Lucy to Macy. Her heart was touched with their thoughtfulness, "I thank ya girls fer thinkin' of me. I was very lonely today, I didn't feel like I even wanted to git out a bed."

Lucy ran to the coat closet and found Ms. Beulah's coat, gloves and scarf. She handed them to her, "Well, we come to fetch ya to eat with us."

Ms. Beulah's face lit up with pleasure, "That's 'bout the nicest thing a body has done fer me in a long time. I'd love to come with ya. Oh, by the way, I heered 'bout the dance. Had me a good chuckle 'bout that."

Macy winked at her, "Yeah, them polk berries shore did make a purple color jist like you said they would."

They all shared a mischievous giggle.

"Ma's been a makin' us fix a batch of lye soap ever since," Macy told her.

Ms. Bevins laughed again, "I tell ya what, go to the barn and hitch up the horse and buggy. We'll take us a ride to yer cabin."

The girls squealed with excitement and ran out to the barn. They led the horse out of it's stall, put the harness on and hitched it to the buggy. They led the horse around to the front of the house and yelled to Ms. Beulah that they were ready. She came out of the house and they all climbed in the buggy. Ms. Beulah flicked the reins; the horse took off in a trot.

"Ya know, girls, I feel's like singin' a song," she started singing. "Jingle bells, Jingle bells." Macy and Lucy joined her singing as loud as they were able. They arrived in time to help set the table.

When the table was set and the dinner arranged, everyone sat down and bowed their heads. Lucy's father started the blessing. for the food.

"We thank ya Lord, for this time with friends and family. We thank ya for this harvest and the table ya have set before us," he paused and looked around the table. "Now, I want each of us to say somethin' we are thankful for."

Lucy's mother looked at everyone sitting at the table. "I'm thankful fer family," she looked at Ms. Beulah. "I'm also thankful for good friends."

Macy's mother spoke next, "I'm thankful fer family also and a fixed home that ain't a chuggin' down the railroad."

Macy's father smiled at her, "I reckon yer right, a fixed home is mighty nice. I'm thankful fer family, theys nothin like family."

"I'm thankful fer turkey," Lucy's little brother Ben said, eyeing the food on the table.

Everyone laughed.

Ms. Bevins looked with tears in her eyes at Macy and Lucy. "I reckon I'm most thankful fer a mop that were ruint with burrs," she told them and everyone laughed again.

Lucy's father picked up the platter of turkey, "Ben, pass Ms. Bevins some turkey."

They ate the meal telling stories and laughing, enjoying the time together.

Chapter 9
Christmas Decorations

Macy and Lucy rode back with Ms. Beulah to her house and helped unhitch the horse. The snow started coming down as they walked back home and by morning, it was almost knee deep.

Lucy woke up first, she jumped out of bed and ran to the window, "Oh Macy, look. Did ya ever see such a site?"

Macy ran over to the window to see what Lucy was talking about. "Why the ground's gone, it ain't nothin' but white ever'where' s. Do ya have school when they's snow ever'where's like this?" she turned to Lucy.

Lucy looked with wonder at the snow covered trees. The beauty of the snow never ceased to amaze her. "Yep, it don't matter ta teacher, he a'las has school. Well, 'ceptin' when we's a workin' fer the fall harvest."

Macy was disappointed, "I's sort a hopin' he'd call it off."

Lucy jumped back in the bed and pulled the covers up around her chin. "Why Macy?"

Macy started getting dressed. "We need's ta git us a tree and fix it up fer Christmas."

Lucy let out a sigh, "Oh, is that all? Pa a' las git's the tree fer us. We don't have ta worry 'bout that."

Macy shook her head. "We ort'ta be the one's git's it this year. Yer pa and my pa got enough ta worry 'bout with clearin' the new ground. I know' s jist what kind I want' s ta git too. One a them big lob lollys," she pulled the covers off Lucy and pulled her out of the bed.

Lucy jumped back in the bed and pulled the covers up around her neck. "Oh Macy, them ole trees are too big. They won't fit in the cabin. They's a grove a cedars not far. We can git's one of them."

Macy made a face at her. "No, I don't care fer cedars, they' s prickly when ya try ta decorate 'em."

Lucy's feelings were hurt. Macy never took any of her suggestions. "Well, them lob lollys, they ain't got no branches on ' em. They's scraggly lookin'," she said under her breath.

Macy pulled Lucy back out of the bed, "Not if'n ya get's the top a one. They's real full and purty at the top."

Lucy started getting dressed, "Well, maybe, but I like the hemlocks better'n them lob lollys. How 'bout we git a hemlock? They' s some purty ones jist over in the holler."

Macy had made up her mind. She shook her head, "We can climb up in the lob lollys and cut the top out of it."

Lucy's eyes bugged out at her, "Oh no, not me. I ain't a goin' up in no more trees.

'Sides it's too cold ta be a climin' trees."

Macy fidgeted around the room trying to make Lucy hurry and get dressed. "Yeah, it'll be fun. We'll do a search this mornin' ta find a big'un and git's it on the way back from school."

Lucy's mother opened the door to their room, "Girls, breakfasts a waitin', come on and eat 'afore it git's cold. Ya got ta git goin' if'n yer gonna git ta school today. I'll be a helpin' yer ma do some fixin's to their cabin today, Macy. I reckon it'll take us all day. I want ya girls to come straight back home from school and start supper."

"We's a comin' Ma," Lucy finished dressing. She hoped Macy would change her mind about the kind of tree they should choose for decorating.

After breakfast, they put on their coats and. shoes and started walking to school.

Lucy stopped walking and sat down on a rock. She wiggled her toes in her new shoes. "My feet are already hurtin'. These shoes ain't broke in yet. I been a wearin'um fer a month now, you'd think they'd be broke in a little better now."

Macy stopped and sat down beside her, "Let me see," she wiggled the shoes. "What ya got ta do is quit a growin' yer feet. That way ya can use the same ones ya had last year."

Lucy rolled her eyes at Macy, "Oh Macy, ya can't stop a growin' your feet."

Macy lifted her overalls so Lucy could see her shoes, "I could if'n I had a mind to. See mine are the same ones from last year."

Lucy put her finger in a hole on the side of Macy's shoe. "Yep, but ya got some holes a startin'. Yer feet's a gonna git cold purty fast when the snow starts getting in and makin' yer feet wet."

Macy stood up. "I'll just wear some extr'y socks if'n it does," she glanced over the hill and became very excited. The tree she had been searching for stood out to her, "Hey look over yonder. Ain't that the purtiest tree ya ever did see? It'll make the best one fer us ta git."

Lucy looked in the direction that Macy pointed. She shook her head, "That one's too big Macy. Why ya can't even reach the first limb." She leaned back to see the top of the tree.

She was determined that was the tree she wanted. Macy told her, "I'll shove ya up and ya can reach the bottom limb ta climb up in it."

Lucy crossed her arms and shook her head again, "I ain't a goin' up in that tree I told ya. 'Sides, I got's a dress on. I can't climb no tree in a dress. If'n ya want it, you'll have ta go up and git it yerself. What ya gonna chop it down with?"

Macy reached into her overalls and pulled out a small hatchet, "I borried yer pa's hatchet."

Lucy grabbed the hatchet from Macy, "Oh Macy, yer gittin' us inta trouble again. Pa'll be awful mad ya, dull his hatchet."

Macy took the hatchet back, "They's made fer chopin' wood, ain't they? Well, it won't dull it none. I swear Lucy, ya don't want ta do nothin' fun."

Lucy looked at the tree again, remembering the last time she climbed a tree with Macy. "Well ya climb it if'n ya want to. I ain't." she told her sternly.

They saw Sam coming up the road. "Hey Lucy, we's done been ta the school. The snow's too deep and teacher's froze in his house. Froze in his house. They ain't a gonna have no classes today. No classes today."

"Thank you Sam. We won't go no farther," Lucy hollered back at him.

Macy tried to understand why Sam repeated everything he said, "I think they's bound ta be somethin' wrong with him."

Lucy shrugged her shoulders, "I don't know. He's jist al'as been like that."

Macy started dragging Lucy down the hill to the tree, "See now, that's a sign, we can git the tree. Come on."

When they were at the base of the tree, they stood with their heads tilted back looking up at it. Macy decided maybe she should be the one to climb the tree and chop out the top.

She made Lucy stand beside the tree, "Now let me climb up on yer shoulders and I can reach the bottom limb. Cup yer hands and let me git a leg up."

Lucy cupped her hands behind her back. Macy put the hatchet on the ground and put her foot in Lucy's hands. She climbed up to stand on Lucy's shoulders.

Macy tried to reach the first limb but it was just barely out of her reach, "It's still a might high, jump a little so's I can reach it."

Lucy was about to fall on the slippery ground. "I can't jump with ya on my shoulders, yer 'bout ta weigh me down. Come on, let's find another one."

Macy jumped and grabbed the tree limb. Lucy was knocked to the ground, "Macy, that 'bout kilt me. Ya better git's it if'n this is the one ya want, on account I ain't a lettin' ya climb up on me no more."

Macy straddled the first big limb. She clapped her hands at Lucy, "Throw me the hatchet."

Lucy looked up at Macy. She shook her head no, "If'n I throw it, it'll come up and knock ya out'a that tree. I'll throw up yer lunch bucket and ya can tie yer belt 'round it. Then ya lower it down to me and I'll put the hatchet in it."

Macy thought that was a good idea. She untied her belt and threw it down to Lucy. "Ok, here's my belt."

Lucy looped the belt around the lunch bucket and tied a knot in it. She threw it back up to Macy. Macy missed catching the bucket and it hit her in the head, with a clunk.

Macy rubbed her head, "Hey, ya idget that hurt."

Lucy gave Macy an angry look, "Well, jist be glad it weren't that hatchet what hit ya in the head. Lower it back down."

Macy lowered the bucket down and Lucy put the hatchet in it. Macy pulled it back up and tied the bucket around her waist with the belt. She began climbing the tree. When she was able see the top, she stopped climbing. Taking the hatchet from the bucket she started chopping the tree.

Lucy looked up the tree, but she wasn't able to see Macy. "I hears ya a choppin', Macy, but I can't see's ya. Are ya alright?" Lucy yelled up to Macy.

Determined to chop the top out of the tree, Macy yelled back down, "It's a might big here. It'll take me a while. Best ta find ya a place ta sit. Or maybe ya can find some berries or somethin' ta decorate with whil'st I'm a choppin' the top."

Lucy found a log and sat down by the trunk of the white pine Macy was cutting. She listened to Macy hitting the tree with the hatchet.

Chop. Chop. Chop.

The cold and sound of the chopping made Lucy sleepy. She closed her eyes.

Chop. Chop. Chop.

Macy persisted in her chopping and in no time had the tree almost cut. She hit it one more time with the hatchet and it started to fall. "Timber!" Macy yelled.

Cold and sleepy, Lucy heard the tree falling and started running. She didn't move fast enough, so the tree top landed on her at the same moment she tried to jump out of the way.

Macy watched the tree land on Lucy and her heart leapt up in her throat. "Oh Lord. I've done kilt her," she said out loud. "Lucy, ya alright? Are ya kilt?" she yelled and started scrambling down out of the tree. When she got to the bottom limb, she jumped to the ground and ran over to where Lucy lay motionless under the tree top.

She started frantically moving the branches to see if Lucy was hurt. "Say somethin' to me Lucy! Are you kilt?" Macy shouted.

Lucy started batting at the branches. "No, I ain't kilt, but that there is the third time ya 'bout did kilt me!" Lucy yelled in an angry voice.

Macy gave a sigh of relief. She didn't know how she was going to explain if Lucy had been hurt again. "Well if'n ya ain't kilt, let's git's this tree back and start decoratin' it. Hurry now, I want to git it fixed 'afore anyone gets home. Come on, Lucy, git up."

Lucy was scratched all over and shivering from the cold, but she knew Macy was determined to make her help. She dragged herself up and dusted the snow and pine needles off her clothes. She helped take a hold of the tree top.

They dragged it a few feet. The tree top was very heavy so Lucy dropped her end and flopped down in the snow, "Macy, this'll be too big fer the cabin. We need ta chop it some more."

Macy dropped her end and looked at the tree top, "No, I like it this way. I know we can do it. Come on, it won't be that hard, help me pull it."

They dragged it a few more feet.

Lucy dropped her end again, "We's a draggin' all the needles of'n it. I told ya, it's too big."

Macy looked at the trail of pine needles behind them, "We kin put that side in the corner. Nobody'll see it."

They dragged the big tree top a few feet at a time and rested. When they got their breath back, they dragged again. Lucy was exhausted when they got the tree top home. They opened the door and tried to drag it inside the cabin. The tree top was too big for the door and it became stuck.

Lucy sat down on the porch step, "See I told ya, it's too big."

Macy looked at the tree, "I kin chop a little off'n it and it'll go through just fine." Macy took the hatchet and cut the limbs that had caused the tree to git stuck.

When Macy finished chopping the limbs, Lucy looked at the tree. She thought it was pitiful looking, "Look at this pitiful tree now, it ain't got no needles in the back and the sides are chopped off. It looks awful."

Macy started dragging the tree through the door, "It won't when we get's it fixed. I saved the strings of popcorn from the square dance and we can git some holly and berries ta fill in the sides. We can even git some apples from the fruit cellar."

Lucy began helping Macy pull the tree into the house, "I ain't a gittin' no apples fer Ma ta lick me over I tell ya rite now."

Macy gave an exasperated sigh, "She won't lick ya. We has ta eat them anyway's, else they'll ruin. We can jist eat them off'n the tree."

They pulled the tree into the big room. Lucy dropped her end and sat down in her mother's rocking chair, "Well, let's me rest a spell. I got ta git my wind back 'afore I do anythin' else."

Macy started back outside, "Alright. I'll go git a bucket ta set it in. We'll decorate when I git's ever'thin' ready to put on it."

Lucy took her shoes off and put her feet up next to the fire, "I wish ya would chop that ole holly tree down. Ma loves that ole tree. I hate's it. All it does is shed them leaves and they dry up like needles and stick yer feet when ya go walkin' in the yard."

Macy thought that was a good idea, "Yeah, they do look mighty purty in decoratin' I'll do that."

Lucy looked worried as she jumped up, "No, ya better not. Ma'll lick me shore ya chop up her holly tree."

Macy pushed Lucy back down in the rocking chair, "I'll jist take a little here and there. I'll make shore it ain't noticed."

Macy went back out to find her decorations and a bucket to sit the tree in. Lucy warmed herself by the fireplace. It took Macy a while to collect all her decorations. She came back in with a bucket and a sack full of holly boughs.

She dropped the sack beside Lucy and opened it, "Look here at all that I found. We can put this bucket 'round the bottom of the tree and then we can sit it up in the corner over yonder." She put the bucket on the bottom of the trunk.

Macy started trying to lift the tree. "Help me push it up," she demanded.

They both took hold of the tree and pushed. It took all the strength they had, but they muscled it up and balanced in the corner by the fireplace.

Lucy stepped back to look at it, "Well, it is purty standin' there big like that in the corner."

Macy smiled triumphantly, "See, I told ya it would be."

Lucy looked at the tree again, "Yeah, but it does look lopsided with them branches gone off'n the sides."

Macy handed the sack of holly to Lucy, "Ya need ta stick this holly in and we'll see if'n that helps."

Lucy took the holly boughs and stuffed them in the sides of the tree. The holly scratched her arm and it started bleeding, "Ouch! I got pricked!"

Macy didn't pay attention to her, "Now, go 'round to the other side and stick some more in there."

Lucy dropped the sack of holly, "Yer the one want's ta decorate with the holly, so ya can finish it. My hand is a bleedin' from these stickers."

Macy stuffed the holly in the tree. The holly scratched her arm also, "Ouch is right, they got me too." She stepped back to look at the decorations. I declare, it looks real purty, if'n I say so myself. Filled in them sides right good don't ya think?"

Lucy stood back and looked at the decorating they had done so far, "I reckon it did." Lucy looked in the sack of decorations to see what Macy had gathered, "What else ya got ta put on it?"

Macy pulled the strings of popcorn out of another bucket, "I got's some popcorn strings from the dance."

They both snickered remembering the polk berries. They wrapped the strings of popcorn around the tree. Lucy went to her room and found some red ribbons. They tied the apples on the tree with the ribbon. They didn't notice the pine needles all over the room. When they were finished decorating, they stepped back to admire the tree.

Macy clapped her hands in excitement, "See's I told ya them lob lolly tops'ud make a purty Christmas tree."

Lucy had to admit, the tree was pretty with all the decorations, "You's right, Macy that lob lolly did make a purty tree." She became excited when she heard footsteps on the porch. "I think I hear Ma on the porch, I think she'll really like it."

The tree started tipping and Lucy panicked as she watched it begin to topple over. "Oh no, Macy, it's falling over!" she yelled.

Lucy's mother had been visiting with Macy's mother and helping her get settled in their cabin. She came in the door at the same moment the tree began to fall. It fell on her and knocked her down.

Macy and Lucy looked at each other and started running for the tree. "Ma, Ma, are ya alright?" Lucy yelled.

Lucy's mother started struggling trying to get out from under the tree. "What in the world? Wher'd this come from? Help me out'a here. Ow, what's in here, stickers?"

Lucy pulled at the tree, "It's holly, Ma. We thought we'd fix a real purty Christmas tree fer ever'one."

Lucy's mother rolled around trying to escape the tree, "Ya best not chopped up my holly tree, Lucille Watson. Hurry now, git this tree off'n me."

They pulled the tree to the side and helped her up. She stood there in silence looking at the mess of pine needles and decorations. She looked around the room, "I don't care how long it takes. If'n yer here till this time next year. I want ever needle picked up off'n this floor."

Lucy protested, "But Ma, we can fix it back up. The tree were jist heavy with decorations. We'll arrange some on the back. Don't you even like it?"

Lucy's mother tried to control her temper, "Lucille Watson, of all the crazy things, jist look around this room. They ain't no needles left on that tree fer ya to decorate. They's all in the floor. Take it outside and git rid of it. When I come back, ya better have this mess cleaned up." She turned around and stormed back out the door. She was going back to Macy's mother's cabin before she laughed or really lost her temper.

Lucy looked around the room, for the first time, she noticed the pine needles all over the floor. "Oh Macy, what a mess. Look at this room. They's not a place don't have a tree sprig on it. We will be here 'till next year. What are we a gonna do?" Lucy wailed.

Macy didn't say a word. She went outside and got a big ax. She came back in and started chopping at the middle of the tree. Lucy took the hatchet and started helping her.

Every time they chopped what was left of the pine needles, more fell off the tree. They chopped it in two pieces.

Lucy looked over at the fire. She had an idea, "Hey Macy, ever' time we chops at this tree, it sheds more needles. Most of the branches are on the top part. Why don't we jist stick the top up the fireplace. It'll burn up and won't git no more on the floor."

Macy looked from the tree to the fireplace, "Yeah, that's quick thinkin', Lucy."

They dragged the bottom trunk over by the door and set it down. They pulled the top to the fireplace, twisted it around and shoved it up the chimney. They stood back pleased with themselves.

WHOOOSH! The sap in the tree caught on fire and the blaze went up the tree like a lightning bolt. The fire and sparks flew out of the chimney and landed all over the room.

"It's a gonna burn the cabin down," Lucy screamed as she ran for the door.

"Grab the bucket and git some snow ta throw on it!" Macy hollered. She grabbed the sack that she had put her decorations in and started batting at the sparks that popped out of the fireplace.

Lucy grabbed the bucket and jumped over the bottom part of the tree. She ran outside and scooped up a bucket full of snow. She ran back inside just as a spark set the other half of the tree on fire.

Macy grabbed the bucket and threw the snow on the tree. It started smoldering and smoke filled the room. She jerked the tree and started pulling it out of the cabin. "Hurry we got's ta pull this'un outside 'afore it catches up. The cabin'll burn shore if'n it does."

Lucy snatched up the smoldering tree and started helping Macy pull it outside. Smoke engulfed them and made their eyes sting. "My eyes are a waterin' and I can't see," she wailed.

Macy yelled at her, "Jist pull backwards, we's almost got's it. Keep pulling, hurry!"

They pulled the log outside and dumped it off the porch in the snow. They ran back inside. Sparks were still flying around the room. Lucy grabbed the bucket and ran back outside to fill it with more snow. Macy batted furiously at the sparks that still popped out of the fireplace.

Sparks settled on the floor and small flickers of flames started up. Macy panicked, "Hurry Lucy, git some more. I can't stomp them sparks fast enough. We's a gonna burn the cabin down, shore."

Lucy ran back inside and dumped the bucket of snow on the fire. The flame hissed as it dwindled to ashes. Little wisps of smoke curled up the chimney.

Lucy wiped the soot out of her eyes and peered into the fireplace, "Is it out?"

Macy stomped and the remaining embers that tried to start up, "It's still a sizzling. Run git a bucket of water."

Lucy ran over to the sink and filled the bucket with water. The smoke began to die down. She came back over to the fireplace and stood poised with the bucket, in front of it. "Reckon it's out now?" she asked as a flicker of flame started up. Lucy threw the bucket of water at it. A puff of soot came out of the chimney, covering both of them. They were black from head to toe.

Lucy sat down on the floor and started crying, "Now what'er we gonna do. We drag this out we'll git the whole cabin black with the soot."

Macy threw her hands in the air, "I don't know, maybe we can get's a sheet ta wrap it in and that'll keep it off'n the floor."

Lucy stopped crying, "They's some old'uns in the chest by Ma's bed. Be shore and not git one a Ma's good sheets though. I'll stay here and make shore it don't start up again." Lucy went back over to the sink and filled the bucket with water. She brought it in the room and set it by the fireplace.

Macy found a sheet, that they wrapped the half burnt tree top in and dragged it outside.

Lucy wrinkled her nose at the strong smell from the burnt wood, "Sheewwweee it stinks now. Nothin' worse than a half burnt log fer stinkin'. Macy, I ain't a list'nin' ta you no more 'bout nothin'."

Macy turned to Lucy and put her hands on her hips. "It were yer idea to stick that tree up the chimney. Yer the cause all this," she accused Lucy.

Lucy put her hands on her hips, "Ya should'a know'd that were a gonna happen."

Macy ignored her, "Hey, we can take yer idea and git us a hemlock tomorry'."

Lucy punched Macy on the arm, “Not me, I’s a waitin’ on Pa ta git one. This has learn’t me a lesson and I ain’t a gonna help ya no more.”

Macy sighed, “I reckon it jist as well. We’ll be a cleanin’ on this mess till next week.”

Lucy slumped her shoulders and looked at the mess, “I’ll get’s the broom and start a sweepin’.”

It took three baths and two days to wash the soot out of their hair, and get the soot in the cabin cleaned up. Lucy’s mother felt sorry for them and helped. She also knew that it was the only way to get the cabin back to normal.

Chapter 10
Lucy Gets a Hair Cut

Macy's brothers went to Gatlinburg for supplies and came back with a new Sears and Roebuck Christmas catalogue.

Lucy and Macy were fascinated by the pictures of merchandise and models, and loved to look at it. They flipped through the pages and circled things they saw that they liked. Both of the girls secretly hoped this Christmas, they would get something they had been wanting.

Macy showed Lucy a picture of a bicycle, "Would ya look at that contraption! I never saw such a thing. I'd really like to have somethin' like that. Ya reckon if'n I was to show that to Ma and Pa, they might git it for me?"

Lucy grinned at her, "I think we'll probably git a lump a coal in our stockin' fer all the meanness we been up too lately."

Macy flipped the page and paused, "If'n yer a talkin' 'bout them girls, Helen and Loretta, it ain't mean if'n they gots what's a comin' to 'em." Macy started turning the pages again.

Lucy looked up at Macy, "No, I's a talkin' 'bout settin' the cabin on fire."

Macy paused from looking at the catalogue and looked over at Lucy. With wide open eyes. "Hey, that wern't our fault. We's just a tryin' ta decorate fer ever'body. They can't be mad for that. How were we supposed to know that tree'ud burn up like that?"

Lucy put the catalogue down and went over to the window, "Ma ain't hardly said a word ta me fer three days now."

Macy nodded her head, "She ain't said nothin' ta me neither but at least we didn't git a lickin' for it."

"I guess so," Lucy sighed and came over to pick up the catalogue. She found her place and flipped the page. She became excited when she saw the picture of the model. "Look here, Macy at this girl. Ain't she got the purtiest hair ya ever did see? I wish my hair were like that."

Macy looked at the picture, "Well, why don't ya cut it like that?"

Lucy exclaimed, "Ma'd lick me shore I go a cuttin' my hair."

Macy looked at the picture again. "I can cut it and it'll look just like this here girls in this picture. If'n it's purty like this, she can't be mad at ya."

Lucy looked from the catalogue to Macy. She didn't believe Macy knew how to cut hair. "Really? How do ya know how to cut hair that way?" she asked.

Macy went over to the dresser and took out a pair of scissors. "It's easy, let me show ya. All's ya got ta do is put a braid in the back and jist cut that off. It'll be short in the back and a might long in the front, look jist like this," she pointed to the picture.

Lucy looked at the picture again, "Have ya ever cut anybody's hair afore?"

"I cut's my hair all the time," Macy rubbed her braided hair under her nose.

Lucy watched Macy flick her hair back and forth across her nose, "Ya do that all the time, rub yer hair across yer nose. Why do ya do that?"

Macy dropped the braid, "Habit I reckon. Ma say's I been a doin' it ever since I was little. Jist got out'a the habit a suckin' my thumb. Now that were a hard habit to break. I's a'feered them girls at school'ud make fun of me, so I quit a doin' that."

Lucy remembered that she hadn't seen Macy with her thumb in her mouth for quite some time, "Yeah, I seen ya had quit a doin' that."

Macy stood up and clicked the scissors together. "Well, ya want's me to cut yer hair for ya or not?" she challenged Lucy.

Lucy looked from Macy with the scissors in her hand and back to the picture in the catalogue. "I don't know. Ma'd be more mad at me than she is now I mess my hair up."

Macy went over to the dresser and put the scissors down. She came over and sat beside Lucy. "I promise it'll look jist like that girl in the picture. I cross my heart," Macy made a motion to cross her heart and held up her hand.

Lucy looked at the picture again. She envied the model in the picture, "Well, if'n ya know how, I reckon it'll be okay."

Macy went over to the dresser and picked up the scissors again. She patted a chair for Lucy to sit down, "Well come over here and sit down, turn around and let me braid yer hair."

Lucy sat in the chair and turned around. Macy braided Lucy's hair in one long braid down the middle of Lucy's head. She took the scissors and began cutting the braid she had made. It was harder than she thought, so she had to cut hard.

Tears came into Lucy's eyes from the pulling. She reached around and took Macy's hand. "Hey what'er ya doin', Macy, yer a pullin' me bald," she cried.

The scissors made a ripping sound as Macy sawed at Lucy's hair. "Hey Macy, that sounds awful. Like yer a cuttin' me bald headed."

Macy shushed her, "Be still. I'm almost done."

Lucy heard the scissors, snip, snip, snip, snip. "Hey, I thought ya said ya was almost done."

"There! Finished," Macy yelled and pulled the braid free.

Lucy looked up at Macy. She was excited, "Well, how's it look?"

Macy stood there looking at the enormous gap she had just made in Lucy's hair. "Well, it didn't 'xaclty go like I thought it would."

In panic, Lucy threw her hands to the back of her head to feel her hair. She felt the short hair and the gaps of uneven hair. She felt the long hair on the sides. "WHAT! What did you do to me, Macy?" Lucy was beside herself with fear.

Macy tried to calm Lucy down, "Well now, it ain't that bad really. One good thing is that it'll grow back soon."

Lucy felt of her hair again, "Oh Macy, my hair feels like it's all gone. Here give me the mirror." She grabbed a small mirror and ran to the big mirror on the dresser. She wheeled around and held the mirror up so that she could see the back of her hair. Her heart dropped to her knees. "My hair's all gone, oh Lord, Ma and Pa's a gonna kill me!" she wailed.

Macy went over and picked up the catalogue. She held up the picture for Lucy to see. "It don't look that bad from the front. See look, the front looks jist like the picture."

Lucy whirled around and held up the little mirror so that she was able to look at the back of her hair, again. "I don't have any hair in the back. How can I go to school without no hair. They'll all make fun a me shore," Lucy moaned.

Macy tried to pacify her, "Ya can wear a bonnet 'till it grows back."

Lucy started crying louder. "We don't wear bonnets in the winter and how am I gonna 'splain this ta Ma?" she sobbed. "I know. Yer gonna have to 'splain to my ma how this happened."

Macy pointed her finger at her chest, "Me? It were yer idea to cut yer hair. Yer the one wanted ta look like that picture in the catalogue. I ain't got's to 'splain nothin'."

"Ya said, ya know'd how to cut it purty," Lucy said between sobs. "How are we a gonna hide this from Ma?"

Macy started looking through the dresser for a bonnet. "I tell ya what ta do, ya put yer bonnet on and tell yer Ma, yer head were cold. It's cold here in yer room anyway's."

Lucy wiped her nose on her sleeve and sniffed, "I don't even know where the bonnets are now. Ma warshed all the summer clothes and put them away."

Macy motioned for Lucy to stay in the room, "Jist wait right here. I'll go and find one for ya."

Macy ran out of the room and Lucy went over to the mirror to look at herself again. She turned from side to side. She did think the front of her hair looked like the picture. It touched her shoulders. But when she held up the mirror to look at the back of her hair, she started crying again.

Macy came back in a few minutes with a bonnet she had found, "I found one. This were hard sneakin' this in here to ya, yer ma was a watchin' to see what I's a doin'."

Lucy grabbed the bonnet and tied it on her head, "Did she see's ya git it?"

"No, I don't think so," Macy shook her head. She spun Lucy around to look in the mirror, "See it looks good with yer hair sticking out the front like that."

Lucy moved the bonnet to arrange it on her head better. She looked at herself in the mirror, turning from side to side. "Ya can't tell much with this on. Maybe Ma'll not notice."

They heard Lucy's mother calling for them, "Girls, this food is a gittin' cold. Come on in here ta supper. Yer Pa's jist got home from cuttin' timber all day with Macy's pa and he's hungry."

Lucy looked at herself one more time in the mirror. "Coming, Ma," Lucy yelled back.

They scurried down the hall and into the kitchen. They flopped down at the table.

Lucy's mother looked up from setting the food on the table and saw the bonnet on Lucy's head. "Lucille Watson, what are ya a doin' with yer best summer bonnet on yer head?" she demanded to know.

Lucy touched the bonnet, "My head was cold."

Her mother came around the table and put her hand on Lucy's forehead. "Are ya gettin' sick? That's all we need for ya to come down with the chills. We'd all be sick shore in jist a little while."

Lucy sat down and reached for a biscuit. "I don't think I am, Ma. It's jist cold in my room," she said hoping her mother would let the subject drop.

Her mother finished putting the food on the table, "Well, it ain't cold in here. Take it off afore ya git it all dirtied back up. I'll find ya a night cap to wear when ya go to bed tonight."

Lucy's heart leapt up in her throat, "But Ma, my heads still cold. Can't I wear it jist fer a little while."

Lucy's mother looked up from putting milk on the table, "For pete's sake, take it off and I'll go find ya a night cap." Her mother left the table and stomped off to find the night cap for Lucy.

Lucy's father passed a bowl of potatoes to her, "Ya heer'ed yer ma, Lucy, take off that clean bonnet and put it on the chair there."

Lucy touched the bonnet, "But Pa, I's hopin' to wear it till she git's back. I'm awfully cold."

"No, go ahead now and do like I told ya," he said and ladled some corn in his plate.

Lucy untied the bonnet and took it off.

He father looked at the huge gap in the back of Lucy's hair and let out a whistle. "Well now, we know's why ya was a wearin' that bonnet.

How in the world did that happen, Ms. Lucille?" he asked.

Lucy hung her head down, "It were Macy's idea."

Macy dropped her fork and choked on a bite of food, "It were not, ya said ya wanted yer hair to look like that girl's hair, the one in the picture in the catalogue."

Lucy darted Macy an angry look, "But ya said ya know'd how ta cut it like that picture, ya said ya knew how."

Lucy's father looked back and forth from Macy to Lucy. "Ya let Macy cut yer hair?" he asked.

"She said she know'd how," Lucy said in a whimper of misery.

Her father started laughing, "And ya believed her? Lucy, I don't know what get's in yer head sometimes. This is a good lesson for ya I reckon. I'll find ya a chapter in the bible about pride a goin' afore a fall after supper for ya ta read."

Lucy's little brother Ben came in the kitchen with her older brother Jeb. They had been out getting wood. Ben stopped abruptly in the doorway when he saw Lucy's hair and Jeb bumped into him. "Hey, what happened to yer hair?" Ben exclaimed. "It looks like one a Jack's mutt dogs."

Jeb went over to Lucy. "Now that's a fact, how come ya cut it that way, little sister? Ya look like you been in a hatchet fight and ya forgot yer hatchet to fight with," Jeb rubbed her hair.

Lucy slapped his hand away, "On a'count I wanted to, that's why. And it ain't none a yer business."

"Well, it's certainly my business," Lucy's mother said from the doorway.

Lucy jumped and turned to look in her direction.

Her mother came over to inspect Lucy's hair. "I see's now why ya got that bonnet out. I'd like ta know what ya was a thinkin'. Please 'splain to me what happened to yer hair," she started tapping her foot and waited for Lucy to answer.

Lucy started crying again, "Macy said…"

Macy cut her off in mid-sentence. "Ya said ya wanted yer hair cut. So's I cut it for ya!" she said loudly.

Lucy's mother crossed her arms, "Ya can't blame Macy, Lucille, if'n it were yer idea. Don't ya know ya can't believe everthin' yer told? Ya should'a know'd Macy didn't know how to cut hair."

Ben started laughing, "That beats anythin' I ever seed."

The tears started streaming down Lucy's face.

Lucy's mother started pushing the strands of long hair away from Lucy's face. "Hush now, cryin' ain't a gonna make it grow back. I reckon I should cut the front some so's it grows back even."

"Oh, Ma! Don't cut it no more!" Lucy screamed.

She dropped the strand of hair and put the night cap on Lucy's head. "Well, I hope ya have learn't ya a lesson."

Lucy sniffed back the tears, "Ma, can I stay home from school, I mean jist till it grows back?"

Lucy's mother shook her head, "No, yer jist gonna have to learn that ya need to think afore ya jump's and does somethin'."

Lucy tried another argument, "But them girls'll make fun a me shore."

Lucy's mother gave her a weary look, "Well, no more'n ya caused them to be made fun of."

"We didn't do nothin' to them girls," Lucy whimpered.

Her mother replied, "Oh, yes, ya did. Don't ya think for a second ya fooled me, Lucille and ya too, Macy. I know ya tricked them girls at the square dance." Lucy's mother handed her a biscuit, "Go on now eat yer supper."

Lucy put her fork down, "I ain't hungry now."

Her mother tapped the table with the spoon, "Eat it anyway. We don't waste 'round here. Ya too, Macy."

Lucy tried to eat but the food had no taste. She pushed it around on her plate until her mother sent her and Macy off to bed.

Lucy and Macy went to their room. They changed into their nightgowns getting ready for bed. They squiggled down under the covers to get warm. Macy poked her head out and looked over at Lucy. "I'm sorry I ruin't yer hair. If'n them girls make fun a ya, I'll just knock'um in the head with somethin'," she blew out the lantern and turned over.

Lucy silently cried herself to sleep.

The morning came way too early for Lucy. She rolled over and felt of her hair hoping she had just had a bad dream.

Already up and dressed, Macy had an idea. "Maybe ya could act like yer sick this mornin'. Can ya cough real loud?" she asked Lucy.

Lucy forced herself to get out of the bed, "She'd not believe me."

Macy chewed her bottom lip, "No, prob'ly not. But, ya could wear a hat, like me."

Lucy put her hand to the back of her hair and felt the reality of the hair cut, "I think it'd be better'n this."

Macy handed her one of her straw hats. "Yeah it will, and if'n them girls make fun'a ya, I'll jist give them what fer," Macy shook her fist in the air.

Lucy knew her cousin would do it too. "Don't start no more trouble Macy. It'll be Christmas soon and I don't want to git a lump a coal in my sock this year. That's jist what we're a headin' fer I reckon," she begged.

Macy sat down on the bed and pulled her brogan shoes on her feet. "Gitting a lump a coal won't be the first time for me," she admitted.

Lucy forgot about her hair for a minute and she giggled, "What did ya do?"

Macy shrugged her shoulders, "Didn't do nothin' Ma jist got plum mad an 'count a I used her best table linen to make a bed and nurse some kittens. They didn't have no ma to take care of 'em."

Lucy laughed at that, "Why even I know'd not to do somethin' like that. How's come ya got the best linen and didn't git no rag or somethin'?"

Macy leaned over to Lucy, "Well, I tell ya, them was the purtyest little critters ya ever did see. I thought I'd get'um somethin' purty to lay on."

Lucy snickered, "Did she git plum mad?"

"I'll say she did. That happened close to Christmas time and I got a lump a coal in my sock on 'count of it. To make matters worse, I had to help Pa chop wood to sell and buy her a new table cloth, to make up for the one I ruin't. Took me a month to git her to speak back to me."

Lucy laughed, "What'd ya do with yer cats?"

Macy stood up, "Give'um away, they's a'las someone a wantin' a mouser."

Chapter 11
Lucy Sings

After they dressed for school and ate breakfast, Macy and Lucy bundled up and headed out for school. Lucy carried one of Macy's straw hats under her arm. She didn't put it on until they were out the door.

Macy nodded at her, "That don't look half bad Lucy. Maybe nobody'll notice."

They made the walk to the school in silence. Each one was absorbed in their own thoughts.

Lucy worked herself into a panic about her hair. The walk seemed to last forever and get longer to her with every step she took. When they turned the curve in the road that went by Ms. Beulah's house, they saw her waiting for them on her porch.

Ms. Beulah's face lit up in a smile when she saw her friends coming down the road. She met them at the gate, "Good mornin' girls. I need to go to the store this mornin'. If'n ya'll hitch up the buggy for me and I'll take ya to school."

Lucy rubbed her hands together. She was glad to be riding in the buggy. "Thank ya Ms. Beulah, it's blusterin' cold this mornin'," she said.

Ms. Beulah smiled at them agreeing, "That it is fer a fact. Go on out to the barn and git the rig and I'll meet ya out front in a jiffy."

They ran to the barn and hitched the horse to the buggy. They were both glad not to have to walk the rest of the way in the snow this morning. Macy led the horse out of the barn and they brought the buggy around to the front of the house. Lucy helped Ms. Beulah up in the buggy.

When they all settled in the buggy, Ms. Beulah flicked the reins and they were off at a trot. She looked over at the girls and gave them a wink, "It won't be long girls 'till it's Christmas mornin'. Yer gonna git's somethin' real nice on 'count a ya bein' such good girls I reckon."

The girls just looked at each other. Macy spoke up, "I don't right'ly know Ms. Beulah, we're sort'a thinkin' we'll git's a bunch a switches or maybe a lump a coal."

Ms. Beaulah had grown to love Macy and Lucy and laughed, "I think ya might be surprised what ya'll git's fer sure."

She drove them all the way to the schoolyard. The two girls jumped down out of the buggy and waved goodbye to her. They scurried in the schoolhouse and sat down at their desks.

Mr. Jenkins rang the bell on the desk. "Quiet now. I have an idea, how would all of you like to put on a pageant for Christmas?" he asked.

All the children clapped. The boys whistled.

He held up his hands for silence, "Good, I think the best story comes from the bible. It is the story of the baby Jesus. I think that is what we should do for our pageant. We'll need a Mary and Joseph. Who wants to be Mary?"

All the girls held up their hands and bounced excitedly in their seats.

Loretta stood up and tossed her hair, "I'm the oldest, I think's I should be Mary."

Helen stood up beside her, "Yeah, I think's she should be Mary with her black hair."

"You mean purple hair," Macy blurted out.

All the children laughed at Helen and Loretta.

"My hair ain't purple now," Helen said and stuck her tongue out at them.

Mr. Jenkins rang his bell again and instructed, "Quiet that's enough. Yes, Loretta, you can be Mary and I think John should be Joseph."

All the boys started clapping and whistled at his suggestion.

Mr. Jenkins said, "Settle down, settle down. We need some angels and shepherds for our play. Who wants to be an angel?"

Helen raised her hand. She looked over at Louise and Olivia Howard, she thought they looked like angels with their white hair and big blue eyes. "I can be an angel. So can Louise and Olivia," she suggested.

Mr. Jenkins nodded approval, "Okay, we've got our angels, now

check see what it is? Go check?"

Mr. Jenkins cleared his throat, "No Sam, that's alright. I think I know what the noise is now. Maybe we don't need everyone to sing in this pageant. We don't have a lot of people and we will only need one person to sing. Everyone else will be in the pageant."

Macy took the hymnal from his hand, "Who's a gonna sing? I'd shore like to sing and not be a shepherd in the play."

Mr. Jenkins thought for a moment. "Um, yes, we need to have you be the director, Macy. You can help me with costumes and the little ones. I need you to help them get their places. Do you think you could do that?" he asked her to redirect her attention away from singing.

Macy felt proud to be asked to be the director. The director sounded like it was a very important job to her. "Oh shore, I can help with that, but I like to sing, I can do that too if'n ya want me too."

Mr. Jenkins cleared his throat, "No, no Macy. The job I have for you is much more important." He turned to the class. "I think what we will do is have auditions after school to see who will to sing for us," he turned back to Ms. Bevins. "Ms. Bevins would it be too much trouble for you come back… say about two, and help us with the auditions?"

She smiled at the class, "No trouble a'tall. Yes I will. I shouldn't be too long getting the things I need from the store and I'll take them home and be back at two."

Mr. Jenkins clapped his hands, "Great! Thank you very much for your help. Now, children while Ms. Bevins is leaving let's get back to our desks and take out our lesson books. We will start getting things ready for the pageant when she comes back this afternoon. I have to send a telegram. I'm going to go to the store with her. You children begin reading the lesson and we will discuss it when I get back."

After Mr. Jenkins and Ms. Bevins left the room, Bob Blaylock went over to Lucy and knocked the straw hat off her head.

He stopped and stared at Lucy's missing and gapped hair. "Would ya look at that? What in the world happened ta your hair?" he asked Lucy.

Lucy grabbed her hat and shoved it back down on her head, "T'ain't none a yer business."

Macy jumped up from her desk and went over to Lucy. "Better leave Lucy alone," she warned.

Bob started laughing, "I ain't a botherin' her. I jist never seed seech a thing afore. Looks like she's been caught in one a them saws down at the mill."

Macy balled up her fist and stated, "If ya want ta know, I cut it fer her. That's the way they cut their hair in the catalogues."

John snickered, "I never see'd no hair cut like that in the mail order books. But if'n ya cut it, that 'splains why it looks that bad."

Lucy started crying. Macy ran over to John and drew her hand back and warned him, "Her hair don't look bad, take that back."

"How kin he take it back when it's the truth?" Helen asked her.

Macy wheeled around to stare at Helen. "Ya stay out'a this, Helen, else I'll whoop ya too." She turned back to John, "Take it back John Taylor."

Lucy tugged on Macy's sleeve and pleaded, "Macy, please don't."

Macy's face became red with anger as she looked at John. "Take, it, back," she said every word slowly with emphasis.

John shoved her backwards. "I ain't a gonna, it's the truth. Lucy looks awful now. Ya done went and ruin't what hair she had."

Macy swung her fist and connected with his jaw. It knocked him across the room.

Loretta jumped up and ran over to John. "John, are ya alright?" she cradled his head in her lap.

Macy started toward him with her fist balled up. Helen stepped in front of her.

Macy drew her fist back again, "Get out'a my way, else I'll knock ya a windin' too."

Helen shoved Macy backwards, "What do ya think yer a doin'? leave John alone. He jist told the truth. Lucy does look awful."

Macy grabbed Helen's hair and pulled it. Helen grabbed Macy's hair back. They both fell on the floor, rolling and pulling each other's hair. They knocked over several desks. Macy got on top of Helen and sat straddling her chest.

"Get off'n me!" Helen yelled at her.

Macy had both hands in her hair pulling it, "Take it back and I will."

Sam and Bob jumped in and tried to separate them. Macy punched Sam in the stomach and he fell backwards into Mr. Jenkins desk. He knocked the books and papers all over the room.

Mr. Jenkins came back from sending his telegram as the fight escalated. He opened the door and an eraser hit him in the mouth.

"What in the world is going on here? Stop this. Stop this instant!" he yelled.

The fight continued. He ran to his desk and began ringing his bell. "Stop it, stop it, now!" he yelled over the noise of the battle.

The room became quiet. Macy still had a hold of Helen's hair.

Helen shoved Macy, "Let go'a me."

Macy turned loose of her hair and stood up.

"What is the meaning of this?" Mr. Jenkins asked them. "Who started this?"

Helen stood up, rubbing her head, "It were Macy. She knocked John with her fist and I tried ta stop her."

Everyone turned to look at Macy.

Macy stepped back from Helen. "They was a makin' fun a Lucy, Mr. Jenkins. That's how's come we was a fightin'. I were jist a takin' up for her."

Mr. Jenkins looked over the class. "Is that true? Who was making fun of Lucy and why?"

Loretta came over to Mr. Jenkins and pointed at Lucy's hat. "Make her take that hat off'n her and you'll see why. She's mostly bald in the back of her head on 'count a Macy cut her hair."

Mr. Jenkins turned to look at Lucy, "What? Lucy come here and take off that hat."

Lucy sat slumped with her head down at her desk. She stood up and walked over to Mr. Jenkins.

He instructed her, "Well go on, take off your hat, Lucy."

She reached up and pulled the straw hat down off her head.

"Oh My," was all Mr. Jenkins could think to say.

Loretta nodded her head, "See I told ya. Ain't that the worst thing ya ever did see?"

Macy went over and stood beside Lucy. She turned to Loretta, "Watch out now, else I'll clobber ya, too."

Mr. Jenkins stopped it before the fight broke out again. "Now, now, there will be no more clobbering. Everyone go back to their seats."

Mr. Jenkins patted her on the back, "You put your hat back on, Lucy. It doesn't look that bad and I know it will grow back soon. Go on back to your desk."

Lucy put her hat on and dragged her feet with every step back to her desk.

Mr. Jenkins rang the bell, "There will be no more fighting or I will have to tell your parents."

At two o'clock, Ms. Bevins came back and Mr. Jenkins dismissed lessons for the day. "Alright, that is enough for today. We are going to see who needs to sing in the play for us. Anyone that wants to sing will need to stay and do an audition. We will choose the person who sings the best."

Macy was the first one to the piano. Lucy dragged along behind her. "I want's to be the first one to try out and sing for ya, Mr. Jenkins."

He cleared his throat. "Um, well, yes, Macy. I need you to help organize the whole play. We'll call you the director's assistant. I think that will take up too much of your time to sing," he said to divert her attention.

Macy sat back down, "Well okay, but if'n ya need me to, now I can sing, too."

Mr. Jenkins looked over at Lucy, "How about you, Lucy? Do you want to try out for the singing?"

"I bet she can't sing a lick," Helen whispered to Loretta.

"Prob'ly not. I'm the one that sings. But I am goin' ta be Mary and I can't sing. I don't care anyway. Let's go on home," Loretta whispered back.

Lucy picked at her dress, "I don't know, Mr. Jenkins, I never tried to sing much."

He motioned for her to come up to the piano. "Come up here and try. Sing a few verses and we will see. How's that?"

Lucy took a deep breath, "Ok, I'll try."

Ms. Bevins smiled and nodded to her.

She started playing and Lucy began to sing, "Silent night, holy night, all is calm, all is bright."

Mr. Jenkins and Ms. Bevins looked at each other as Lucy sang. Helen and Loretta stopped at the door and turned around. All the other children stopped talking to listen at Lucy singing.

When Lucy finished the song, the room was completely quiet.

She looked around at everyone staring at her. Her heart skipped a beat. She thought that she had sung off key. "What? Were it not no good?" she darted nervous looks at everyone who stared at her.

"Why Lucy, ya sang that beautifully!" Mr. Jenkins exclaimed.

"That were beautiful, child. That sounded like the voice of an angel," Ms. Beulah told her.

Macy started clapping her hands. "Why that's the pur'tiest singin' I ever did heer. I'd a not believed it but ya really can sing. Yeah, go on sing us another song."

Ms. Beulah smiled at her, "Yes, do sing another one for us Lucy."

Lucy smiled at them, "What do ya want me to sing?"

Mr. Jenkins got a hymnal and turned to the Christmas songs, "Do you know Star of Bethlehem?"

Lucy took the hymnal from him, "Yes, but I don't 'member all the words."

"Wait right there. I'll get another hymnal for Ms. Bevins to play out of," Mr. Jenkins picked up a hymnal from the back of one of the pews and brought it to her.

Lucy turned to the page and placed it on the piano. Ms. Bevins started playing. "Oh beautiful star of Bethlehem, shining a far through shadows dim," she began singing. When she finished, everyone clapped and cheered for her. Lucy smiled at them with delight.

Macy went over and stood beside Lucy, "I think Lucy should be the only one to sing fer us Mr. Jenkins."

Mr. Jenkins nodded his approval, "I think you are right Macy." He turned to the other children. "What does everyone think? Should Lucy sing for us?"

The students cheered and clapped and that was their answer.

"Okay, that is settled. Lucy, you stand here on the pulpit. We will put a curtain up and no one will see you singing. It will be as if an angel is singing for us."

"That shore is a good idea, Mr. Jenkins," Macy said. "That way she won't get 'sceered like she a'las does 'bout ever'thin' 'sides her hair won't be grow'd out by then and we'll have to hide her."

On the way home, Lucy made Macy promise not to tell their parents. She wanted her singing to be a surprise for everyone.

Chapter 12
Christmas Play

For two weeks, the children practiced their play. Lucy and Macy kept the secret of Lucy singing. They had a hard time keeping Lucy's secret, but they managed not to tell.

Mr. Jenkins decided that the best time to put on the pageant would be the Sunday before Christmas. Macy and Lucy stayed behind after church with all the other children that day to help decorate and get set up for the play. They started working on the props for the play. Mr. Jenkins brought a stained glass star for the wall above the manger.

When Lucy saw the star, she loved it. She turned the star over in her hand looking at it. "I think that's the purtiest thing I ever did see, Mr. Jenkins."

Mr. Jenkins took the star to find the best place to put it, "I found it at the Christmas craft fair in Gatlinburg. I thought we should put it on the wall behind the manger and shine a light on it. That way, all the colors will reflect on the manger at just the right moment in our play."

Macy climbed up on the pew behind the pulpit. "I think it'd be purty right here above the manger," she motioned for the star and Mr. Jenkins handed it to her.

"Now, hold it up as high as you can," he told Macy. Then he stepped back to look at where she was holding the star.

Macy held the star up over her head, "How 'bout this?"

"Yes that's perfect. Hold that and I will shine the light on it to see how it looks."

Mr. Jenkins held up a lamp and shined it at the star. The colors danced across the pulpit.

Loretta and Helen were setting up the manger scene. "That's just beautiful Mr. Jenkins," Loretta told him.

Helen bounced around the manger barely able to contain her excitement about the play. "We never did nothin' like this afore, it's fun. Don't ya think so Loretta?" Helen turned to her.

Loretta arranged her chair around the manger, “I do think this is fun. Mr. Jenkins?”

He stepped off the ladder, “Yes, Loretta.”

Loretta went over and looked up at the star. “What’cha gonna do with that star when we’s done?”

Mr. Jenkins stopped decorating and looked up at the star, “Well, I hadn’t actually thought about that, maybe we will use it for the top of our Christmas tree when we decorate it.” He turned to the other children. “Sam if you brought the hay for the manger you can bring it in now. Make sure you arrange the manger in the middle of the stage. We will need a chair beside it for Loretta.”

Sam went out and came back in with the hay under his arm, “I shore did and I ‘membered ta bring the manger, too. Manger, too.”

Mr. Jenkins turned to the stage, “Ok, where are our props of animals. Olivia, you put the animals your father carved for us around the manger. Thank him for us. That was a lot of work. They look great.”

“I will Mr. Jenkins, he say’s ya can keep’em after the play if’n ya want.”

“That is very nice of him Olivia. I’ll thank him after the play myself.” He turned to Macy, “Macy, you gather up our shepherds and the little ones that are the sheep and help them with their costumes.”

Macy liked being in charge. “All the shepherds come with me to git fixed with yer shepherd outfits,” she rounded up the little ones and marched them behind the curtain.

Mr. Jenkins went behind the curtain to find Lucy, “How are you doing, Lucy? No stage fright I hope?”

Lucy fidgeted nervously, “Long as I can stay behind this curtain, I’ll be fine. I jist don’t like when I get’s stared at.”

He patted her on the head, “Good girl, we are all counting on you.” He went back out on the stage to see how the other children were doing. “Helen you and Olivia find Louise and get the halos fitted on your heads. We don’t need angels with their halos falling off, now do we?”

Helen giggled, “No, we shore don’t. I’ll go get’em fixed.”

They worked hard to make sure everything they needed worked. They took a break and stopped decorating. They munched on sandwiches Ms. Beulah had brought with her. After they finished eating, it didn't take them long to finish getting ready for the play.

While they made their last adjustments to the decorations, they heard the people begin coming into the church. Macy peeked out through the curtain, "It's almost time, I see folks startin' to come in."

Lucy wiped her sweaty hands on her dress,"I'm a startin' to git nervous, Macy. What if'n nobody likes my singin'?"

Macy encouraged Lucy, "They's all a gonna think yer singin' is special Lucy. It's as purty as I ever did heer."

Ms. Beulah came over to them. "Macy is right Lucy, ya can sing as purty as a songbird. Nothin' to be nervous 'bout."

Mr. Jenkins came over to Lucy and Ms. Beulah, "Are we ready?"

"We's as ready as we ever gonna be," Macy spoke up for them all.

"Ok , I'll go get us started," he parted the curtain and stepped out from behind it. He addressed the crowd that had gathered. "We want to thank everyone for coming tonight to our pageant. The children have all worked very hard to present this to you. We all hope you enjoy it. We have a special treat. Ms. Lucy Watson will be our angel singing from behind the curtain," he announced to them.

Ms. Beulah began playing the piano and Lucy began to sing. A murmur of appreciation went through the crowd. They became silent as they listened to Lucy sing Oh Little Town of Bethlehem.

After the song, they pulled the curtain back and Macy began reading the bible. She turned to the gospel of Luke and began reading from chapter two, "And there were in the same country shepherds abiding in the field keeping watch over the flocks by night."

Sam and the other shepherds came out from behind the curtain. Ben and the little ones came out with them dressed as the sheep.

"Baaah, Baaah, Baaaah," they made the noise and skipped across the stage.

A sound of laughter went through the crowd.

Macy continued reading, "And lo the angel of the Lord came upon them and the glory of the Lord shown 'round about them, and they were sore afraid."

Mr. Jenkins shined a light at them from behind the curtain. The shepherds and sheep fell on their knees.

Helen, Olivia and Louise stepped out from behind the curtain and went over to the kneeling shepherds.

Macy continued, "And the Angel said unto them."

Helen took up the story, "Fear not: for behold I bring you tidings of great joy, which shall be to all people. For unto you is born this day in the City of David a Saviour, which is Christ the Lord. And This shall be a sign unto you, you shall find the babe wrapped in swaddling clothes lying in a manger."

Macy took her turn reading, "And suddenly there was with the angel a multitude of heavenly host praising God and saying. Glory to God in the highest and on earth peace good will to men."

Lucy began singing, "Hark the herald angels sing."

The shepherds stood up at the end of the song. "Let us now go even unto Bethlehem, and see this thing which has come to pass, which the Lord has made known to us. Made known to us," Sam said the lines he had rehearsed.

The shepherds all went behind the curtain and Lucy began singing, "Away in a manger, no crib for his bed."

The curtain was pulled back to show Loretta and John beside the manger.

Macy began reading again, "And they came with haste, and found Mary and Joseph and the babe lying in a manger."

The Shepherds came back on stage and kneeled down at the manger.

Macy continued, "And the shepherds retuned, glorifying and praising God for all the things that they had heard and seen, as it was told unto them."

"Oh beautiful star of Bethlehem," Lucy sang.

The shepherds left the stage and changed into the three kings while Lucy sang the carol. As they marched back to the manger scene as the three wise men. Lucy began singing, "We three kings of Orient are."

The kings marched over and put the gifts down in front of the manger. Mr. Jenkins shined the light on his stained glass star. The light reflected the colors across the stage and on the manger. As the light reflected around the room, the children joined Lucy in singing, Oh come all you faithful.

"The end," Macy said and pulled the curtain across the stage. Their audience began clapping in appreciation.

Mr. Jenkins went out on the stage, "We would be pleased if you join us in singing Silent Night."

Lucy stayed behind the curtain and started the song. All the children came out on the stage and took a bow. Soon the church rang with the song. One Christmas song led to another one, everyone stayed and sang songs well into the night.

After the play was over and they were leaving to go to their homes, Mr. Jenkins motioned for Lucy, "Lucy, we have all decided that we want you to have the star. You sang beautifully for us." He took the star from the wall and handed it to Lucy.

Lucy looked at the star in wonder. "Thank ya," was all she was able to say and she started crying.

"Hey, what you a cryin' fer?" Macy asked her.

Lucy wiped her eyes and sniffed, "I jist never had anythin' as purty as this."

"That is thanks enough for me," Mr. Jenkins told her.

Lucy wrapped the star in her costume. She didn't want to break it. She carried it gingerly all the way home. She put it in her chest at the foot of her bed. She changed into her nightgown and climbed in bed. She turned and blew out the lantern, "Macy, I been a thinkin'."

"What 'bout ?" Macy asked her.

"Ms. Beulah, she don't have nobody to git her presents or nothin'. I think I'm a gonna wrap up this star for her. Do ya think she would want it?"

Macy had been thinking of Ms. Beulah, also, "I reckon she would like that. I been a thinkin' we should carve her a manger scene with my pa's whittlin' knife."

Lucy liked that idea, "Yeah, that'd be good. That way, she could shine a light on it like we did at the play. I think it'd be purty on her fireplace with all them other doo dads she has. I can help ya whittle."

Macy rolled over, her eyes were heavy with sleep. She yawned, "We'll do that tomorr'y. We can find some cedar branches to carve. That's way, it'll smell good fer her, too."

Lucy yawned also, "I loves ta smell cedar. That's a good idea."

"Goodnight, ya did sing as purty as I ever did heer tonight," Macy whispered as she fell asleep.

Lucy smiled with pleasure, "Thanks, Ma and Pa said so too. Goodnight Macy." Lucy noticed Macy had fell asleep. Her feet were cold, so she slipped them up next to Macy.

Macy jumped, "Hey, what'che a doin' to me? Them feet's as cold as ice cycles."

Lucy giggled, "Sorry, I thought ya were asleep."

Macy scooted over away from her, "Well if'n I were, I wouldn't be now. Keep'em yer feet's on yer side a the bed."

Lucy giggled and soon she was asleep, too.

Chapter 13
Christmas Fun

The next morning, the girls were up with the first rays of sun to find the cedar limbs. They bundled up with coats and gloves and went in search of the right tree.

"I love this snow. Ya ever eat snow cream?" Macy asked Lucy.

Lucy smacked her lips, "Yeah, I like it, Ma uses the cream from the milk to make it."

Macy picked up her pace and walked faster, "If'n we get's some snow, ya think she'll make us some?"

Lucy trudged through the snow behind her trying to keep up, "I reckon she will if'n we ask her."

Macy had an idea, "I got's a big barrel lid in the barn. Want ta go ride down the hill in the snow on it?"

Lucy loved to sleigh ride, "Yeah, that'd be fun. I like to slide on the snow."

Macy started running for the barn, "Me too, we'll have ta pick a place that ain't got too many trees. It ain't no fun to go slidin' down the hill really fast and run into a tree."

"I know's jist the place. Come on," Lucy ran for the barn.

They opened the door to the barn and heard a loud and strange noise.

"MRREWWWOOOWW!"

Macy stopped suddenly and Lucy ran into her nearly knocking her down. "Hey what'cha doin'?" Lucy demanded. She peeped around Macy. "What did ya stop so sudden fer?"

Macy motioned for her to be quiet, "I heer'ed a crazy noise."

Lucy became very quiet and strained to hear, "What did it sound like?"

Macy shushed her again, "I don't know like somethin' pitiful."

"MRREEWWOOOWW!"

Lucy jumped back, "What in the world is that?"

Macy looked around the barn, “I don’t know, sounds like a cat, or maybe a skunk.”

“I never heer’ed no skunk afore,” Lucy told her.

Macy tiptoed toward the corn crib. “Me neither but that was a crazy noise,” she whispered to Lucy

“MRREEWWOOOWW!”

Lucy pointed to the corn crib, “It’s a comin’ from over there. Under the corn crib.”

“Let’s go see.” Macy took her by the hand and they sneaked over to the corn crib.

Lucy stepped back, she was afraid, “What if’n it’s a skunk.”

Macy let go of Lucy’s hand. “Just be ready to run,” she whispered.

They kneeled down and looked under the crib. A yellow and white striped cat stared back at them from underneath.

Lucy was disappointed, “Why it’s jist a kitty cat.”

Macy stood up, “That’s the ugliest cat I ever did see. It’s head is bigger’n its body.”

Lucy peered at the cat, “Reckon that’s why it’s a makin’ that awful noise?”

Macy lost interest when she found out the noise came from a cat. She went to the get the barrel lid, “I’d yell like that too if’n I’s that ugly.”

Lucy stood back up, “I feel sorry for it. Maybe we ort’ta git it some milk or somethin’, it’s prob’ly hungry.”

Macy stopped and came back over to the crib. She bent down to look at the cat. “It prob’ly is, here kitty, here kitty,” Macy crooned to the cat.

The cat slipped back and hissed at them.

Macy stood up, she decided they better leave the cat alone. “That done it, that there is a wild cat and I don’t want nothin’ to do with it. Come on let’s leave it alone,” Macy told Lucy.

Not willing to give up, Lucy whined, “I can’t stand the thought’s a it being hungry. Let’s git’s some milk for it first, okay?”

Lucy made her feel sorry for the cat, “Alright, go get’s it some milk. I’ll just stay here and see where it goes.”

Lucy ran to the spring shed and dipped up a can of milk. She ran back to the barn. "Where's it at?"

Macy sat on a hay bale, watching the corn crib. "It's still under there. Put the milk down and let's step back and see if'n it'll come out."

They poured the milk in a saucer they found and backed up to the door of the barn. The cat smelled the milk and slowly came out from under the crib. It kept a wary eye on Macy and Lucy.

"That is the ugliest cat I ever did see," Macy whispered.

"Yes, it is. Maybe it's starvin' and that's how come it's ugly," Lucy whispered back.

Lucy liked the color of the cat, "It's head is twice as big as it's body, but it's a purty color though. Yeller and white stripes. Most all our cats are tabby or calico."

Macy decided they should keep the cat. "I thinks we ort to keep him. We can name him Tiger, on account a he looks like a tiger."

Lucy decided she liked that idea to keep Tiger. She didn't want to scare the cat, so she whispered to Macy, "Did you ever really see a tiger?"

Macy shook her head, "In a picture book, I did. They look's like this here kitty."

Lucy liked the name, it suited the cat to her. "That'd be a good name for it then. We can tame him down with milk and some scraps. Reckon he'll be warm 'nough in the barn?"

Macy looked around, "I reckon so, he can sleep in the hay and we'll come feed him ever'day."

Lucy thought of her mother, "Don't tell Ma though Macy, else she'll make us git rid a him."

Macy backed out of the barn and shut the door, "No, I won't say nothin'. We best be a gettin' if'n we's a gonna be sleigh ridin' today."

Lucy followed her out of the barn, "Yeah, it git's dark awfully early. I git's cold real quick like' too. We'll do one slide down the hill and then we'll find us them cedars to make the carvin's fer Ms. Beulah." Lucy had an idea, "Hey, I know, we can get's some mud from them dobbers nests and make some a the things for the manger."

Macy put the barrel lid under her arm and they started off to find a place to slide. Yeah, that'd be a good idea. Them dobbers make the best clay for their nests."

Lucy followed Macy down the trail, "I know where some is in the loft in the barn.

"We'll git it when we git back."

They went to find a hill to slide down. Lucy remembered the best place to ride, "I know's jist the rite place to ride, it's over near the bridge. Ever'body rides down there. Ya jist have to be careful and not go in the river."

Macy walked in front of her, "The river's most likely froze by now. If'n it is, we can skate on it."

Lucy stopped, "I never did that afore."

Macy waited for Lucy to catch up with her, "What?"

Lucy trudged through the snow in front of Macy, "Skate on the river. I's a'las a'feered a fallin' in."

"I think yer a'feered a ever'thin'," Macy followed Lucy.

Lucy ran to the river. She stopped and looked at the ice with a wary eye, "Is it fun? To skate I mean?"

"Yeah, it's a lot a fun. I can show ya how. All ya do is take a run and go and slide," Macy searched for the right place to skate.

Lucy trudged along, trying to keep up with her, "What if'n ya fall?"

Macy decided she had found the right place to skate, "If'n ya keeps yer balance ya don't. It hurts if'n ya do."

Lucy didn't like the thought of falling on the ice. "I think I'll jist watch ya skate."

They trudged back up to the top of the hill that overlooked the river. Macy put the barrel lid down and sat down on it, "Ya git behind me Lucy and hold on."

Lucy sat down behind Macy. "Now rock back and forth and give a big shove," Macy told Lucy and started rocking on the barrel lid.

They teetered on the top of the hill. Macy pushed forward and they were off.

Swooosh down the hill they went. Lucy started giggling. "This is fun!" she yelled.

"Hang on," Macy shouted as they went from the bank and onto

the frozen river, sliding across the ice. They slid all the way to the other side, they plowed into the creek bank.

Lucy stood up. "That was fun," she dusted the snow off her clothes.

Macy stomped her foot down on the ice to test it. It didn't crack, so she decided it was thick enough to slide on. "Now watch me," she started running and slid across the ice with her arms out for balance. "See, that's how ya do it. Ya try it now. Do it jist like I showed ya."

Lucy started running. Her feet flew out from under her on the slick ice. She tried to keep her balance and ended up falling on her face. She rolled over and sat up, "Ouch, that hurt."

Macy watched the fall in horror, she ran over to see if Lucy was alright. "That ain't the way yer 'posed ta do it," Macy jerked Lucy to her feet. "Try again. This time ya need ta hold your arms out like I show'ed ya and ya won't fall."

Lucy took another run across the ice. "Like this?" she yelled.

"Hold yer arms out," Macy hollered back.

Lucy slid for a little distance and lost her balance again. This time she landed on her backside.

Macy ran over to her, "How's come ya fell that'a way? Are ya alright?"

Lucy's backside felt numb. She tried to sit up. "I can't feel my legs," she whimpered.

Macy helped her to stand up, "It ain't no wonder, that ain't the way yer 'posed ta do it."

The ice began to crack with a hollow crunch underneath them. "Oh no, it's a bustin' up, come on Lucy afore it breaks," Macy yanked her up by the arm and dragged her to the safety of the bank.

The snow had made its way into the holes in Macy's shoes making her feet wet. She began to shiver from the cold, "Lucy, I'm a gettin' cold we's best be a goin' back in now. Where did ya say we could find the cedars?"

Lucy trekked her way up the hill, "At the top a this hill, they's a grove of 'em."

Macy followed behind her, "We need's the one's that are already dead."

Lucy's ankle began to throb and she started limping. Her front and her backside both throbbed. Macy took her by the arm and helped her along the trail. They located the cedar trees, then gathered several limbs they thought they could use. They hurried back to the cabin and rushed in with their cedar limbs.

Lucy's mother stopped them at the door. "Jist what do ya girls think yer a gonna do with all them sticks?" she asked them.

They put the cedar limbs on the floor. "We thought we'd carve Ms. Beulah a manger with Mary and Joseph for Christmas," Lucy told her.

Lucy's mother pointed to the door, "That's sweet a ya girls but ya ain't a gonna be a messin' up my floor with no whittle shavin's. Ya can do yer carvin' in the barn, while yer at it, ya can milk Flossy for me."

Lucy's eyes flew open, "Oh Ma, I hate that old cow. She's the dumbest critter I ever did see."

Her mother went back to scrubbing the stove, "It's been my 'sperience that if'n I heer som'body say an animal is dumb, it's on 'count that critter done out foxed'um."

Lucy huffed at her, "She never out foxed me, she's jist plain on'ry!"

Her mother turned them around and pointed to the door. "Ya go on and out fox her then." She put her hands on her hips, "Don't ya neither one be mean to that cow, else I'll have yer hide. Now go on, git's."

They bundled back up and went out to the barn. Lucy dreaded another encounter with Flossy, "Macy, ya do the milkin' fer me, okay? That ole cow is mean and I hate's her."

Macy followed Lucy to the barn, "I will, that old cow don't sceere me none. She better watch out, else I'll knock her in the head with somethin'."

Lucy giggled, "I tells her I'm a gonna do that all the time. She don't pay no attention ta me. Last time she knocked me over with that dirty tail a hers."

They opened the barn door and went inside. Lucy saw Flossy munching on hay in her stall, "At least, she's in the barn. Last time, she's outside and I had to catch her. She's the awfulest thing to catch ever was."

They went over to the stall. Macy found a bucket and filled it with water. She placed it under Flossy and sat down to wash the udder. Flossy didn't even flick her tail.

Lucy couldn't believe what her eyes were seeing, "Would ya look at that, she's a gonna let ya milk her. Let me try."

Macy moved and Lucy sat down beside Flossy. As soon as she got settled, Flossy hit her in the mouth with her tail and knocked her over.

Lucy got up and shook her fist at Flossy, "OOOOHHHHH I hate's ya."

Flossy, let out a big beller as if she was laughing at Lucy.

"Here, let me do it," Macy pulled Lucy out of the way and took her place.

Flossy went back to munching on her hay.

"MMMMRRREEEOOOOWWW!"

"Hey, sounds like Tiger is still here," Lucy said as she dusted herself off. "Here kitty kitty," she crooned to the cat.

Tiger came out from under the stall door.

Lucy laughed, "He shore is scrawny."

Tiger came closer.

"Maybe, he wants some more milk," Lucy told Macy.

"Watch this," Macy started squirting the milk from the udder at the cat.

The milk hit Tiger in the head and he ran back under the door.

The two of them laughed at him.

While Macy milked Flossy, Lucy went to the loft and found the dirt dobber nests. She scraped the mud off the wall and into a bucket. "They's lots'a them dobber nests up here. We kin make a lot a figures from all this mud."

Lucy climbed back down the ladder and took the bucket of milk from Macy. Macy stood up and patted Flossy on the neck, "She ain't mean. Lucy yer jist not a doin' somethin' rite."

They left their cedar limbs and clay in the barn and went in for supper.

For two days they worked on their gift for Ms. Beulah. Whittling the cedar limbs into figures of animals and mixing the clay into the manger. They carved sheep and cows. Lucy made a cat out of some of the clay she had gathered.

"They ain't no where's in the bible that says they's a cat at the manger," Macy told her.

Lucy kept on shaping the clay into a cat. "They could'a been. Ever barn has a cat. Well, she can put it somewheres else, if'n she don't want to put it with the manger," Lucy told her.

They found a wooden box and Lucy wrapped the star she had been given in some white writing paper. She tied the package together with a ribbon. They placed the figures they had carved around the star in the box and tied the outside with a ribbon.

The next day was Christmas Eve. Macy and Lucy became very excited because Ms. Beulah promised to come and spend the night with them and eat dinner on Christmas. They hid their gift for her under the tree in the back. They didn't want Ms. Beulah to see it until Christmas morning.

Christmas Eve was full of laughter and cooking. Lucy and Macy sneaked in the kitchen and sampled the pumpkin pies and applesauce cakes their mothers were making. They gathered pine branches and made a wreath for the fireplace. They hung it up and put their stockings beside it.

"Are ya girls a hopin' Santa'll put somethin' in them stockin's?" Macy's father asked them.

"Oh Pa, we don't think they's a Santa. We's too big for that," Macy told him.

He knocked the tobacco out of his pipe, "What ya a hangin' them stockin's for if'n ya don't believe no more?"

"I believe in Santa," Ben said.

"What ya want Santa ta bring ya, Ben?" Macy's father asked him.

Ben thought for a moment, "I don't know, I want's some hard candy. I love's the peppermint sticks."

Macy's father put more tobacco in his pipe and took an ember from the fire to light it, "Have ya been good?"

Ben dropped his head, "I's been sort'a good."

"I reckon that's 'bout the truth," Lucy's father said laughing.

Ben perked up, "If'n Macy and Lucy don't believe, ya think Santa mite give me their candy?"

"He mite fer a fact. I reckon them girls prob'ly will git's a bundle a switches," Lucy's father laughed. "What we need's ta do is gather 'round the fire and read the Christmas story from the bible."

Lucy made a face at her little brother. She turned to her father. "We need's ta wait fer Ms. Beulah," Lucy told him.

They heard sleigh bells, a horse and buggy outside.

"I think I hear her now," Lucy ran to the window.

"Maybe it's Santa," Ben bounced around the room with excitement.

"It's too early fer Santa, he only comes after ya go ta sleep tonight," Lucy's father winked at him.

There was a knock on the door. Macy and Lucy raced to the door and flung it open.

Ms. Beulah hugged them both. "Merry Christmas!" she said merrily. "How are my girls? Excited for Santa to come?"

"These girls don't believe in Santa," Lucy's father went over to welcome her.

She took off her coat and handed it to him, "Nonsense, I believe in Santa. Ya girls jist wait 'till mornin'. Then ya'll see."

Lucy fluttered around Ms. Beulah. "Ya kin stay in my room with us Ms. Beulah. It git's cold in my room, but we's got's lots a covers on the bed," Lucy told her.

Ms. Beulah gave her a big hug, "I don't mind the cold girls. It's mighty comfortin' to be with friends and not by yerself at Christmas."

"We're mighty glad to have ye Ms. Bevins. These girls ain't talke'd 'bout nothin' else but yer stayin' with'em," Lucy's mother said as she came into the room.

"Please all of ya call me Ms. Beulah,"she encouraged them. "I've brought some chocolate candy and a few more things that are still out in the buggy."

"Ya jist sit right down Ms. Beulah. Jeb, ya and Ben go git's Ms. Beulah's horse settled in the barn and bring in her packages," Lucy's father told them. "As soon as they get back, we'll read the Christmas story from the bible and have us some supper."

Lucy's mother wiped her hands on her apron, "Supper's almost ready, mind ya now, all ya young'uns stay out'a the cakes and pies. They's fer tommorr'y."

The fireplace crackled merrily sending warmth and light through the cabin. "Jack, ya and Louis go help them and bring in some wood for the fire," Macy's father sent her brothers to help.

Jeb made sure the horse had hay and was settled in the barn. He gathered the packages Ms. Beulah had brought with her. Then he noticed the bicycle in the back of the buggy. He handed a few of the smaller packages to his little brother Ben and sent him back to the house before Ben saw the bicycle.

Louis and Jack carried armfuls of wood and stacked it beside the fireplace. Lucy's mother called for everyone to come to the table to eat.

When dinner was over, they all gathered around the fireplace. Lucy's father took his bible up in his lap and turned to the Christmas story. He started reading and everyone listened intently to what he read.

After Lucy's father finished reading, her mother found a hymnal and turned to the Christmas carols. "Lucy, how 'bout ya start us in some songs," her mother encouraged Lucy to sing for them.

Lucy smiled in pride and embarrassment, "Which one ya want's me ta sing?"

Her mother settled down by the fireplace in her rocking chair, "Let's start with Silent Night."

Lucy's father motioned for her to wait. "Let me git my gitar, it'll jist take me a minute," he went to the wall and took his guitar down.

He came back in and started playing. They sat around the fireplace enjoying the fellowship of family and company. They sang all the carols they knew.

The evening began to get late. "Alright'y, I reckon ya young'uns ort'a be a gettin' in bed. Else Santa can't come," Lucy's mother told them with a wink.

Ben jumped up and scrambled off to his bed in the loft. Macy and Lucy helped clear the dishes and showed Ms. Beulah their room.

They piled more covers on the bed. The two girls bounded with excitement to have Ms. Beulah spend the holiday with them. They jumped in the bed and made a place for her. They all snuggled under the quilts together.

"Ms. Beulah, ya have ta watch Lucy. She's got the coldest feet ya ever did feel and she'll stick them rite on ya if'n you fall asleep first," Macy warned.

Ms. Beulah chuckled remembering being a girl and having cold feet. "That's alright Lucy, ya can stick yer feet on me if'n ya want's to," she smiled at Lucy and Macy. "Goodnight my girls."

Macy and Lucy fell asleep fast. Ms. Beulah laid awake thankful for the girls that had come to mean so much to her.

The next morning, at first light, Macy and Lucy jumped around the room with excitement. They shook Ms. Beulah and woke her up.

Macy ran to the door and back to the bed, "It's Christmas morning, Ms. Beulah. Wake up!"

She opened her eyes and smiled at them, "I was awake already. So ya think's maybe ya believe's in Santa this morning after all?"

"Let's go see!" Macy said happily. "Come on! Hurry!"

Ms. Beulah laughed at them, "Ya girls go on and I'll be along in a minute, let me git dressed."

The two ran into the living room and stopped. There on the fireplace were two bundles of switches.

Ben was sucking on his peppermint candy. "See, I told's ya they's a Santa. I got's a piece a peppermint and a apple and a orange. Ya didn't get's nothin' them switches is fer ya," he snickered at them.

Macy and Lucy dragged slowly over to the fireplace. The bundles of sticks had a little tags on them. Macy picked one of the bundles up. She turned it over and read the tag. It read For Macy from Santa.

Lucy picked up the other bundle. She turned the tag over and read it. For Lucy from Santa.

"Don't jist stand there take's the string off'n them bundles. We can use them to start the fires with," Lucy's father told them barely able to keep a straight face.

"That jist prove's to me they's a Santa. I reckon ya girls got what ya deserved for all the meanness ya been up to," Macy's mother told them. Then she turned her head to keep them from seeing her laugh.

Lucy's father burst out laughing, "Go on now, open'em up and put'em in the kindlin' box."

Lucy had come almost to the point of tears.

Macy and Lucy untied the bundle of sticks. When they fell apart, they saw the hard candy and oranges in the middle of them.

Everyone broke out laughing.

Lucy looked up and smiled in relief, "Oh Ma, ya know'ed it all along."

Lucy's mother answered, "I did for a fact. Santa told me what he was a gonna do. He said to tell ya if'n yer mean next year they really won't be nothin' but switches for ya."

Macy popped a piece of candy in her mouth, "This is the best candy I ever had."

Lucy agreed. "Look'i here, oranges! I loves oranges, too," she said giggling.

Ms. Beulah came in the room and joined in the laughter.

Lucy jumped up and ran over to her. "Ms. Beulah, we got's ya somethin' fer Christmas. Wait right there," Lucy told her.

Lucy ran over to the tree and retrieved the box they had made. She took it over and handed it to her. "Me and Macy made this fer ya. Merry Christmas."

Ms. Beulah became overwhelmed. Her heart soared with love for the girls. She started crying.

"Open it," Macy and Lucy said together.

She opened the box. When she saw what was inside, words failed her. She felt a lump of emotion in her throat.

Lucy became worried, "Don't ya like it? It's my star they give me for singin'. We carved ya the manger and Mary and Joseph all by our self."

She put the present down and hugged Macy and Lucy. "I love it, girls, I reckon this is the best Christmas present I ever did git's." she hugged them again. "I reckon I brought ya girls somethin' for Christmas, too. It's a present fer both of ya and it's out in the barn."

Macy and Lucy jumped and squealed with eagerness. "What is it?" Macy blurted out.

"Let's go to the barn and see," Ms. Beulah told her.

The whole family followed them out to the barn. They opened the door and went in. A shiny red bicycle leaned up against Flossy's stall.

Macy ran over to the bike and stood it up. She went all around it testing the pedals and looking it over. She turned to Ms. Beulah beaming. "I seen them contraptions in the Sears book. How did ya know I wanted one?" Macy asked her.

"Santa told me," Ms. Beulah said. "Go on, try's it out." She encouraged Macy.

Macy straddled the bike, "What's do I do?"

"I think's ya git's on and put yer feet's on the pedals, that is what makes the wheels go round," Ms. Beulah told her.

Macy put her feet on the pedals and started peddling. "Whoooaaaa!" she yelled as she crashed into Flossy's stall.

Flossy started kicking and bellowing, Macy jumped up and ran out of the way of the cow's wrath.

Macy's mother ran over to her and helped her up, "Maybe ya should wait 'till it's spring to ride that contraption afore ya 'stroy yer Uncle Big's barn."

Macy dusted herself off and motioned for Lucy, "It's the best Christmas present ever, come try it out Lucy."

Lucy ran over to the bicycle, "Ya'll have to show me what's ta do."

Macy helped her on the bike, "It's easy, jist put one foot on one side and the other foot on the other side, push down and it'll make the wheels turn."

Lucy tried to peddle, as soon as she tried to make it go, the bike tipped over. "Hey!" she yelled.

"No, that ain't the way ya do it. Here, let's me show ya," Macy took the bike from her and started peddling. "Like this. Oh, oh, oh, look out!" she yelled as she crashed into the hay stack.

"I'm purty shore that ain't the way yer 'posed to do it, Macy," Lucy said laughing at her.

Lucy's mother shook her head and closed her eyes every time they crashed into something, "I reckon both ya girls'll have all winter ta practice. Come on now ever'one, let's go in and eat our dinner."

The girls stayed behind admiring the bicycle. They lowered the kickstand and set it in the corner of the barn.

Lucy beamed with delight, “I think’s this is the best Christmas I ever had. Don’t ya, Macy?”

Macy took a feed sack and covered the bike, “Yeah, it’s the best one fer me, too. Not on ‘count a the presents, I’m jist glad we’re in one place now and not a travelin’ all the time. I’m glad for ya too, Lucy. This is the best Christmas ever fer me.”

Lucy hugged her cousin, “I’m glad for ya too, Macy. I reckon I finally got’s me a sister now.”

Macy turned away before Lucy saw that she was almost to the point of tears. “Come on. Ma’s a gonna git’s us if’n we don’t come eat,” she took Lucy by the hand and they went in to eat their Christmas dinner.

Chapter 14
Baptizing the Cat

With snow coming down every day from January to April, the winter seemed to last forever to Macy and Lucy. They spent the days going to school, trying to make friends with Tiger, and learning to ride the bicycle.

The first day of May, they were in the barn practicing riding. Lucy had gotten the hang of it faster than Macy and she peddled all around the inside of the barn. Lucy saw Tiger dart under the corn crib. She stopped peddling and stepped off the bike. She pushed it over to Macy and propped it up with the kickstand, "Macy, I have an idea. That ole cat, he's just a tryin' my patience. He know's we's want's to make friends. I think he's jist being stubborn and don't want to be friends with us. What do ya think we ort'a do 'bout him?"

Macy went over to a hay bale and sat down. She pulled a piece of hay out of the bale and popped it in her mouth between her teeth. "I've been a thinkin' 'bout that, too. Maybe if'n we git's some ham from the smoke house and let him get a whiff of it, he might come out to get's the ham. If'n he does, he can see we jist want to be friends. He might git's so's he'll come to us instead a runnin' and a hidin' ever' time we's come's in the barn."

Lucy sat down beside her. She bent down and looked under the corn crib. She saw Tiger sitting under the boards. As soon as he saw Lucy looking at him, Tiger hissed at her and backed farther away. "I think's he's just on'ry. He know's we want's to be friends. Ain't we's been a sneakin' him scraps from our plates all winter."

Macy bent down and looked at Tiger. "Yeah, but that's just milk and cornbread mostly. I think he git's a smell a that ham, he won't be able to resist it. Ya know's, it's almost warm enough that yer Pa'll be a leavin' the barn doors open. If'n we don't tame him, most likely he'll run off and we prob'ly won't see him again."

Lucy didn't want Tiger to leave, "He's turned into a right purty cat.

I would'a never thought it. I mean as ugly as he were with that big ole head he had."

Macy stood back up and laughed, "He were ugly at that, but his body has caught up with his head and now he's big all over. I never seed a cat that color afore neither."

Lucy looked from Tiger to Macy, "He's almost got's color like yer hair, Macy. We jist gotta try ta tame him."

Macy agreed. She liked the cat also, "Okay, but if'n yer ma know'ed we's a sneakin' ham for a cat, she'd likely not let's us have no supper."

Lucy giggled, "She'd be mad as fire at that shore."

Macy had an idea, "Come on, let's slip 'round the side and chunk off a little piece for him, so's we's can see then what he does."

They opened the barn door and looked to see if anyone was watching them. When they decided the coast was clear, they sneaked out to the smoke house. Lucy stood as a lookout while Macy retrieved the ham. Lucy peeped around the wood building and looked toward the cabin. She didn't see anyone. She whispered to Macy, "Hurry Macy, I don't see Ma."

Macy came over and softly said through the crack in the door, "I chunked off a good piece. Look again, is yer ma anywhere's in site?"

Lucy peeped around and looked again, "No, come on, hurry."

Macy opened the door and they both ran to the barn. "Here Tiger, here kitty," Macy called to the cat and waved the ham in the air.

Lucy started calling for Tiger, "Kitty, kitty. Come on now, see's what's we've got ya."

They went around to the corn crib and bent down to look under it. They didn't see Tiger. Now they became worried. "He's usually under here. But I don't see him now. Ya don't reckon he's already left do ya, Macy?" Lucy chewed on her lip.

Macy handed the ham to Lucy. She climbed the ladder to the loft, "He mite'a left, it's been gettin' a little warmer ever'day and the snow's all gone now."

Macy looked down from the loft in time to see Tiger come running at Lucy. "Hey, look out!" she yelled as the cat came barreling out from under Flossy's stall hissing and growling.

Lucy turned in time to see Tiger running at her. "Run!" she heard Macy yell down at her. She turned and started running for the door, forgetting to throw the ham down. Tiger had smelled the ham and was running after her to get it.

Macy scrambled down the ladder and ran to help Lucy get away from the snarling cat.

Tiger jumped on Lucy's leg, he took hold with his claws and climbed up her all the way to her shoulder. Scratching and clawing all the way. "He' s a tryin' ta eat me alive," Lucy screamed. She threw the piece of ham and it landed near Macy.

Tiger jumped off Lucy's shoulder and ran toward Macy.

The hissing cat hit Macy in the legs and knocked her feet out from under her. She fell face first on the ham. Tiger jumped on her back trying to reach the ham. "Help git's him off'n me, Lucy. He's a scratchin' my legs all to pieces!" she screamed.

Lucy ran over to her, but she was afraid to touch Tiger, "He's after that ham, roll over and git off'n it."

Macy rolled to the side and the determined cat grabbed the piece of ham. He headed for the nearest corner and ran into Lucy knocking her down. He began gobbling the ham growling and hissing at them between bites.

Macy helped Lucy up, "Are ya alright?"

Lucy dusted the hay off her coat, "Yeah, jist scratched up a little bit. Did he git's ya bad, too?"

"Clawed his way from my ankles to my head. Look here," she showed Lucy her bleeding scratches.

Lucy knocked the hay out of her hair. She looked over at Tiger, who was growling and gulping the ham as fast as he was able. "I never seed a cat as mean as him. Maybe we's ort'a quit feedin' him and let him leave," Lucy decided.

Macy had had enough. "What he needs is some manners and I'm jist about the one to teach' em to'im," Macy said as she picked up a feed sack.

Lucy looked from Macy to the growling cat, "What's ya a gonna do with that?"

Macy shook the feed sack out to make it as big as she could, "I'm a gonna throw it on him and catch' im." She handed one side of the sack to Lucy. "Here get the end of it and when we get's close, we'll pounce on'im."

Lucy dropped her side of the sack and backed up, "Maybe this ain't such a good idea. We jist ort'a leave'im 'lone."

Macy was determined now to catch Tiger, "I ain't a gonna let him beat me. Come on if'n yer scared, let's git a wash tub and throw on him. That way he can't scratch us up."

Lucy dropped her end of the sack and ran for the door. The wash tub sounded safer to catch the cat with than the feed sack, "I know's where's one, it's in the corner behind the crib."

Macy looked over her shoulder at Lucy, "Hurry and git it, then. I'll stand here and if'n he move's I'll try to catch him with the feed sack. Hurry afore he finishes his ham."

Lucy scurried out of the barn to find the wash tub. She dragged it back to the barn. "Will this'un work?" she asked Macy as she came back in the barn. Macy nodded.

Macy took hold of one side of the wash tub and Lucy picked up the other. They held the tub in position and crept close to Tiger. The cat was busy eating the ham, but he growled in warning at them. They kept inching toward him. When they came close enough, they threw the tub over the cat and ran over and flopped down on it. Tiger started going crazy under the tub, hitting the sides and hissing and meowing. Even with them sitting on it, the tub started moving as the cat banged against the sides so hard.

Macy pushed down harder, "I never see'd nothin' throw a fit like he's a throwin'. He's plum wild."

Lucy pushed down with all her strength on the tub, "He's a goin' crazy under there. How'er we gonna get'im out from under here without him a gettin' away or a killin' us?"

Macy had been thinking about that very thing, "I know's, let's put this feed sack down next to the ground and lift the tub up a little bit. He'll try to run out and run right in the sack."

Lucy wasn't sure she liked that idea, "What's ya gonna do when he git's in the sack?"

Macy became aggravated at Lucy's questions, "I don't rightly know, maybe we can sort'a pet'im some and tame'im down a little."

Lucy began to try to talk Macy out of her plan, "What if'n he don't tame down?"

Macy looked at Lucy and sighed, "I hadn't thought of that. I reckon we'll jist have ta let him go."

Lucy had another idea, "I know's, we could baptize him."

Macy became very interested, "What's that?"

Lucy thought of the best way to explain. "Well, when they has the revivals, the preacher he git's a lot a the people and takes'um to the river. He dunks'um down in the river and they come's up not mean no more."

Macy didn't believe Lucy, "What does that's do to make'um not mean no more?"

Lucy shrugged her shoulders, "I don't know, it jist does."

The cat made another try to get out from under the washtub and Macy pushed down harder it. "I don't believe that," she shook her head at Lucy.

Lucy made a motion to cross her heart with her finger, "It's the truth, ask Pa. They baptize a lot a people ever' year when they's has the revival."

Macy became more intrigued, "Yeah, I believe's that. But what does the water have to do with'um not a bein' mean no more?"

Lucy shrugged her shoulders again, "I don't know, I jist know's it works. Maybe it'ud work on Tiger."

Macy looked at the tub, the cat had settled down, "I reckon it's worth a try. What do we need ta do?"

Lucy tried to remember how she had seen the preacher baptize, "Ya git's a little cloth, and ya put's it over his nose, that's so as the water won't choke him. Then ya dunk him under. When he comes up out'a the water, he prob'ly won't be mean."

Macy thought the baptizing might work, "Okay, let's try it. Ya go git's a handkerchief and I'll sit here's on the tub 'till ya git's back. He ain't a bellerin' like he was. When ya git's back, we can see if'n we can git him in the sack."

Lucy ran to the cabin. She opened the door and sneaked around to her mother's bedroom. She found a handkerchief in the dresser drawer. She tiptoed through the house. When she came out of the house, she ran back to the barn as fast as she could.

She opened the door and went over to where Macy sat on the wash tub, "Is he calmed down any?"

Macy took the handkerchief from Lucy and stuffed it in her pocket, "Yeah, he ain't made a peep ever' since ya been gone. All we have ta do is get's him in the sack now. Ya git one side and I'll hold to the other." Macy handed the sack to Lucy, "Now, put's it down real close. We'll lift the tub jist a little, be prepared though fer what he mite do."

They held the feed sack open and settled it down near the tub. They lifted the tub slowly. Whooosh, the cat ran full force into the feed sack. "Hurry close the top," Macy yelled. They pulled the top shut and tied it with a hay string.

Tiger started clawing and scratching. His claws poked through the feed sack and Lucy let go of the sack, "Boy, would ya listen to that. I never heered sich a goin's on."

Macy held the feed sack with both hands, she shook the sack. "Ya settle down now Tiger. There ain't no use ya a makin' such a fuss. Yer caught now."

Tiger clawed and scratched at the feed sack, hissing and growling.

Macy shook the sack again, "Ya jist quit that Tiger. We ain't aimin' to hurt ya none," she headed for the barn door. "Come on, Lucy, the faster we git's him baptized, the better off we'll be."

Lucy remembered how cold the river was this time of year. "That water is gonna still be cold. Reckon we can baptize him in the shallow part a the river?"

Macy wanted to do the baptizing right. "I don't know, tell me again how they do it. Do they dunk'um all the way under?"

Lucy nodded her head, "Yeah, they do, they's dunks'um backwards."

Macy stopped walking. She whirled around to look at Lucy. "Backwards! How does that work?"

Lucy shrugged her shoulders, "I don't know, but that's how I a'las seen it done."

Macy turned around and started for the river. "Well, we want's to do it rite. Backwards it is."

As they came to the river, Tiger had settled down some. They waded out in the water, up to their knees. They were in a hurry to get him baptized and didn't stop to take their shoes off.

The cold water took Lucy's breath away."Ooohhhh it's cold," she said between chattering teeth.

Macy had been concentrating on opening the feed sack. She looked up at Lucy. "Yeah, I can hear's yer teeth a bangin' together. This won't take long though, I reckon. They don't hold's 'em under long do they?"

Lucy helped Macy untie the top of the sack, "No. It happens real quick, they dunk 'em under and then rite back up. How in the world are we a gonna dunk him backwards?"

Macy thought for a minute, "We'll open the sack jist enough fer him to stick his head out. Then you slap the cloth over his nose and I'll dunk him."

Lucy liked that plan. She nodded her head in agreement, "Yeah, that'll work."

Macy started to open the top of the sack. She looked over at Lucy, "Ready?"

"Ready," Lucy nodded. "He shore needs baptizin'. That's the meanest cat I ever did see."

Macy handed Lucy the handkerchief and began to make an opening in the top of the sack. "I hope's it helps. Ya got the cloth ready?"

Lucy put the handkerchief in her hand, "Yeah, I'm ready."

When they opened the top of the feed sack, Tiger stuck his head out, hissing, growling and biting at them.

Macy yelled at Lucy, "Slap it on 'im!"

Lucy tried to put the handkerchief over Tiger's nose. When her hand came close to him, he bit her and would'nt let go.

Lucy screamed, "AAAAAAYYYYEEEE! Help he's got me, Macy and won't let go. Hurry dunk him fast."

Macy plunged Tiger under the water and the feed sack came loose. Tiger scratched and clawed and came out. He clawed his way up Macy's overalls and up on her head trying to get out of the water. "Help, Lucy. git this wild cat off'n me!" she screamed.

Lucy tried to help her, but she lost her footing, falling backwards in the water.

Macy screamed louder, "Grab him and throw him off. He's a eatin' me alive!"

Tiger kept hissing, growling and scratching Macy. Lucy managed to regain her footing. She was soaking wet, but she ran over to help pull the scared cat off Macy. Tiger jumped from Macy to Lucy. He then began biting and scratching her.

Lucy started dancing around in the water trying to throw Tiger off of her. "Help, Macy, help! He's a eatin' me up."

Macy ran over to her. She grabbed for Tiger. He clung to Lucy. "Turn him loose, ya dope," she yelled.

Lucy fell backwards in the water again. Tiger latched on to her. "I have turned him loose. He won't turn me loose!" she screamed.

Macy ran over to Lucy and grabbed the frightened cat. She flung him down in the water. He started swimming toward them. "Run, Lucy, run. Here he comes again!" Macy yelled.

They started running. Lucy slipped on the slick rocks and fell in again. She grabbed Macy trying to keep from falling and pulled her down in the river too. Tiger jumped on Macy and bit her one more time. They were close to the bank and he jumped to land and took off through the trees.

Macy helped Lucy up, "Are ya alright?"

Lucy began trembling, "Yeah, ya alright?"

Macy shook her fist in the direction Tiger had run. "That dern cat 'bout eat me alive. Look here at the scratches," she said. "Yer a bleedin' all over yer arms too, Lucy."

They sloshed through the water to the bank. Lucy flopped down. "Well, I reckon that baptizin' only works on people."

"We found that out the hard way." Macy rubbed her head. "I reckon we'll git rabies from that old cat!"

Lucy's eyes flew open wide. She hadn't thought of that. "Ya don't think he has rabies do ya?" Lucy panicked.

Macy helped Lucy to her feet, "I ain't seen him slobber none. But he's 'bound to have somethin' makin' him that mean. Come on, let's see's if'n we can sneak back in our room without yer ma a catchin' us."

Terrified now, Lucy felt as if she might faint. She stumbled, "She'd whoop us shore she know'ed it."

Macy steadied her. They started limping back towards home. "I reckon if'n we're a gonna git's the rabies, it'll show's up perty soon."

Lucy stumbled along beside Macy. "Maybe we should tell Ma."

Macy shook her head. "T'ain't nothin' they can do fer us now if'n we git's the rabies."

Lucy spit in the direction the cat had taken, "I hope's yer brother's coon dog git's that old cat. I ain't a gonna feed him nothin' else no more."

Macy decided she didn't want anything else to do with the cat herself, "I ain't either. He can fend for hisself."

Chapter 15
Fight with a Bat

Macy and Lucy limped their way back to the cabin. "My feet are hurtin' somethin' awful they's so cold," Lucy said through chattering teeth.

Macy stopped to look at her, "Yeah, ya look kind a blue around the mouth."

Lucy saw that Macy's lips were turning blue. "Yer's are too Macy. What we gonna do if'n Ma sees us?"

Macy put her arm around Lucy, "I don't know. Try to make up somethin' I reckon."

Lucy limped along beside her she wanted Macy to tell her what she was going to say to her mother, "What will that be?"

Macy didn't know how she was going to explain and she became aggravated at Lucy question. "I told ya, I don't know. We need's ta sneak in and git out'a these wet clothes a 'fore she sees us though," Macy told her.

Lucy was cold and her head was beginning to hurt, "I don't feel good."

Macy held Lucy with her arm and stared walking again, "Me neither, but we'll be home in a minute. I'll git's us some coffee. It'll make us feel better."

They came to the edge of the woods and stopped to see if anyone was in the yard. Macy peeped around a tree. "I don't see yer ma, hurry let's git in the cabin and git some dry clothes on."

Lucy stopped and thought for a minute, "Wait, look through the winder and see if'n she's in the kitchen."

Macy looked again. "I don't see'er. Wait, I heer her. She's in the chicken coop. Come on, hurry," she dropped Lucy's arm and started running.

Lucy ran hobbling every step trying to keep up with Macy. They ran in the door and straight to their room.

"That was lucky," Macy said and flopped down on the bed.

Lucy pulled at her wet clothes, "Pa don't believe in luck, he says ever'thin' happens fer a reason."

Macy nodded her head in agreement, "Well, the reason yer ma was out in the chicken coop was fer us. That we didn't git a whoopin' I reckon."

Lucy started coughing, "I feel too bad for a whoopin' that's the truth."

Macy helped Lucy pull off her shoes. "Ya ain't blue no more. Yer red all over."

Lucy fell back on the bed. "I don't feel sa good," she whimpered.

Macy's looked at her worriedly, "Oh no, I bet ya got the rabies."

Macy's announcement caused Lucy panic; she became very afraid and couldn't catch her breath. "Reckon we's a gonna die?" she cried.

"I don't feel sa good myself," Macy complained.

Lucy crawled under the covers and pulled them up over her head, "I'm miserable."

Macy was right behind her, "Me too."

Macy jumped in the bed and pulled the quilts up over their heads. They snuggled close together and then they fell asleep.

Lucy's mother came back in from gathering eggs. She noticed the trail of water from the door to the girls room. "Now what are them girls up to?" she put the eggs down and followed the water trail. She opened the door to Lucy's room, "Girls, what ya been a doin'?" There was no answer and she was about to leave the room when she heard Lucy start coughing. She went over to the bed and pulled the quilts down. "What are ya girls a doin' in the bed this time a day?" she demanded.

Lucy moaned, "I don't feel good."

"Me neither," Macy said and started coughing.

Lucy's mother reached her hand out and felt Lucy's forehead and then Macy's, "Why yer both a burnin' up with the fever."

"We's got the rabies and we's a gonna die," Lucy wailed.

"Rabies!" Lucy's mother stepped back. "How's come ya think you gots the rabies?"

"We tried ta baptize that ole cat and he eat us up," Lucy told her.

Lucy's mother shook her head in disbelief. "Baptize a cat? What in the world are ya a talkin' 'bout?"

Lucy coughed and moaned in misery, "We found a old yeller cat and we been a feedin' him all winter. He didn't want to make friends with us. We thought if'n we baptized him, hit'ud make him not sa mean."

Lucy's mom pulled the covers back up around them, "I reckon ya went in the river to do it too, I'm a guessin'?"

"Yeah and he 'bout eat us up. Knocked us both in the river, Aunt Linny," Macy told her.

Lucy's mother tried not to laugh, "Were he a foamin' at the mouth?"

"No not yit, he were just mean," Lucy answered.

Lucy's mother coughed to keep from laughing, "We'll have to send for the doctor. If'n ya got the rabies, I reckon we'll jist have ta lock ya up 'till we can figure out if'n yer a gonna die or not." She went out of the room and shut the door. She leaned against the door and started quietly snickering.

Lucy was even more miserable, "See, even Ma thinks we got's the rabies."

Macy pulled the covers back up over their heads. "She's a gonna send for the doctor. Maybe they's somethin' he can do."

Lucy covered her head all the way. "Ya said they's nothin' they could do. We's a gonna die shore. I know's it," she whimpered.

Lucy's mother heard them. She ran outside before she laughed. She didn't want the girls to hear her.

Lucy heard her mother running, "See, Ma's done run to git the doctor. I reckon she think's we got the rabies too."

They fell back to sleep and were awakened by Lucy's mother and the doctor.

Dr. Wilson sat his bag on the nightstand and took out his stethoscope, "Hello girls. Lucy your ma tells me you think you got the rabies."

She sat up in the bed. "Are we a gonna die?" she asked him.

"Well, let me see, open your mouth and say aaahhh," the doctor looked in her throat.

She opened her mouth and Dr. Wilson pressed her tongue down. "AAAAHHHH. Shewee that little wood stick tastes awful," she said when he took it out of her mouth.

The doctor laughed at her. "I know it does," he turned to Macy. "It's your turn Macy. Open up."

Macy opened her mouth. "AAAHHH," she said for him. Macy made a face and swished her mouth around trying to get the taste of the wood out of her mouth. " Ya know, that does taste bad," she told him.

He pulled a thermometer out of his bag, "I know it does. Stick this under your tongue." He popped it in Macy's mouth. Here's one for you Lucy. Keep it under your tongues and keep your mouths closed."

He looked at his watch and when it was time to take the thermometers out, he went over to Macy, "Now let me see, you first, Macy." He took her thermometer out of her mouth and went over to Lucy, "Okay now you, Lucy." He checked the readings, "Uh huh, yep, it's just what I expected. You both have the strep throat."

"What's that?" Macy asked.

"Is it rabies?" Lucy wailed.

"No, it's not rabies and you're not going to die," he laughed. "But, you're going to be sick for a while." He turned to Lucy's mother, "The best thing to do is make them stay in bed. Give them lots a water and chicken broth. I'll leave some medicine with you. I want you to make sure that they take it twice a day. I'll be back to check on them in a week." He closed his medical bag and stood up to leave. Lucy's mother followed him to the door.

When her mother and Dr. Wilson left the room and shut the door, Lucy looked at Macy and smiled. "We ain't got's the rabies," she clapped her hands.

Macy shook her head, "I reckon it wouldn't show up that fast anyways. We might still have it."

Lucy panicked again, "I didn't think'a that. Oh Macy, I just know we got the rabies now."

Macy was afraid and said, "Yep, jist have to wait now and see. Ya feel any diff'rnt?"

Lucy buried her face in the pillow, "No jist hot, and achy all over. How 'bout ya?"

Macy sighed, "I reckon I feel the same. I think's I'll jist try ta sleep some."

"I reckon that'll be the best for right now," Lucy said. She pulled the quilts closer under her chin and went back to sleep.

Lucy woke up and the day had turned to night. The room was very dark and silent. She heard a noise in the attic.

Scratch, scratch, scratch.

She shook Macy, "Macy, are ya awake?"

Macy didn't answer.

"Oh no, are ya dead?" Lucy shook her harder.

Macy woke up, "Hey, what'cha a doin'?"

Lucy let out the breath she had been holding, "I thought ya was dead."

Macy sat up, "No, I's a sleepin'. What'd ya wake me up fer?"

"It's dark out," Lucy whispered.

Macy punched her pillow and lay back down, "I kin see that. What'd ya wake me up fer?"

Lucy snuggled close to her, "I heerd a noise."

"What'd it sound like?" Macy asked her.

"I don't know a kind a scratchy noise," she heard the noise again. "Wait, there it is again. Did ya hear it?"

Scratch, scratch, scratch.

Macy listened for the noise, "Yeah I do, what is that?"

Lucy scooted over next to Macy, "I never heered nothin' like that afore."

Macy reached for the lamp, "It sounds like somethin' a scratchin' up on the ceilin'. Maybe we ort'a light the lamp, see what it is. Where's the matches?" Macy asked her.

"In the table on yer side," Lucy put the pillow over her head.

Macy felt around and found the table. She opened the drawer but she wasn't able to find the matches. She climbed out of bed to find them.

Lucy stuck her head out from under the quilts, "I don't hear it now."

Macy shushed Lucy, "SHHHH, listen."

Scratch, scratch, scratch.

Lucy thought of Tiger and almost panicked again, "Reckon that crazy cats a tryin' ta git in here and eat us up?"

"I think it sounds like a coon," Macy listened for the sound again.

Scratch, scratch, scratch.

Lucy started to become very scared. "It's somethin' a tryin' ta git in here," she wailed. She felt her hair move and thought Macy had hit at her. "Hey, what'd ya hit me in the head fer?"

Macy was looking for the matches, "I didn't hit ya in the head. I'm over here lookin' fer the matches."

"You did too, I felt ya do it," Lucy accused her.

"I did not, SHHH. Listen," Macy tiptoed back to the bed and they tried to be quiet. "I don't heer nothin' now. I reckon it's gone."

Lucy turned her head straining her eyes in the dark to see the other side of the room. She felt her hair move again. "Hey, ya hit me again. Stop it," she demanded.

"I never hit ya," Macy felt something go by her head. "What'd ya hit me fer Lucy? I done told ya I never hit ya."

"I didn't hit ya, Macy. I thought ya hit me," Lucy told her.

Macy found the matches and came back to the table to light the lamp, "I felt somethin' go by my head." She struck the match and lit the lamp. The room became light with a soft glow as she turned up the flame in the lamp.

Macy immediately saw what had been making the noise they were hearing. She screamed, "IT'S A BAT! RUN! HIDE! IT'S A BAT!" She jumped in the bed, grabbed the quilts and threw them over her head. She rolled up in the covers causing Lucy to fall on the floor.

"Hey, Macy unroll and let me in the bed afore it gets me!" Lucy screamed and pulled at the covers trying to get Macy to let her back in the bed. The bat flew by her again. "EEEEEEEEEYYYYYYYY!" she squealed and grabbed the sears catalogue. She ran to the corner and hunkered down. She opened the catalogue and held it over her head.

Macy peeked out from under the covers, "Is it gone yit?"

"NO! It ain't gone, it's a tryin' ta git me. Let me in the bed!" Lucy started for the bed. The bat made another pass around the room. Lucy ran back over to the corner and held the catalogue over her head.

Macy ducked back under the cover. "Go git your Pa!" she yelled.

Lucy was cowering in the corner. The bat flew by her again. "I can't, it's got me pinned down."

"Well, yell fer him!" Macy screamed at her.

"I can't, my throat hurts too bad. Help Macy, it's a swarpin' down at me!" Lucy dodged the bat.

"Crawl over and open the door. Maybe it'll fly out!" Macy was panicking.

Lucy tried to yell back at Macy but her voice cracked with the effort, "Ya crawl over and open it. I ain't a movin'. Ya got the covers to hide under, all I got's this book."

Macy crawled over to the door with the quilts wrapped around her. She opened the door and ran back to the bed. Lucy jumped under the quilts before Macy was able to roll back up in them. They lay very still.

"Reckon it's gone?" Lucy whispered.

"Peep yer head out'n see, fraidy cat," Macy begged her.

Lucy wasn't about to come out from under the quilts. "I ain't a gettin' out from under these covers, you'll roll back up in'um. You peek out'n see. I reckon yer a'feered too, Macy. I'm the one was fightin' it off over in the corner while you'us a hidin' under the covers."

"Let's look together," Macy pushed the quilts down and peeped out from under them.

"Do ya see him?" Lucy asked in a soft voice.

"No, I reckon he's gone," Macy whispered back.

"Look good, I don't want him to git us," Lucy stayed under the covers.

They heard Lucy's mother scream. They knew the bat had flown out of the room.

"He's done went in'ta the big room. Hurry shut the door!" Macy yelled.

Lucy jumped up and ran over to the door. She slammed it shut and ran back to the bed. "Did he git ya Macy? I know we'll git rabies shore if'n that bat touched us."

Macy felt her head, "No, I don't think so. Did he git ya?"

Lucy shook her head, "No, I don't feel nothin'."

They were too sick to get up so they settled back down and were asleep in no time.

Chapter 16
Rock Fight

When Macy and Lucy woke up, they heard voices coming from the big room and kitchen. They put on their housecoats and snuck down the hall to see who was visiting.

Macy put her finger to her lips to signal Lucy to be quiet. They peeped in the room.

"Who's that?" Macy whispered to Lucy.

Lucy looked around Macy, "I don't know. I never seed him a 'fore."

They listened again, and heard Lucy's mother talking, "I'm mighty glad ya come, Mr. Talbot, our girls will be at school jist as soon as they git's over the strep throat."

The man stood up and headed for the door. "I'm making my rounds to all the houses. Mr. Jenkins will be leaving before the spring classes and I wanted to introduce myself to everyone and meet my students."

Lucy giggled, "He shore does talk funny."

Macy shushed her again, "I reckon he must be a foreigner. I never heard talk like that a 'fore."

Lucy looked around Macy at the stranger, "He shore does look funny too. Would ya look at that big nose. I never seen a person that skinny a 'fore."

They heard Lucy's mother tell the man that they would be at school as soon as they felt better.

Macy stepped back, "I think that's the new teacher."

Lucy looked again, "I hope not. I like Mr. Jenkins."

"Mr. Jenkins must be leavin'," Macy started back for their bedroom.

Lucy followed her and they jumped back in the bed. They heard Lucy's mother coming and they pulled the covers up around their head. She came in the room with a tray of breakfast.

She put the tray on the night table, "Girls, git up now and eat somethin'. I've got good news. Yer gonna git a new teacher when ya go back to school."

Macy popped her head out from under the covers, "We heard him a talkin'. He sounded like a foreigner."

Lucy's mother chuckled, "He said he was from Minnesota. I reckon they speak a mite different that we do. But I liked him. Ya girls will too. Ya jist have ta give him a chance. He seemed like a nice young man."

Lucy sat up, "If'n we kin understand what he's a sayin' we mite."

Her mother poured them some milk and handed them the tray of food. "School will be starting next week. The doctor says ya'll be well enough to go when it does. Finish all this food, it'll help ya feel better. Come in by the fire if'n ya feel like it when yer finished."

The next few days Macy and Lucy began to feel better. They spent those days playing checkers while they sat by the fireplace. As the first day of school approached, they became anxious to see the new teacher.

They were up before the sun the first day of school. They were excited and the walk to the school seemed long to them. The closer they got to the school the faster they walked. The bell was ringing as they came in the schoolyard and they ran the rest of the way. They went inside to their desks and sat down.

Mr. Talbot cleared his throat nervously. He wanted to make a good impression on his students. He had only graduated the correspondence school a month ago this was his first post as teacher. He made his way to the front of the class and wrote his name on the blackboard. "Good morning, students."

A giggle went through the room. He turned around. The room became quiet.

He continued, "My name is Mr. Talbot."

Macy had never heard speaking like that and she wasn't able to stand it anymore, so she began laughing out loud. All the other kids joined in.

Mr. Talbot rang the bell on his desk. "Please tell me what is so funny?" he asked the class.

Silence.

He put his hands on his hips to keep them from shaking, "Well?"

A murmur of snickers went through the classroom.

"Alright, suppose someone tell me what is so funny," he pointed to Macy. "You seem to be the one most amused, suppose you tell me."

Macy looked around to make sure he was speaking to her, "Who me?"

Mr. Talbot tapped his ruler on the desk, "Yes, you. Stand up and state your name."

Macy stood up. "Macy Watson," she stated and glared at the teacher.

Mr. Talbot came over to Macy's desk, "Alright, Macy Watson, please take off your hat and explain what is so funny."

Macy hesitated for a moment but she took her off her hat. She was beginning not to like the new teacher with his uppity ways. "I reckon we jist never heered anyone speak like ya do," she explained the laughter.

All the children laughed again.

Mr. Talbot nodded, "Oh I see. It's my northern accent you think is funny. Well, there are different accents all around the United States. We need to learn about them. I think then, the first lesson will be to write all the states in order. Take out your geography books. Macy, you come up here to the chalkboard and write the states on it for the class."

Macy decided she didn't like the new teacher at all. She wasn't going to do anything he said to do. "No, I don't want to," she crossed her arms ready for a standoff.

Mr. Talbot stammered, he wasn't prepared for a confrontation this early. The correspondence school didn't have anything in the curriculum that addressed this problem. He began to lose his patience. "Either you come and write the states or you can stay in for recess."

Macy sat back down, "I choose stayin' in."

He was surprised and paused, "Very well, since you don't want to have recess, you can stay in the rest of the week while all the other children take their breaks."

Macy's face turned as red as her hair. She made up her mind and she refused to give in to the new teacher. Every day for the next week, she sat at her desk with her arms crossed and a scowl on her face while the other children went out to play. Every day, after recess, Mr. Talbot asked her if she was ready to write on the board and every day she refused.

Lucy felt bad for Macy and stayed in with her. The other children all made fun of them for staying inside. They came by the window and pecked on it. When Macy looked in their direction, they stuck their tongues out at her and ran off. She silently vowed they would be sorry for pestering her.

Macy had had enough of their fun making, so on Friday, she sent Lucy outside with the other children. "Lucy, what I want ya ta do is go out at recess today and pile up rocks in little piles all over the yard."

Lucy was worried about what Macy had in mind, "What ya want me ta do that fer?"

"Jist do it, okay? You'll see next week," Macy told her.

"Big rocks or little rocks?" she asked Macy.

Macy had a plan, "Oh git all kinds. Not too big though."

Lucy was beginning to suspect what Macy was going to do. "Oh Macy, ya go chunkin' rocks at them girls, yer gonna git in more trouble than jist missin' recess."

"It jist ain't them girls, John and Sam and all them boys are gonna git it too. I reckon ya know I can chunk rocks better'n anybody."

"But Macy, they ain't the ones a makin' ya stay in. It's teacher," Lucy didn't want any part of Macy's plan. She tried to talk Macy out of it.

"Look at them girls. They been snickerin' at me all week. They's gonna be sorry fer it. Go on out and do like I say. Don't let no one see what yer a doin' though," Macy forced her to go outside.

Lucy sat on a log by herself for most of the recess. She watched as the other children went to the window to taunt Macy. The more she watched them taunting Macy, the angrier she became. She decided to do what Macy asked her to do. She moved all around the schoolyard making mounds of rocks. She piled some mounds behind trees and some behind the school. She even made piles of rocks behind the big rocks in back of the school. She didn't make the mounds very big. She didn't want to draw any attention to them. Lucy knew that Macy was going to get them in trouble again, but she felt sorry for her and decided to go along with the plan.

The next week on Monday, Macy and Lucy made sure they arrived at school early. Lucy helped her write all the names of the states on the black board. They printed their names on the board at the bottom. They wanted Mr. Talbot to know they had been the ones to write the states.

When Mr. Talbot came in the room, he was pleased and thought he had handled the situation with Macy in the right way. He told Macy she had regained her recess privileges.

At recess, Lucy showed Macy where she had made the mounds of rocks. They didn't notice Helen and Loretta following them. They stopped at a large mound of Lucy's rocks. Helen tossed her hair and walked over to them.

"I know'ed you'd give in, Macy. I'd a not give in, if it were me," Helen bragged.

Macy bent down and picked up a rock. "I jist put them states on the blackboard on account I wanted to come outside today. I know'ed all them states all along."

Loretta nodded her head at Helen, "Yeah right, we know'ed you'd give in. If it'd been me, I'd a never give in. Shows ya ain't got no backbone."

Macy rolled the rock over in her hand, "Yer such a cry baby, Helen that you'd a went to the blackboard right off. You'd a not lasted the week like I did."

Helen pushed Macy, "I'd a not got in trouble in the first place."

Macy's face turned red. She tightened her fist around the rock she held in her hand. "Better not do that again," she warned.

John and Sam noticed something was about to happen. They decided to go see what was going on. As soon as they came over to the little group of girls, Loretta took John by the hand. She stuck her nose in the air and turned to walk away, "Come on, John, I'm tired a talkin' with these babies." They turned around and started walking away.

Macy let the rock fly from her hand and it hit Loretta in the shoulder with a thud. She picked up another rock and cocked her hand back to throw it. Loretta and Helen started running for the school house. Macy threw the rock and this one hit Helen in the middle of her back. Helen ducked behind a tree with Sam. John picked up a rock and sent it sailing back at Macy. He picked up another rock and jumped behind a tree.

Macy and Lucy dashed behind the nearest tree and the rock John had thrown missed them and hit the tree. Macy threw another rock at John just as he peeped around the tree. The rock hit him smack in the mouth and knocked his tooth out. Macy threw all the rocks in that pile and ran over to another one. She started throwing them at Helen and Sam.

John darted behind the big rocks in the back of the school. He discovered Lucy's rock pile there. He started throwing those rocks back at Macy and Lucy. Lucy started helping her cousin throw the rocks. One of Lucy's rocks hit Helen again as she ran screaming to the schoolhouse to get the teacher.

Mr. Talbot stepped in the schoolyard with Helen behind him. A flying rock hit him in the side of his head. "What is the meaning of this? Stop it right this instant!" he yelled.

Rocks continued to fly. He ran over to John and grabbed him by the arm, "Stop this nonsense immediately!"

John dropped the rock he had in his hand. Macy threw another rock and it landed right in the middle of John's stomach. He doubled over from the blow.

Mr. Talbot ran over to where Macy and Lucy hunkered down behind the tree. "Macy and Lucy Watson, you stop throwing rocks this instant," he demanded.

Macy knew she had been caught. She stood up and dropped the rock she had in her hand.

Flustered, Mr. Talbot yelled. "Everyone back in the school house right now." He pointed to the school.

The children dragged themselves back in the school and sat down at their desks. Macy's face flushed red with anger. She sat very stiff backed at her desk. Lucy slumped down in her chair. She was very afraid of the consequences to come.

Mr. Talbot came in behind them and went to the front of the room, "Who is going to explain what happened?"

Helen stood up, "The whole thing started on account a Macy and Lucy. They jist started throwin' rocks at us for no reason a 'tall."

The teacher then turned to Macy, "Is that true? Did you start throwing rocks at these girls?"

"They was a makin' fun a me and Lucy," Macy balled her fist up, ready for another fight.

Loretta jumped up, "We did not, we weren't a doin' nothin' to make ya throw rocks at us. John, he never did nothin' 'cept walk over to where we was a talkin' and look at him, his mouths a bleedin' and his tooth is knocked out."

Mr. Talbot decided this was a great opportunity to teach the children about court and having a trial. "I think this needs to go to court and have a trial. This is a case of Loretta and Helen's word against Macy and Lucy's. John too, he has his tooth knocked out," he explained the process of a trial. "The way this works is, Helen, Loretta and John will charge Macy and Lucy with assault. John, Helen, and Loretta will try to prove what Macy and Lucy did. Macy and Lucy will be the defendants. They will have to make a defense in a trial."

Lucy started shaking. She leaned over and whispered to Macy, "Oh no, Macy, we are a goin' to jail."

Macy shook her head. "No we ain't, teacher says they have to prove their charges."

"They can, we did throw rocks at them," Lucy whispered back.

"Shhhh, I want ta listen how ta do it," Macy hushed Lucy. She listened to Mr. Talbot intently. As he talked, she began to understand what the trial process would be. She determined that she would be the one to win the case.

The next week they prepared for the trial. Macy elected to be her own lawyer. Mr. Talbot sat at his desk, to preside as the judge. Loretta and Helen wanted to be the lawyers for John and he decided that they could be on his team. They arranged the chairs so that the rest of the class could sit as the jury.

They studied how trials were conducted and how the process worked. After a week of study, everyone involved felt that they were ready for the trial to begin.

Loretta and Helen took their turns presenting their case. They called all the children in the schoolyard to testify starting with Sam.

Helen marched around the chair where he sat and proceeded, "Now

Sam, tell us what ya saw the day John got his tooth knocked out."

"We saw all ya girls a talkin' with Macy and Lucy. Me and John figured we'd go over and see what'cha was a doin', was a doin'. 'Bout the time we walked over to where ya where the rocks started flyin', started a flyin'."

Helen stopped pacing and turned to him, "Tell us who was a throwin' them rocks?" She turned and looked at Macy and Lucy.

"Macy were the one I reckon. Macy I reckon," Sam rubbed his head and fidgeted in the chair.

Helen turned and smiled triumphantly at the jury. "No further questions for this witness," she announced to them.

Mr. Talbot nodded to Macy, "Do you want to cross examine this witness?"

Macy stood up. "I shore do," she walked over to Sam, "Now Sam, did ya actually see me throw the rock that hit John in the mouth or any rock for that matter?" she questioned him.

Sam scratched his head, "Well no, I jist seed one hit him, didn't see where it come from, where it come from. We's all runnin' and dodge'un them rocks. Dodge'un them rocks."

Macy put her hands on her hips, "So ya mean to tell us that ya didn't actually see who throwed the rock that hit John? Anyone in the schoolyard could've throwed that rock then, rite?" she asked with a raised voice.

Sam dropped his head, "Well, I reckon that's rite, I didn't see who throwed the rock. Throwed the rock."

Macy slapped her desk. "Well, tell us who were a throwin' rocks that day?" she challenged him.

Sam twisted uncomfortably in his chair, "I reckon ever' body was a throwin' rocks, throwin' rocks."

Macy turned to the jury and raised her voice to a shout. "So John could'a been hit by a rock throwed by anyone that were a throwin' rocks?"

Sam put his head down, "When ya say it like that, I reckon so, reckon so." Sam squirmed in his chair.

Loretta jumped up, "I object!"

Macy whirled around to her. "To what?" she shouted.

Mr. Talbot banged his ruler on his desk, "That's enough of that, Macy. I'll ask those kinds of questions. "

Loretta sat back down. "I don't know I jist object. That's what the book says yer 'posed ta do when ya don't agree with what's a being said."

"Overruled. Just because you object, doesn't mean you will be granted the objection. You have to have a reason to object," Mr. Talbot said pleased. He was happy that the children had caught on to the trial process as quickly as they had.

The trial continued for two days. Loretta and Helen called every child to the witness stand. Every child said the same thing, they didn't see who threw the rock that hit John when Macy cross examined them. Macy even wrangled a confession out of John. She caused him to admit that he didn't see who actually hit him with the rock. Macy pointed this out in her closing statement and the jury came back with a not guilty verdict for her and Lucy.

Mr. Talbot, who had been very pleased with the way the children caught on to the way a trial should be conducted had a nagging doubt that he had made matters worse. He believed that Macy and Lucy had started the rock fight. He also believed, they had been the ones to hit John in the mouth and knock his tooth out. His conscious bothered him that he had taught the children a bad lesson. He decided to make Macy and Lucy to pick up rocks and carry them out of the yard as punishment for their part in the rock fight.

Chapter 17
Chiggers

Mr. Talbot gave Macy and Lucy the task of clearing the schoolyard of the rocks. The girls gathered rocks once a week for the next two months at recess. This was their punishment for starting the rock fight.

Lucy dumped a bucketful over in the ditch. "I think this yard is a growin' rocks. Or else somebody's a pickin' um up and puttin' um back in the yard at night," she said as she wiped her hands on her dress.

Macy dumped her bucket, "I know I'm mighty tired of that ole teacher. We won the trial case but he still punished us."

"I reckon it's on account a we did start the rock fight. I feel bad for John. He looks funny with his tooth knocked out," Lucy then set her bucket down and started putting more rocks in it. "Maybe if'n we say we are sorry, he'll let us quit this work."

Macy huffed at Lucy, "Ya are a dummy. That'd be admitting we done the rock chunkin'." She picked up her bucket and followed Lucy around the schoolyard. "I ain't a gonna pick up rocks much more."

Lucy turned her bucket upside down tipping the rocks out and sat on it, "I never thought'a that."

"I did. He's a wantin' us to admit it. He'll not git me to admit it. Even if I have to pick up rocks forever," Macy sat down beside her in the dirt.

The bell started ringing to signal recess was over and time for classes to begin. They picked up their buckets and put them beside a rock pile. They followed the rest of the children back in the schoolhouse.

Mr. Talbot waited for the class to settle down. When they did, he began writing the new assignment on the blackboard. "We are going to do a science experiment. I want everyone to make a collection of bugs and identify them."

Loretta raised her hand.

He stopped writing and acknowledged her, "Yes, Loretta?"

She made a face, "How are we gonna do that? I hate bugs."

He held up a mason jar, "This is what is called a kill jar. You take some cotton balls and soak them in rubbing alcohol. The cotton balls are then placed in a jar with a tight lid on it. After you catch the insect, drop him in the jar and close the lid. The insect will then suffocate. The next step after the insect dies, is to take a stick pin and pin the insect to a piece of cardboard. Identify the insect on the cardboard with both the common name and the scientific name out of this science book." He picked up an insect identification book that he had brought with him.

Loretta made another face, "Do we have to do that? I hate bugs."

"Yes, we do, and it will count as a big part of the science grade you receive at the end of the year. We will pair up with partners. Everyone choose a partner to help with the collection. We will begin collections right away. The season is getting late in the summer. We will have to gather them quickly. Most of the insects will be gone before too long."

He passed out the jars. They placed the alcohol and cotton in the jars. When all the jars were prepared, the class followed Mr. Talbot outside to begin collecting the insects. Macy and Lucy thought it was great fun. They took the little nets Mr. Talbot gave them and started running after butterflies.

Lucy noticed a green dragonfly and ran after it wielding her net over her head. She waved the net at the dragonfly and caught it in her net. She ran back to Macy dropped it in the jar, "Macy, Mr. Talbot ain't so bad. We never done anything like this before and I think it's fun."

Macy slammed the lid down on the jar, "Ya forgittin' the work we been a doin' pickin' up rocks? I been in trouble ever since he come here. I don't like him."

Lucy looked in the field beside the schoolyard, "All the good bugs are a flyin' around over yonder in the chigger weeds."

Macy picked up a black beetle, "Yeah, I know, but I ain't a goin' in and gettin' them chiggers all over me. Ya can if'n ya want to."

Lucy's eyes flew open wide. She had been bit by chiggers enough to know she didn't want anything to do with them. "I ain't that stupid. No one else is goin' over there either."

Mr. Talbot came over to Macy and Lucy, "How are you girls coming along with your collection?"

Lucy held up the kill jar for him to see, "We got two, a dragonfly and a beetle, that's all so far."

He looked over to the meadow beside the school. The softly blowing summer breeze made the meadow alive with brilliant colors: white Queen Ann's Lace, yellow Golden Rods, and scarlet Iron Weeds were mixed with the purple berries of the Polk. The flowers looked to him as if they were colorful fairies dancing in the breeze. "What about over there? I see many insects buzzing around those beautiful flowers. What are those white flowers? I have never seen any like them."

Lucy started laughing. "Oh them's, OOOWWW!" she yelled as Macy stomped her foot.

Macy smiled with a wink for Lucy, "I'm sorry, Lucy, I didn't mean to step on ya." She turned to the teacher, "Them flowers are called Queen Anne's Lace. They grow this time a year. They don't last long, they'll be gone in a few days."

Mr. Talbot looked at the lacy flowers. "They are certainly beautiful for a wild flower. I think they would make a beautiful bouquet," he thought of Nancy, the girl he was to marry. "I have a visitor coming to visit and go to church with me this weekend. I think I'll pick her some of those flowers."

Lucy giggled and Macy elbowed her in the side, "I think that'd be a great idea, Mr. Talbot. Any girl'ud like a purty bunch of flowers like that."

He looked again at the flowers, "Right, that was my thinking also. I think I'll pick her some. Continue your collecting girls." He went to find a vase for them.

When he got out of hearing, Lucy let out the breath she had been holding, "Oh Macy, Mr. Talbot's gonna git eat up."

Macy laughed, "If'n he's dumb enough to go in them weeds, I say let him. Besides, he's got it a comin'."

"Ya know he's gonna be real mad when he finds out about them critters. We'll be in more trouble than we are now," Lucy kicked at a rock in the yard.

Mr. Talbot retrieved a pair of scissors and went in the field of Queen Anne's Lace to gather the flowers. One by one the children noticed him and came to the edge of the field to watch. John and Sam began laughing. They could not believe he was actually walking around in the chigger weeds.

Loretta came over to John, "Somebody ort to tell him what is a gonna happen."

John shook his head and smiled, "Yeah, they should, but it ain't gonna be me. This is too great."

Loretta looked from John to the teacher. "I feel sorry for him, when them chiggers git a hold on him, he is gonna be miserable," Loretta shook her head.

Mr. Talbot picked flowers for the rest of the evening while the children chased and collected insects. When he had a basketful of the wildflowers, he called the children back to the school. He helped them begin putting the insects they had collected on the cardboard. While they were doing the boards, he put some of the flowers in vases and he tied some of the flowers in the window to dry.

Mr. Talbot began showing the class how to identify the insects with his insect key. A small red welt began to itch and he scratched it. He thought he had been bitten by a gnat or mosquito. In a few minutes, another welt began itching. He didn't pay a great deal of attention to the welts until all at once his skin was covered in them. They began getting bigger and itching painfully. He thought he was having some kind of allergic reaction to the flowers and began to get worried that he was going to have more complications than the itching.

He was afraid to go for the doctor himself. The welts were multiplying and he began to panic. "Someone quick, go for the doctor!" he yelled as he began to scratch uncontrollably.

"I'll go, Mr. Talbot, I'll go," Sam ran out the door.

Mr. Talbot grabbed a ruler and stuck it down the back of his shirt to scratch the welts that were developing down his back. The itching and burning became intense. He grabbed the rubbing alcohol they were using in the kill jars and ran to the outhouse. He tore off his shirt and began rubbing the alcohol on his arms and torso. He began to feel the itching around his belt and down his legs. He grabbed his shirt and began running for the doctor.

Sam had ran to Dr. Wilson's and they met Mr. Talbot halfway.

"Oh doctor, I'm having some kind of reaction to the flowers I picked earlier today. Hurry, before I go into some kind of shock. Do something!" Mr. Talbot yelled.

Dr. Wilson took one look at him and knew what was happening. "What kind of flowers were you picking?" Dr. Wilson asked him.

He pointed toward the meadow, "Those wildflowers over there in the meadow, the white ones."

Dr. Wilson looked in the direction he pointed. He began chuckling, and then it escalated into a fit of laughter.

Mr. Talbot became angry. "What are you laughing at? I need some help, I'm in misery and I could die!" he yelled as he scratched at the welts.

Dr. Wilson tried to stop chuckling long enough to tell him what was wrong with him, "Mr. Talbot, you have a bad case of chiggers."

Mr. Talbot stopped scratching and panicked again. "What in the world are chiggers? Is it dangerous?" he said with a voice a couple octaves higher than he usually spoke.

Dr. Wilson tried to hold in the laughter. "Not dangerous, but you are going to be in misery for a few weeks. Chiggers are a tiny mite. They live in the grass and on those flowers this time of year. Their bite lasts for a few weeks, but you are going to think it's months," Dr. Wilson tried to contain his amusement.

"This isn't funny, I'm on fire," Mr. Talbot began scratching again.

Dr. Wilson stopped laughing and tried to console him, "No it isn't, and the worst thing you can do is scratch the welts. You need to go right now and take a bath, in case there are more chiggers on your skin and clothes. Wash your clothes good or better yet throw them away. I'll send over some salve to rub on the welts. I'm afraid it won't help much though. I'm sorry."

Mr. Talbot turned and ran for his house. The children had gathered around and they all began laughing.

Dr. Wilson turned to them. "Why didn't you warn him about those chiggers when you saw him getting in those weeds?" he asked them accusingly.

They stopped their snickering. Dr. Wilson understood what they had done and stared at them. "You should all be ashamed of yourselves!" he scolded them. "Go on home all of you. I'm sure Mr. Talbot will have a lot to discuss with all of you."

Macy and Lucy took their insects and began walking home. "Ya know that he's a gonna be really mad at us don't ya, Macy? He's a gonna blame us and we are gonna be in trouble," Lucy fretted.

Macy stopped walking and turned and looked back at the school. "I hadn't thought of that and I never thought them chiggers would'a eat him up like that. I figured only one or two would'a got him. He must a really stunk or somethin' for them bugs to git him like they did," Macy concluded.

"Maybe, but I never smelled him stinking, did you?" Lucy asked her.

Macy shook her head, "Well, no, but Pa says that bugs only bite stinky people or lazy people."

Lucy giggled, "Yeah, my pa says that too. I reckon Nanny used to tell them that when they's young'uns. Ya know, Macy, he's a gonna really make it hard on us."

"Yeah, but not for a while. He ain't a gonna be able to do nothin' fer awhile except scratch them chigger welts. I reckon it'll be worth it," Macy started laughing.

Lucy joined her and they giggled all the way home.

Chapter 18
Insect collection

All the next week, Macy and Lucy worked hard catching the bugs for their insect collection. In misery, Mr. Talbot missed a week of teaching. He sent word to the students to continue with their collecting and he would help with the identifications as soon as he was able to be back at school.

The forest was humming with bugs this time of year; summer was ending and soon the cold would drive them away. Macy and Lucy ran through the groves of pines with their nets, chasing anything that moved. They chased butterflies around the edges of the meadows, not daring to follow them in amongst the wildflowers. They didn't want anything to do with chigger bites themselves. They giggled every time a butterfly escaped their net by flying into the meadow thinking of Mr. Talbot.

At the end of the week, they had collected over a hundred insects and pinned them to the cardboard. When they finished pinning the last insects, they stepped back to admire the collection. They were pleased with the collection and was ready to take it to school with them the next day. The girls put them on the table in the living room and covered them with a cloth.

Macy was up early and dressed to go to school. Before she woke Lucy, she went in to the kitchen to find some breakfast. She went to the living room to check on the insect collection. She lifted the cloth and stared at the cardboard. The pins were still in the cardboard but most of the bugs were gone. The heads of some of the bugs still hung there with the pins still in them.

She ran back to the bedroom and shook Lucy, "Hey git up, hurry somethin's happened to the bugs."

Lucy opened her eyes and jumped out of bed. Macy led the way and they raced to the living room. Macy stopped at the door of the living room. Lucy stepped around her and stood in the doorway staring at the empty cardboard. "What happened?" she turned to Macy.

"How should I know? I bet it were yer brothers done somethin'," Macy accused.

"Why would they do somethin' ta our bugs? They knowed we had them for school?" Lucy plopped down on the floor in a heap.

Macy tried to make sense of the missing insects, "I don't know, did ya make'um mad at ya fer some reason?"

Lucy thought for a minute, "No, we ain't had no spats in over a week." She stood to her feet and started pacing around the table. "What are we goin' ta do? How are we goin' to ' splain this to teacher?" she grumbled.

Macy lifted the cardboard off the table. As soon as she picked it up, they both knew what had happened to the bugs. They looked at each other and then back to the evidence on the table and stared at the mouse droppings underneath the cardboard.

Lucy let out a big breath, "This is worse than I thought. How are we gonna 'splain this? Mr. Talbot's prob'ly already mad at us for all them chigger bites he got. He won't believe us when we tell him a mouse ate our bugs."

Macy kept staring at the destroyed bug collection, "Ya keep askin' me that, how should I know? I never know'ed a mouse'ud come in here and eat all our bugs. I reckon he'll fail us and we'll have to stay back a grade next year."

Grasping for something to do Lucy had an idea, "Maybe we could catch some more bugs right fast."

Macy let the cardboard drop on the table. Some of the mouse droppings rolled in the floor. "They's no way ta catch butterflies now. This is September; it's a fixin' ta frost. They won't be nothin' but beetles and they probably will be way down in the ground now. 'Sides, we got to have'em at school today and it took us a long time ta catch all them bugs a 'fore."

Then Macy had an idea. She jumped back from the table, "I know, we'll jist take the mouse droppings with us to school and show Mr. Talbot what happened."

Lucy brightened up, "Macy, that's a good idea. He'll have to believe us that way. But what are we a gonna git ta take them in? I shore ain't a gonna touch them stinkin' droppin's."

Macy headed for the kitchen with Lucy close behind her, "Let's go look in the dish cupboard, they's bound to be an old bowl or somethin' we can use."

They went over to the cupboard, rummaged around and found a small bowl with a chip near the bottom. Macy picked it up, "Look at this one, it's real old and got a chip. I reckon we can use this'un. Yer ma'll never notice this'un bein' gone."

Lucy looked at the little bowl, "I never see'd that one a ' fore. No, she won't even notice this'un is gone."

They went back to the living room table. Lucy lifted the cardboard and Macy took a knife she had brought with her from the kitchen and raked the mouse droppings in the bowl. She took the knife back in the kitchen and flopped it in the sink, "Make sure we tell yer ma to wash that knife good a 'fore she uses it."

They decided to use a feed sack from the barn to carry what was left of the insect collection. They didn't want the wind to blow what was left of the bugs away. Macy thought she'd better carry the bowl of mouse droppings. She didn't trust Lucy; she thought Lucy might spill the evidence. Macy carried the bowl all the way to school herself and Lucy carried the bugs.

They arrived at the school before any of the other children. They went straight into the school and directly to Mr. Talbot, who sat at his desk. Macy plopped the bowl of mouse droppings down on the desk right in front of him. Mr. Talbot saw what was in the bowl and jumped up.

Before he could say anything Macy began explaining, "Mr. Talbot, look here at our bugs collection." She took the sack from Lucy and opened it up. "We had all kinds of critters for ya ta help us identify and look here what happened. A mouse got in the house and ate ever' one of our bugs."

Lucy pointed to the bowl of mouse poop. "Yeah, we weren't able to catch the mouse but we brought his leavin's so ya could see we was a tellin' the truth. We figured it's too late to catch anymore bugs, but ya can see what's left of the ones we had," Lucy told him.

Mr. Talbot regained his composure, "Yes, I see that Lucy. You can take the bowl of," he paused. "Stuff out and dump it in the yard. We'll work with the insects you have and see if we can figure out what they were." He picked the bowl up off his desk with his fingers and handed it to Lucy. "Go on now, take that outside and dump it. Be sure and leave the bowl outside," he told her as she walked toward the door.

Lucy took the bowl outside she still didn't want to dump her evidence so she set it down by the steps.

As soon as the other children arrived with their collections, Mr. Talbot had the class spend the day trying to figure out what each of the insects Macy and Lucy had collected were. They made comparisons to find out if anyone had caught a similar insect. At recess all the children went outside to eat their lunch.

Chapter 19
Chewing Tobacco

They took a break from identifying the bugs and Macy and Lucy found a place to eat in the shade of the big oak tree behind the schoolhouse. Macy noticed that John and the rest of the boys were making trips from the big rocks behind the schoolhouse to the outhouse. She decided to go see what they were doing.

"Do ya see them boys a goin' back and forth behind the outhouse?" she asked Lucy.

Lucy had been watching them too, "I do, wonder what they are a doin'?"

Macy stood up, "Let's go see."

They snuck through the yard and peeked behind the outhouse. The boys all sat around in a circle. They watched as John spit something out of his mouth.

Macy came out from behind the outhouse, "What are ya guys a doin'?"

Fearing they had been caught, they all jumped and turned around. "We ain't doin' nothin' and 'sides if we were it wouldn't be none of yer business," John breathed a sigh of relief that it wasn't the teacher.

Sam winked at John and poked him in the arm, "We are a chawin' baccer, chawin' baccer."

Macy looked close at the brown spittle in his mouth, "What does that mean?"

John reached in his pocket and pulled out a plug of chewing tobacco. He winked at Sam, "Baccer, ya know, like yer pa chews."

Lucy made face, "My pa don't chew nothin' like that."

He handed it to Macy, "Ya take a bite off'n it and chew it 'round in yer mouth and ya spit out the juice. Like this." John made a big to do about rolling the tobacco around in his mouth. When he was ready, he spit the brown juice out on the ground.

"That looks nasty," Lucy made a face of disgust.

"It's good. Try it. Try it," Sam said.

Macy looked at the plug of tobacco John held out to her, "Lucy is right, that looks nasty."

John picked up a grasshopper that was crawling by him. He squeezed it gently and it formed a brown ball of spittle in its mouth. He showed it to Macy. "Look here, even the hoppers chew baccer. It's good, but I reckon yer chicken to try it ain't ya, Macy?" he dared her.

Macy took the plug of tobacco from him. She rolled it around in her hand. It felt oily. She put it up to her nose and sniffed. A mixture of sweet and pungent aroma made her cringe.

John started laughing, "She's a chicken to try it I reckon."

All the boys started laughing. Macy didn't want them to get the best of her, so she put the tobacco in her mouth and bit off a piece. The taste was strange and made her eyes water. She swallowed some of the juice before she could spit it out. She started coughing and swallowed some more.

All the boys began laughing at her. She turned red from getting angry and then she turned pale. Macy started feeling sick at her stomach.

Lucy watched in fear as Macy's face turned from red to a green color, "Macy, ya look like yer a turning green, are ya alright?"

"I don't feel sa good," Macy's head began spinning, she was sick at her stomach, dizzy, and began rocking back and forth.

Lucy put a hand on Macy to steady her, "Ya better sit down Macy. Over here on this rock." Lucy helped her over the rock.

Macy put her hand on the tree to steady herself. The trees looked to her as if they were spinning. She still hadn't spit the tobacco out of her mouth. She swallowed some more of the juice. Her skin turned a pale color. She started sweating and became very nauseated. She sat down and dropped her head. With a spinning head, she fell forward onto the ground. Lucy helped her sit back up. Macy still had the tobacco in her mouth. When she realized that she did, she spit it out and started throwing up.

Lucy ran over to the boys, who were laughing at Macy, "This ain't funny, ya know'ed that'ud make her sick. I'm going to tell teacher on ya."

John jumped up and grabbed Lucy by her arm and twisted it behind her. "Ya tell and you'll regret it," he warned.

Lucy tore her arm away from him and ran back over to Macy. Macy was lying on the ground, "Macy, are ya alright? Ya look sort of green."

Macy sat back up and looked over at the boys that were still laughing at her, "I'm sick." It was all she could say and she started throwing up again. Lucy helped her to sit up again. Macy grabbed her stomach and doubled over with the nausea. She put her head down between her knees. "I'm a gonna git even with them boys if'n it's the last thing I do," she said weakly and started throwing up again.

When recess was over, Mr. Talbot rang the bell to signal the children to come back inside. Lucy helped Macy get back inside the school. John seized Lucy by the arm again. "Ya better not be a tattletale, else you'll be sorry," he pinched her arm and let it go.

Lucy helped Macy to her desk. Macy put her head down again as waved of sickness rushed over her. She silently vowed to get even with John for the tobacco. Then she started throwing up again.

Mr. Talbot noticed how sick Macy was and came over to her. He took one look at her and sent Lucy for the doctor.

Lucy found the doctor at the general store and begged him to come with her. As soon as Dr. Wilson looked at Macy, he knew what was wrong. He had seen enough chewing tobacco sickness to recognize the signs, "Macy, you have been chewing tobacco, haven't you?"

"Yeah," was all she could manage to moan.

Mr. Talbot was shocked, "I never heard of such a thing, a young lady like yourself chewing tobacco. Macy you should be ashamed of yourself."

Macy moaned in misery. "I never chewed no baccer a 'fore this."

Dr. Wilson snorted at her, "You shouldn't have chewed any this time." He gave her some bicarbonate soda to drink and sent her home with a note about what had happened. "Now you give this note to your mother Macy, I will be asking her about it," he warned her.

Macy leaned against Lucy all the way home only stopping occasionally to throw up. When they arrived home and Lucy's mother read the note, she sent for Macy's parents. Macy's mother became very upset. She refused to let Macy explain. She decided that as punishment, Macy should spend the fall with relatives in Kentucky harvesting tobacco.

With every wave of nausea and thoughts of working in the tobacco, Macy vowed she was going to get back at John and the other boys.

Chapter 20
Macy's Lemonade

The next day at recess, Macy leaned up against the big oak tree behind the schoolhouse. A plan of just how to get even with John Taylor for making her sick on that tobacco began to form in her mind and all she needed was to talk Lucy into helping her. Macy waited for Lucy to come out for recess.

"I been thinkin', I'm a gonna go inta business for myself," Macy stated and popped the end of a piece of grass between her teeth.

"What ya got planned Macy?" Lucy asked a little breathless. She knew Macy's plans usually ended up with the both of them in trouble.

"I'm gonna start a lemonade stand," Macy stated.

"Aw Macy, that ain't gonna work. Ya seen that Nancy Boggs try that last summer down by the Old Mill in Pigeon Forge. She took all her money she'd been a savin' and lost it ever' bit," Lucy said, a little disappointed and relieved at the same time.

"Yeah, but she weren't sellin' what I'm a gonna be sellin'," Macy smiled. "I'm a gonna git my brother's special brew to put in mine."

Lucy gasped, "Macy, ya don't mean moonshine do ya? Ya ain't gonna try to sell lemonade with moonshine in it are ya? Why yer brothers would whup the tar out'a ya they find out ya stole some of it."

Macy stood up and dusted her overalls, "They'd better not if'n they want us ta do all that there totin' the water for it when they make it. The way I figure it's half mine anyway. I work jist as hard as they do ta make it."

"But Macy, what if'n teacher finds out?" Lucy asked looking from side to side to see if anyone was listening.

"I been thinkin' on that. I got that all figured out. If'n you'll help me I'm gonna give ya twenty percent of ever thing we make," Macy crossed her arms and waited for Lucy to respond to her generous offer.

"Ya mean yer gonna give me all that jist for helpin'?" Lucy looked at Macy a little weary. "What else am I gonna have ta do?"

"Not a thing, ya do half the work and I'll give ya twenty percent of what we make," Macy waited for her answer.

"I don't know, Macy, I'm a'feared we gonna git caught," Lucy shook her head. They usually did get caught.

"I saw that purty blue dress in Mr. Summer's store winder. I bet we make a'nough ya can buy that dress, Lucy," Macy knew that was sure to hook her.

Lucy had shown Macy the dress that morning as they walked to school, how she would love to have it. Maybe Macy's idea would work. That dress sure was pretty.

"Ok Macy, I'll do it. What ya need me ta do?" she asked with a mischievous look. The recess bell rang and the two girls made their plans as they scurried back inside. The next day, Macy gathered up all the money she had and went to Mr. Summer's store. She bought all the lemons he had in stock.

Lucy was busy setting up the booth. They made it from an old soap box and a piece of plywood. Macy had sneaked into the root cellar that morning and stole a jug of her brother's best moonshine (which meant the newest batch). At recess she went about making her special lemonade.

Their first customer to come by their stand happened to be John Taylor. "I heered ya was makin' some refreshments, Macy," he grinned. The lost tooth from the rock fight caused his words to come out in a whistle when he talked.

Macy smiled sweetly at him. This couldn't be working out any better she thought, "I am for a fact, would ya like ta try a free sample?"

Sweat ran down his face as John eyed the lemonade, "Well now that's right hospitable of ya, Macy, I don't mind if'n I do."

Macy smiled, filled a glass and handed it to him. Before he was able to take a drink, Macy warned him, "It's my great, great, great grandpa's own special concoction. It's got magic in it. If'n ya been a lyin', it'll make ya cough and sputter and spit them lies right out'a yer mouth."

John took the glass from her and looked at the lemonade, "I don't believe ya, Macy, there ain't no such a thing as lemonade that can tell if'n ya been a lyin'."

"Well now, jist try it and we,ll see," Macy tested him.

John lifted the glass and smelled of it. He took a big swig of the spiked lemonade and his face began to turn red. He began to gasp for air and thump his chest. The spiked lemonade caused his insides to burn fiercely. He turned his head before Macy could see the color he was turning. He tried hard not to let her see his reaction to the drink.

Macy leaned across her lemonade stand, "Are ya alright, John? Ya look a little pale. Ya ain't been lyin' 'bout nothin' have ya? Cause if'n ya have, yer gonna have ta cough them thare lies right out else this'll burn yer insides ta pieces."

John sucked in another breath and regained some of his composure. "I'll be jist fine. Ya made it too tart that's all. I don't care for sour lemonade," he managed to squeak out.

Ya want some more, John?" Macy asked sweetly.

He put his glass down and looked over at the big rock where the rest of the boys sat eating their lunch. "No, but I got some figurin' ta do. I know that Sam Creech been lyin' to me 'bout what happen' to my new pocket knife. I'm a gonna see if this stuff works. How much for another glass?" John knew he had been tellin' lots of whoppers and that lemonade of Macy's made him 'bout cough his eyes out. It was bound to be some kind of truth serum. He decided to see if he could find out now what Sam had done with his knife.

Macy smiled with glee, she realized John had taken her bait, "Well now, this is special lemonade here John, but I guess I kin let ya have a glass for a dollar."

John stepped back, "That ain't fair, Macy, that's too much."

Macy pulled the glass of spiked lemonade back toward her. "Ya want to find out if'n he's a lyin' or not, don't ya?" she challenged.

"Yes," John replied. Maybe it would be worth it to catch that Sam in his lies, he thought.

Macy pushed the glass back toward him, "Then, it's a fair price. I reckon ya better take him out by the outhouse though, jist in case he's been a lyin' somthin' awful and he gets sick." She didn't want any attention to be drawn to her little plan.

John took the spiked drink from Macy and paid her the dollar. “Alright Macy, but ya fill that there glass to the top. I want my money's worth,” John said as he looked around to locate Sam.

Macy giggled with glee as she watched him hurry off to find Sam. “I think We're gonna git real busy in a shake, Lucy. We better git ready,” she laughed again. This was going to be fun.

All of the boys in the school took turns buying each other Macy's lemonade trying to see if one or the other of them had been lying. The spiked lemonade burned them tremendously all the way from their mouth to their stomach when they drank it.

They decided Macy was right. It had to be some kind of lie testing drink.Lucy looked and saw Mr. Talbot coming their way. She gasped, “Oh no, here comes Mr. Talbot! What're we gonna do?”

“Ya jist keep yer mouth shut. I'll handle this,” Macy warned. “Remember now, I'll do all the talkin'.”

Mr. Talbot came over to her lemonade stand, “Hello Macy, looks like you're doing good with your lemonade stand.” He looked hopefully at the sweet brew on the table.

“I am for a fact. Ya'd think this time a year the day'ud be cold, but it's a mighty hot today, I reckon this is Indian summer. I'm jist nearly sold out,” Macy told him.

Mr. Talbot nodded his head. “Yes I heard a few people talking about Indian summer. I had not heard this time of year called that before. Do you have enough for me a glass, Macy? I am feeling the heat myself,” he said as he wiped his forehead with a handkerchief.

Lucy held her breath and her face turned red.

Macy bent down and retrieved a glass of un-spiked lemonade that she had in a bucket of water. “I shore do, let me see now, ahhh here's the thing. A new glass I been savin' jist for ya. Had it in this here bucket of nice cool spring water,” Macy handed the glass to him.

Lucy gasped for air, “But Macy, it's got, OOOOOCH!!!” Lucy wailed as Macy stomped down hard on her foot.

Mr. Talbot took the glass and began to sip it. Lucy nearly fainted.

When he finished, he handed the glass back to Macy, “Well Macy, that was good. How much do I owe you?”

"That was free for ya, Mr. Talbot. I've near got twenty dollars from selling this today," Macy shook her can of money.

Mr. Talbot was pleased for her, "That is wonderful, Macy. One day you might be a business owner. Set your sights high, you can achieve anything if you put your mind to it. Thank you for the lemonade. Only ten minutes to go in recess, you better start putting your things away."

Macy took the glass and stowed it away under the soapbox, "I'll be shore and do that, Mr. Talbot."

When he walked away, Lucy let out the breath she had been holding. "He shore must be a drinker. Why that didn't even make his face red," she said as she rubbed her throbbing foot.

Macy rolled her eyes at Lucy, "That's cause there weren't nothin' in it, stupid. I had that made all day jist in case he came by."

Lucy looked at her with admiration, "Ya shore are a thinker, Macy."

Macy looked around. She didn't see any of the boys anywhere, but could hear them laughing out behind the outhouse. "We better git rid of the rest of this stuff before anyone realizes what it is."

"Ok what're we gonna do with it?" Lucy asked as she looked around for a some place to dump it.

Macy looked over at the creek, "We better take it to the crik. If we dump it here, it'll most likely kill the grass."

Lucy nodded in agreement.

Mr. Talbot rang the bell to signal recess was over. The children began filing back in the schoolhouse. The boys, however, came in a little slowly.

Not long after the class had begun, John went up to the teacher's desk. "I ain't a feelin' too good, Mr. Talbot, can I be excused?"

"It is May, not can. May I be excused. What is wrong John?" Mr. Talbot stood up and looked at John's face. He turned John's head back and forth. "Let me see, why you are pale as a ghost," he looked around the room. He noticed that all the boys were sick. "What have you been doing?" he demanded.

"Ain't been doin' nothin' 'sept drinkin' Macy's Lemonade. She must of posined us," John said weakly.

Macy jumped up and argued, "Why I never done no such a thang.

Mr. Talbot, ya had some, did it make ya sick? What was ya doin' runnin' back and forth to the outhouse at recess, John?"

John let out a burp. Mr. Talbot smelled the moonshine and gasped. "Why, you are drunk, John Taylor," he accused.

John burped again.

That smells like corn liquor," Mr. Talbot stepped back.

About that time, Tim Creech, Sam's little brother, jumped up and started running around the room. He let out war hoops and patted his mouth like he was an Indian on the warpath. It didn't take long before he was joined by all the other boys.

Bob jumped across Helen's desk and yanked her hair, "Now pilgrim, I'm a gonna scalp ya." Helen let out a scream.

"I'll save ya! Save ya!" yelled Sam. "I'm the calv'ry. The calv'ry," he charged at Bob.

The potbellied stove was in his path. Sam won; the stove broke apart as he tackled it. Soot went everywhere; most of it landed on Helen's face and made it completely black all over.

"How dare ya do that ta my sister!" Bob yelled at Sam.

Bob tackled Sam and they started fighting. Lucy ran and hid under Mr. Talbot's desk. Macy sat back and watched the chaos with glee. This was even better than she could have imagined it would be.

The teacher stood helplessly watching with his hands on his head. The correspondence school never said anything about this either. "You boys stop this instant!" he yelled. But, they could not hear him, over all the noise of the battle.

Mr. Talbot had had enough. He went to his desk and grabbed his ruler. He began banging it on his desk and yelling for the commotion to stop. After several minutes, everyone in the room became quiet. The only sound was the girls sobbing and sniffing.

Sam wobbled over to Mr. Talbot's desk. "I ain't feelin' too good teacher, ain't feelin' too good," he turned around threw up all over Loretta.

"AHHHHIEEEE!" Loretta screamed. She jumped up and started running for the door.

"Loretta, stop!" Mr. Talbot shouted.

She kept on running. The teacher banged his ruler on the desk. "Now everyone calm down. One of you girls run to the mill and bring all these boys fathers back with you. The rest of you go on home," he dismissed the girls.

Macy and Lucy got up to make their way outside. Macy tossed her head and grinned at John as she went by him. They decided to hide behind the big oak tree, to see what would happen.

Mr. Talbot remembered what Macy had said about the boys being around the outhouse at recess. He decided to go to the outhouse and see if he would be able to tell what they had been doing. He found the jug that Macy had planted for him to find. He had it with him when the girls came back with all the boys fathers. He showed it to them and tried to explain what had happened.

Macy and Lucy giggled as they watched all the boys git their britches burned, with the switches their fathers had brought with them. They laughed with glee all the way home. John looked up and saw Macy laughing at him. He realized what she had done.

The next morning, Macy and Lucy rounded the big curve in the path that led to school. John, Sam and all the other boys were waiting for them. They stopped walking and Macy bent down and picked up a rock.

Macy drew her hand back, "Ya better leave me 'lone, John Taylor or I'll chunk this here rock at ya and knock another tooth out."

John's face glowed red with anger. "Yer gonna pay for yesterday, Macy Watson.

Git her boys!" John hollered and they all ran toward Macy.

Macy let the rock fly. It hit its mark right on John's cheek and made a cut on his face. He didn't let it stop him. Macy cursed as they jumped on her. She began kicking and biting and scratching. Sam hollered and jumped up after Macy landed a hard blow to his leg. She let her fist fly and it connected with John's left eye. Two of the boys had Lucy pinned to the ground. It took all of the rest of them to subdue Macy. It took four of them to hold her and two of them to hold Lucy.

"You hold'um good now, boys," John instructed as he picked up a hand full of mud. He rubbed the mud in Macy's hair and all over her face. He went over to Lucy and stuffed a big ball of mud in her mouth.

He stood back and laughed at them. "Now boys, be ready to run," John knew what would happen when they let Macy up.

They let Macy go and she came up scratching. "I'm a gonna git ya, John Taylor," Macy hollered as the boys ran off.

Her shirt was torn and she could feel her eye beginning to swell. She touched her mouth; it was bleeding. Lucy spit, trying to get the mud out of her mouth.

Macy went over to her. "Are ya ok, Lucy?"

"This tastes awful, like dirt," she spat again.

"That's on a'counta it is dirt," Macy wiped at her eyes.

Too dirty and banged up to continue on to school, they hobbled back home. They snuck in the back door as quiet as they could.

"Lucy, is that you?" Her mother called to her. "What are ya doin' back home?"

Lucy winced, "Yes, it's me, Ma, I didn't feel so good, so I come back home."

"Did Macy come back with ya? Come in here to the kitchen and let me see," her mother yelled.

"Yeah, Macy came back too. I'm jist gonna go lay down, Ma, okay?" Lucy yelled.

"No, ya come in here first. There's a bad sickness goin' round. Ya come in here and let me see ya both," her mother demanded.

They came into the kitchen with their heads hung down.

She looked at their bloody and bruised muddy faces. "Why, both ya girls have been in a fight," Lucy's mother was not shocked.

Lucy started crying. "It were'nt our fault, Ma, honest. John Taylor jumped me. I jist fought back, that's all."

She started tapping her foot and shook her head at them. "It ain't never yer fault. That's a'las yer excuse. I don't believe ya this time. Ya must'a done somethin' ta provoke'um. Go to yer room and wait for yer pa. He's a gonna give you a good whoopin' fer fightin' this time."

"Yes Ma," Lucy said and they both hobbled to their room.

That night, Macy laid on her right side in the bed. It was the only place that didn't hurt. Her left eye was black and swelled, her backside was still stinging from the spanking her pa had given her. She had bruises all over from the fight that day.

When she got to hurting too awful bad, she'd take her coffee can of money and look down in it. She felt better when she thought of all that money. Nearly twenty dollars after she gave Lucy her part. A full month's wages for the men that worked at the mill. She thought that maybe she would hire one of her brothers to do her chores with some of it until she felt better.

She looked over at Lucy, who was asleep. Lucy had refused to speak to her the rest of the evening. The thought of getting even with John for the tobacco, and the sound of that money helped Macy to sleep. She drifted off, thinking of how she was going to spend her money. A thought came to her that she might buy herself a horse.

Chapter 21
Horse Trading

Macy and Lucy dragged themselves out of bed the next morning and went in the kitchen for breakfast. Lucy's mother took one look at them. She couldn't believe the scrapes those two girls had gotten into and just shook her head.

On the walk to school, Macy decided to tell Lucy of the plan to buy a horse. "Ya know what I been a thinkin' Lucy?" she turned to look at Lucy, who had not said a word to her all morning.

"I don't care," Lucy said and kept on walking.

Macy held her hand out to Lucy, "What are ya still mad at me fer? I know we got in a lot of trouble but don't all the money we made make up fer it?"

Lucy gave her an angry stare. "Look what that money cost me. I got bruises all over. My pa done give me a lickin' and them girls are a gonna make fun of us all day."

"But I got an idea," Macy began.

Lucy cut her off, "I don't want to hear it."

Macy stopped her, "Yeah, ya do. Listen to me, I am a gonna buy us a horse with my part of the money. That way, we can ride to school. When summer comes, we can take the horse and go to Gatlinburg. We might even ride down to Pigeon Forge."

Lucy liked the idea of not walking and she decided she might forgive Macy, "Hey, that's a good idea Macy, I'll give ya my part back and it can be part mine too."

Macy clapped her hands in excitement, "Now yer a talkin'. Why, we might even go to Sevierville on our horse."

Lucy stopped walking again, "Where are we a gonna buy a horse?"

Macy already had a horse in mind that she wanted, "From John and his pa. They's the only ones got horses to sell. I see'd a real purty red horse they was a ridin' the other day."

"You think they'd sell it to us?" Lucy was very excited now.

Macy paused for a moment, that thought had not occurred to her that she might not be able to buy a horse. "I don't see why not. We got the money to buy it, don't we? They want to sell horses, don't they? We'll go right after school and see about hit. Do ya got your money with ya?" Macy asked her.

"Yeah, I brought it. I were a gonna buy that dress. I think a horse'ud be better," Lucy reached in her pocket and handed Macy the money.

Macy grabbed the money and stuffed it in her pocket, "Ya jist let me do the talkin' when we go to buy the horse, ok?"

Lucy looked at her skeptically, "Well ok, but do ya know about horses?"

"Shore I know's about horses. My pa and brothers use mules to haul the logs all the time. They can't be no different than the mules," Macy told her.

Lucy stopped. She had a sinking feeling in her stomach. "I don't know."

Macy threw her hands up. "Do, you, know, 'bout, horses?" she said emphasizing every word.

Lucy shook her head, "No, not really. I jist know how ta ride'um."

Macy took Lucy by the hand and they started for school, "Ya jist let me do the talkin' then. I'll git us a good one."

They forgot about their injuries and ran the rest of the way to school.

Excited about the thought of buying a horse, they planned all day about all the things they would do with their horse. They had a hard time concentrating the lessons and ended up in trouble most of the day.

After school, they ran all the way to John Taylor's place. John's father watched them run up the driveway as he worked on a broken harness in the barn. Macy and Lucy saw him in the barn and began to run faster. They were almost out of breath when they reached the barn.

Macy stopped in front of him and bent over to catch her breath.

Lucy stopped behind Macy and peeked her head out from behind her, "Hi, Mr. Taylor."

He stopped working, "Hello girls, what brings ya over here taday?"

Macy looked around and saw a red horse running in the paddock behind the barn. "We come here ta buy us a horse."

Mr. Taylor stopped working and put his tools down. He wiped his hands on his overalls. "Do ya know what kind a horse ya want ta buy."

Macy could not take her eyes off of the red horse, "We want one like that'un over there." She ran over to the paddock to take a better look at the horse.

John saw the girls from the window and came out of the house to see what was going on.

He walked over to where they were. "What are ya doin' here Macy Watson?" he demanded.

She turned from the paddock, "We want to buy one a yer horses." She turned to Mr. Taylor, "We got twenty dollars and we know we kin git a good one fer that much."

He took his hat off and wiped his forehead, "Now what are ya girls a gonna do with a horse? Don't ya know that having a horse is a big responsibility?"

Macy turned and looked at the red horse running in the field, "We know that. We'll take good care of our horse. We want's a horse ta ride ta school. We thought we'd use it to ride to town ever' now and then too. How 'bout that red horse yonder? Is it a good'un?" Macy asked him.

John stepped in front of his father, he turned and winked at him. "Now that there is the best horse we got. I reckon we can't be a sellin' her," he told Macy.

Macy looked back at the horse. "So, she's a filly then. I reckon I'm a tradin' horses with yer pa, not you John Taylor," Macy spat at him.

John tried to contain his laughter. He determined he would pawn that crazy filly off on Macy. He managed to maintain a straight face and put his hands in his pockets, "That there horse just happens to belong to me, and if'n ya want her, I reckon I'm the one ya got ta deal with."

John's father realized what John was doing. He shook his head and turned to walk back to the house.

Lucy looked at the filly. It made laps around the paddock, running and rearing. "Looks like she might be a handful to me," Lucy whispered to Macy.

John walked over to the fence. He put his foot up on the bottom rail. "Well, I reckon she's the best bloodline we got. She's a racer from Kentucky. She's a beauty, ain't she?" he suckered Macy.

Macy looked longingly at the filly. "She's purty, that's fer shore," Macy told him. Macy put on her bargaining face and turned back to John, "How much are ya a asking fer her?"

John knew he had Macy hooked to buy the crazy horse. "Well now, I tell ya, Macy, I ain't real crazy 'bout sellin' her. I was a gonna raise me a foal off'un her and maybe take it to the races. Ya can win a lot a money on them races ya know," he baited her.

Macy looked at the prancing filly, "Can ya ride her?"

"Well, she's what ya'd call green, but I reckon with jist a little trainin' she'll do alright." John paused to make Macy think he didn't want to sell the horse, then he continued, "I reckon I jist better keep her." He turned to walk away.

Thinking that John didn't want to sell the filly, Macy became determined to have her. She put her hand out and stopped John. "I tell ya what I'm a gonna do. I got the whole twenty two dollars from yesterday and I'd be willin' to give ya all of it for that filly. Ya know they ain't a horse alive worth more'n that. 'Sides, wouldn't ya like ta git yer money back?" Macy challenged him.

He rubbed his forehead and gave Macy a stern look, "I ort ta take that out'a yer hide, Macy Watson."

"Well, sell me that filly and we'll be even," Macy confronted him.

John tried to keep a straight face. He knew if Macy bought that crazy filly, he would be more than even. "Alright, Macy, ya got a deal. I tell ya what, we got some old saddles and bridles in the corner over there. Pick ya one of them out and I'll throw it in with the deal," he held out his hand. "Shake on it?"

Macy shook his hand, "It's a deal."

She counted out the twenty dollars and handed it to John. As soon as she did, John could not control his laughter anymore and he doubled over with a belly laugh.

Macy put her hands on her hips. "Why are ya a laughin'?" she demanded.

"Yer a gonna find out soon enough," John said between breaths.

John pointed to the saddles. He told the girls to choose any of them that they wanted and he turned to let them try to catch the filly themselves.

"Hey, what's her name?" Macy yelled after him.

John turned around and doubled over still cackling "We call her Fireball." Then, he went in his house and slammed the door.

Macy and Lucy looked at each other. "Fireball?" Lucy asked Macy.

"John were jist a tryin' to scare us, Lucy. Look at her, ain't she the purtiest horse ya ever did see? Now she's all our'n," Macy said as they walked over to the fence.

Lucy looked at the filly that was still running back and forth in the paddock and she had a sinking feeling in her stomach. "I think we mite'a made a mistake," she said under her breath.

They went in the barn and found a halter and a lead rope. They came back with them and opened the gate to where Fireball was still running. The horse started running faster when she saw Macy and Lucy. Fireball made a mad dash to escape through the gate that they had just opened. Macy slammed it and Fireball changed direction knocking Lucy down.

"For heaven's sake Lucy are ya alright?" Macy asked and helped her up.

Lucy dusted herself off. "I'm alright, but how in the world are we a gonna catch that horse?" she asked Macy.

Macy watched the filly run. "She's 'bound ta git tired in a minute. She's been runnin' ever since we got here," Macy told her.

Lucy stared at the filly and she noticed the horse was already wearing a halter, "Well, at least she's got a halter on. That'll make it a little easier ta catch her."

Fireball ran at them again. Lucy jumped behind Macy, and the feisty horse ran by and kicked at them.

Macy became blind to anything but the beauty of the red filly. The filly had her tail up, as she pranced around the ring.

Lucy peeped out from behind Macy; she was already afraid of

Fireball. "I catch Flossy with some feed. Maybe we can catch her with some feed," she said.

Macy just kept looking at the filly. "That's a good idea Lucy. Go in the barn and find a bucket. I'll stay here and watch her."

Lucy gladly made a dash out of the field and into the barn to locate something to feed the filly. She searched around and found a barrel of oats. She dipped up the oats in a bucket and brought it back to Macy.

Macy took the bucket and started shaking it at Fireball. "Look here what I have for ya," she crooned sweetly to the horse. She shook the bucket making sure that Fireball noticed the feed. The filly stopped running. "See, I told ya. She's smart," she told Lucy.

Fireball smelled the oats and started to come over to Macy. The horse nervously put her head in the bucket to grab a bite of the food. As soon as she took a mouthful, she ran back to the other side of the paddock.

Macy shook the bucket again. "Now ya know ya want somethin' to eat. Come on, that's it, come on," she crooned to the horse and put her hand in the bucket to rattle the feed.

Fireball nervously pranced over to Macy. She snorted and backed up. She advanced again toward Macy blowing and snorting. Macy held her ground. She stood there not moving waiting for Fireball to come to her. The filly stretched her neck out and put her head in the bucket of feed. She snatched a bite of the oats, turned and ran back to the opposite side of the field. The horse stood there munching on the feed and looking at Macy.

Lucy shook her head. "We ain't never a gonna catch that horse," Lucy told Macy.

Macy looked up and saw John laughing at her from his window. "Oh yeah, we are. I tell ya what we need to do. This paddock connects with the barn. Let's open the gate and let her run in the barn. We'll pin her up in one of the stalls and then we'll catch her."

Lucy liked that idea, "Yeah, that's a good idea Macy, she can't git away then. That's how I catch Flossy." Lucy went over to the gate and opened it.

Macy started walking up to Fireball with the bucket of feed. Fireball ran past Macy, through the gate and into the barn. The girls came up behind her with their arms out herding her toward the open stall. "Lucy, ya stand in the door so as she can't run by ya and I'll shoo her in this stall," Macy instructed.

Lucy looked behind her at the open door of the barn. "Why don't we close the door to the barn, she'll jist run by me and git away. We'll never catch her then," Lucy shouted.

"That's a good idea. I reckon we better do that," Macy decided. She put her bucket down and they both ran to push the big door shut before Fireball escaped. They came back in the barn. Macy picked up the bucket of oats and started toward the horse.

Every time they even became remotely close to her, Fireball ran past them to the opposite end of the barn. Determined not to give up, they were able to herd the filly in one of the opened stalls. As soon as Fireball ran in the stall, Macy and Lucy slammed the door behind her. Fireball realized she had been caught and immediately settled down. She started munching on some hay she found in the stall.

"See I told ya she was smart. She knows she's caught now and look how calm she is," Macy told Lucy.

They opened the stall door and Fireball went to the back of the stall and snorted at them. Lucy backed up, "Go on in there if ya want to, Macy, I'll jist stay here and make sure she don't run back out the door."

Macy took the lead rope and the bucket of food and inched inside the stall. Fireball turned her backside toward Macy. Macy backed up. She didn't want to get kicked. Macy stood in the doorway of the stall and rattled the bucket of food. Fireball came over to steal another bite. When she put her head in the bucket, Macy snapped the lead rope on her. Fireball jumped and tried to run to the back of the stall, but Macy had a good hold on the rope and Fireball knew she was caught. "I got her caught. Ya go git us one of them saddles Lucy," Macy yelled.

Lucy dashed off to find a saddle. "I'll git one but there ain't no way I'm a gonna git on that horse," she warned.

Macy lead Fireball out of the stall, "I don't want ta ride her here neither, that John'ud make fun if'n we got bucked off. We'll jist lead her home. I'll lead her and ya carry the saddle and bridle."

"Okay," Lucy was glad that Macy didn't want to ride Fireball.

Realizing she had been caught, Fireball walked beside Macy with no trouble all the way home. Macy put her in a stall in the barn. Lucy put the saddle on a hay bale and flopped down beside it. Her arms ached from carrying the saddle.

"See, she's a good horse. She jist didn't like being at John's barn. I don't blame her, I wouldn't like it either," Macy patted Fireball on the neck.

Lucy rubbed her arms to stop some of the pain, "Maybe, she does seem different, don't she."

Macy felt very proud of their horse. "I reckon we can git Pa to help us train her. Pa has trained mules all his life. They make them mules pull the wagons to git the logs ta the train. I bet he can help us with her," Macy gave Fireball some hay to munch on.

Lucy smelled the aroma of food cooking. "Smells like Ma is a makin' somethin' good fer supper," Lucy sniffed the air.

Macy's mouth watered from the smell of the food, "Yeah it does and I'm starving. We'll ask Pa to help us in the morning." Macy shut the stall door and they ran in the house to see what Lucy's mother was cooking.

They helped Lucy's mother set the dishes and food on the table. The sat down and Lucy ladled ham and potatoes on her plate. At the moment Lucy stuffed a bite in her mouth, they heard a terrible crash coming from the barn.

Macy jumped up and spilled her plate, "Fireball!"

Lucy's father jumped up. "Fire, what's on fire?" he grabbed his hat and ran for the barn.

Macy and Lucy were right behind him. They opened the barn door and Fireball made a dash for it. Lucy's father grabbed the halter as the filly ran by him, preventing her from escaping. He stood there looking at the damage. The side of the stall Fireball had been in, had been kicked down and the corn bucket was turned over. The hoes and shovels were all knocked off the wall and Flossy was bellowing.

He looked from one girl to the other.

Lucy looked from him to the filly. "This is Fireball, Pa, we bought her from the Taylors today," Lucy said meekly.

"What a mess," he said looking at the damage. He turned to Macy and Lucy, "I'm jist not believin' that yun's went and bought a horse. Where did ya git the money fer it? Don't ya know that a horse is a lot of trouble, even a good one. This one seems to be a might crazy. Didn't ya girls think about how yer a gonna take care of a horse? Where are ya gonna git the money to feed a horse? What were you a gonna do with her?" The questions kept forming in his mouth.

Lucy's mother came to the barn. She stopped inside the door. "Oh my, what happened here?" she waded through the damage.

Lucy's father put Fireball in another stall and shut the door. "Looks like these girls done went and bought a horse," he told her.

Lucy's mother crossed her arms and turned to Lucy. "Where did ya git the money to buy a horse, Miss Lucy?" she demanded. She put her hands up, "No, I don't want ta know. You'll jist have ta take her and git yer money back."

"But Ma," Lucy started to say.

"No, but Ma. How are ya gonna take care of a horse? Who's gonna feed it? Not me. Look at this mess, why she's wild," she scolded.

"John Taylor won't give our money back, Ma," Lucy cried.

Macy went over to Fireball and petted her on the neck. "Look how pretty she is, Aunt Linny, Me and Lucy were a gonna ride her to school so as we wouldn't git sick no more a walkin' in the snow," Macy tried that argument on Lucy's mother.

Lucy's father was at a loss for words. He shook his head. "Well, I suppose if'n she were to plow or hitch to a buggy we might could keep her," he consented.

Lucy brightened up, "Oh I know she will, Pa. Uncle Little can help us train her."

Macy took up the argument. "Yeah, that's right. Ya know Pa's got a way with horses. Ever'body knows how good he is."

Lucy's father looked at their eager faces. "Ya ask yer pa in the mornin' then, Macy. If'n he kin train her to be useful I reckon she can stay. "He looked from their happy faces to the filly, "She's a pretty thing, ain't she?"

"Oh, yeah, she is. I know she'll work good as soon as Pa kin work with her," Macy bubbled with excitement.

Lucy hugged her father, "Thank's Pa."

He shook his head; he began to believe Lucy and Macy were capable of anything. "Mind ya now, she has to pull her weight, else she can't stay," he warned them.

Lucy and Macy squealed with delight. The two girls gave their new horse some extra hay. They ran in the cabin to find some blankets, so they could snuggled together and spend the night in the barn. They wanted to make sure that the wild filly didn't destroy anything else. They giggled and planned all that night and through the weekend how they would ride her. One of their plans they made was to ride Fireball to school. They wanted to show her off on Monday morning.

They spent the night before school sleeping in their own bed. The girls were so excited the two of them awoke before daylight. They threw the their blankets off, got dressed and ran all the way from Lucy's cabin to Macy's parent's cabin. They bounced around with glee as they begged Macy's father to help with Fireball. He took one look at their beaming faces and could not refuse to help them.

Known for his way with horses and mules, Macy's father thought it very funny that the girls had bought themselves a horse, so he was excited to see her. He took one look at Fireball and knew she was going to be a problem. Very nervous, the filly ran to the back of the stall. She snorted and turned her back to him. He eased up to Fireball and put his hand on her neck. He felt her tense. "My advice ta ya girls is ta take this filly back and git yer money back. She's way too flighty ta make any kind of workin' horse," he told them.

"They won't give us our money back, Pa. They told us that when we bought her," Macy whined." Ain't there nothin' ya can do?"

He rubbed his beard. He looked at the nervous filly and then back to Macy and Lucy. "I might could git'er so's she'd let me ride her, but I don't know about anybody else. This filly is a racer and belongs at the race track, not plowin' fields. I'm sorry, girls, but ya should'a come to me first a 'fore ya spent yer money," he told them.

"Will ya jist try, Pa?" Macy pleaded.

He looked at their pleading faces and gave in, "Alright, we can try but I done see'd horses like this'un. She can't be tamed to do farm work. Go and snap the lead rope on her then. Let's take her out to the little field, we'll see what she does."

Macy took the bucket of oats and quietly snuck over to Fireball. She snapped the lead on the filly and led her outside. She turned Fireball loose in the small paddock out behind the barn. Fireball started running and snorting. They watched her for about fifteen minutes and the filly kept running and prancing. She didn't show any signs of calming down.

"Macy, ya go in and try ta catch her," Macy's father handed her the rope.

Macy opened the gate and went in the paddock. Fireball stopped running, she pranced up to Macy. Macy turned and smiled at her father for the accomplishment. She hooked the lead on the halter and turned beaming at her father and Lucy. As soon as she turned, Fireball took off running. Macy still had a hold of the lead rope and it jerked her off her feet. She hit the ground, falling on her backside.

Her pa and Lucy ran over to see if she was alright, "Flossy, done that to me, Macy, 'ceptin' I fell in a belly flop not on my backside. I got the wind knocked out'a me. Did it knock the wind out'a ya?"

Macy sat up, "I'm alright. I jist weren't ready for her to do that." She stood and wiped the dirt off her overalls.

"With that filly, ya better be ready for anythin'," Macy's pa shook his head.

Fireball snorted again from the other side of the field and she trotted over to them. "I think this filly knows exactly what she's a doin'. That makes her worse than one that's jist scared. Ya girls ort ta take her back and see if'n ya can git yer money back," he warned them.

Macy's heart skipped a beat at the thought of taking the filly back to John. "I'd jist die if'n I had to do that Pa. That John Taylor'ud make fun a me. I'd never live it down," Macy wept.

"Well, I can help ya some, but I got work ta do. Ya git yer brother's ta ride her for ya, I reckon ya can try that," he went out of the barn to find Lucy's father.

Macy and Lucy worked every day for week trying to get the saddle on Fireball. Each time they tried to put it on her, the filly ran to the other side of the field or the back of the stall and knocked the saddle off before they were able to cinch it on her.

Frustrated, Macy asked her brother's to help with the horse. They told Macy and Lucy that if Fireball would pull a cart, they would buy her from them. Macy's brothers hooked Fireball up in a harness and hitched her to the cart. As soon as they flicked the reins, the horse took off in a run. She ran over the moonshine still they had set up and parts of it went flying all over the mountain.

Fireball ran all the way from the top of the mountain where they had the still, to the barn, with the cart wheeling and bouncing behind her. Macy and Lucy ran after her yelling for her to stop. When she made it to the barn, she stood trembling.

Macy and Lucy tried to calm their horse. They unhitched the cart and waited for Macy's brothers to catch up with them. Macy's brothers vowed that the girls had to pay them back for everything Fireball had destroyed.

The two of them put Fireball in a stall and sat down on a hay bale.

"Oh Macy, what are we a gonna do? I think we ort'ta jist take her up to the top pasture and turn her loose a 'fore she does anything else to us," Lucy said.

"I don't know. I reckon we could take her ta the sale," Macy said.

"Ain't nobody a gonna buy that crazy horse. We are a gonna be in a lot a trouble and we already owe a lot a money on 'count a her. We best jist take her and turn her loose," Lucy dropped her head and wiped a tear that had escaped her eye.

Macy sighed, "I reckon yer rite, Lucy, I jist hate that John got the best a me."

They petted Fireball to try to calm her down. When she stopped shaking, Macy hooked the lead rope on her halter. She began leading her to the upper pasture to turn her loose. The horse seemed to be tired, so Macy and Lucy decided to try one more time to ride her. Fireball stood still while they put the saddle on her and tightened it up. Macy put her foot in the stirrup and swung up in the saddle.

Lucy stood staring, "Would ya look at that, why she's a gonna let ya ride her. Maybe they's hope fer her yet. I reckon that's the secret, ya have ta make her real tired."

Macy rode Fireball all around the inside of the barn. "Open the door, Lucy, and let's take her outside ta see what she'll do."

"I don't know. What if she runs off with ya?" Lucy warned.

"I'll jump off if'n she starts anythin'. Open the door," Macy motioned for Lucy to open the barn doors.

Lucy opened the door and Fireball walked very calmly out of the barn. Macy rode her around in the paddock. Fireball didn't do anything crazy. "Come on Lucy, climb up here with me. We'll take her around the field," Macy told her.

Lucy ran over and put her foot in the stirrup. But as soon as she settled in the saddle behind Macy, the horse started bucking. She reared and bucked, jumping all over the yard. Then she bolted. She ran as fast as she was able, with Macy and Lucy hanging on for dear life.

"Stop her, Macy, pull back on the reins!" Lucy yelled.

"I am. She won't stop!" Macy screamed back.

Lucy reached around Macy and took hold of the reins, they both pulled back on them with all the strength they had. Fireball stopped abruptly and sat down. She sat down with her front feet between her back legs, much like a dog sits.

Lucy slid off the back of her and Macy stepped off, too. Fireball sat there not moving, just looking around.

Macy went around to the front of the horse and tried to make her stand up. Fireball refused and sat there staring at Macy.

"Ya git up or else I'll find a stick and beat ya black and blue," Macy yelled at Fireball. "Lucy git behind her and push. I'll pull the reins and see if'n we can git her to git up."

Lucy stared at Fireball, "I never see'd a horse do that a 'fore. I see'd mules do it but not horses." Lucy went around the back of Fireball and pushed.

Macy pulled and Lucy pushed. Fireball just sat there looking around. "I ort ta jist take a stick to ya, ya crazy horse. Ya git up or else yer a gonna regret it," Macy shook her fist at Fireball.

The filly sat very still.

Lucy looked up the road and saw Sam and John walking toward them, "Oh no, Macy, Look who's a comin'."

Macy looked down the road and shook her head, "I swear I can't believe this is a happenin'. Hurry, Lucy, come 'round on this side of Fireball and sit down. Lean up against her."

"What good will that do?" Lucy asked.

Macy pulled Lucy by the arm and jerked her down beside the horse. They both leaned up against Fireball. "Ya jist keep yer mouth shut. Let me do the talkin'," Macy warned her.

John and Sam came over to where Macy and Lucy leaned against Fireball. "Havin' trouble with yer horse, are ya?" he asked Macy and started laughing.

Macy looked up at him, "Oh, we ain't a havin' no trouble. We are jist a sittin' here in the shade on 'count a this Indian summer gits mighty hot in the evening."

John stopped laughing, "I don't believe ya. They ain't no way ya trained this filly ta do that."

Macy stood up. "It's the truth. My pa's done helped us train this horse. He says she's the smartest horse he ever did see. Ever'body knows how good my pa is at trainin' horses. He taught her to sit down like this and let us rest in the shade," Macy told John.

Lucy giggled.

John looked skeptically at Macy. "I don't believe ya. If'n ya got her that trained, make her git up," he disputed.

Macy's heart skipped a beat until she remembered she had a piece of peppermint in her pocket. She reached in her pocket and rubbed the candy. She took it out of her pocket, careful not to let John and Sam see the peppermint. She went around the front of Fireball and let her smell the candy.

"Okay, ya can git up now, Fireball. We're ready ta go," she waved the peppermint close to Fireball's nose.

The horse stood up to get the treat. "See I told ya. She's the best horse ever," Macy patted Fireball on the neck.

"Let me see ya ride her," John challenged.

Macy turned to Lucy, "Alright, Lucy, ya come git on her and show John what she'll do."

Lucy's mouth dropped open and she started to shake her head. Macy grabbed her and pinched her arm in warning. Macy held Fireball and pushed a trembling Lucy up in the saddle.

The filly stood there not moving. Lucy clucked to her and she walked a few steps. Lucy held her breath afraid of what Fireball might decide to do.

Macy saw Fireball twitch her tail and gather herself. She realized that the horse was acting like she was going to sit back down. "Okay, Fireball, ya can sit back down now," Macy yelled.

Sure enough, Fireball sat down and Lucy stepped off her.

"See I told ya. She's jist the best horse ever. I reckon I can't thank ya enough, John, for sellin' her ta us. We jist love her," Macy beamed at John.

John looked at Sam, "Well, I'd a never believed it. Make her git up again."

Macy went over and petted Fireball's head waving the peppermint under her nose. The filly stood back up to get the treat.

John didn't think that the horse could've ever been trained. He looked at the now calm filly in shock. He decided he didn't want Macy to have her, "Well now, Macy, ya've done a good job with that horse if'n I do say so. I tell ya what, I'd be willin' ta buy her back from ya."

Macy took her hat off and slapped it against her leg. She put it back on her head and turned to John, "Well now, John, I tell ya, we done put a lot a tranin' in this here horse and I ain't crazy 'bout sellin' her now."

John decided he wanted the horse back. He knew Macy would brag to the other kids about what a good horse she had trained Fireball to be. He reached in his pocket and took out some money. "I tell ya what, ya sell'er back ta me right now and I'll give ya thirty two dollars that'd be a big profit fer ya," he flashed the money at Macy.

"Well, I don't know," Macy looked at Lucy. "Lucy yer a half owner. Ya wanna sell John yer half?" she asked Lucy.

Lucy was not able to say anything. She couldn't believe John was actually going to give them more than they paid to buy that crazy horse back. She nodded her head yes.

"I guess that just leaves me. I ain't a really wantin' ta sell my half, but I reckon if Lucy will sell hers, I can sell mine. I reckon ya better jist go on and take her now. I'd be too sad to take her back home and then ya come git her," Macy handed the reins to John.

"It's a deal then," John took the reins and handed Macy the money.

He put his foot in the stirrup and swung up on Fireball. John was shocked at how calm the normally crazy filly had become.

"Hey John, let me ride with ya, with ya," Sam ran over to the horse.

John took his foot out of the stirrup and Sam climbed up behind him. As soon as he settled down behind John, Fireball took off in a bolt of bucking, rearing and running.

"I forgot ta tell ya she don't like to ride double," Macy hollered after them.

The two girls looked at each other and they doubled over with laughter.

"Can ya believe how stupid John was?" Lucy giggled. "Ya tricked him good, Macy."

"Well it serves him right. He tricked me to buy her in the first place. I say good riddance," Macy clapped her hands.

"Me too. What are we a gonna do with all that money?" Lucy looked at the stack of bills Macy held.

"I reckon I'll need it when I go to work this summer in Kentucky. I reckon we ort'ta save all this money. They might be somethin' ta buy when I git there. Maybe a good horse this time."

Lucy had heard her mother and father talking about a family reunion. " I reckon at the end of the harvestin' they's gonna be a family git together in Kentucky. We're a gonna git ta ride the train. I can't wait ta go. It'll be a great adventure!" Lucy was excited.

"Yes, a great adventure," Macy and Lucy laughed all the way home. They were proud of tricking John into buying that crazy Fireball back from them. They planned the things they were going to do on their adventure to Kentucky.

CPSIA information can be obtained at www.ICGtesting.com
Printed in the USA
BVOW08s1326200815

414298BV00001B/1/P